"Do you think my sister is in danger?"

"She has her husband to protect her."

"And I have you, haven't I, Captain Briggs?"

He nodded and moved closer to her. "Aye. But the sooner we get to London, the better."

Christina pressed her back against the door, facing him. "Captain Briggs. When we get there . . ."

He pivoted slightly and placed his hand against the doorjamb, quite near her head. A dangerous gleam came into his eyes.

He spoke quietly, his voice deep and rich. "I have no idea what will happen, Lady Fairhaven."

He touched her hair with his free hand, his eyes roving the contours of her face. His breath feathered against her cheek, sending spears of heat through her.

"Do you h-have any sort of plan?"

"Aye." He cupped her jaw with his hand and ran his thumb across her lower lip just before he kissed her.

Romances by Margo Maguire

BRAZEN
SEDUCING THE GOVERNESS
THE ROGUE PRINCE
TAKEN BY THE LAIRD
WILD
TEMPTATION OF THE WARRIOR
A WARRIOR'S TAKING
THE PERFECT SEDUCTION
THE BRIDE HUNT

Margo Maguire

Brazen

AVON
An Imprint of HarperCollinsPublishers

This is a work of fiction. Names, characters, places, and incidents are products of the author's imagination or are used fictitiously and are not to be construed as real. Any resemblance to actual events, locales, organizations, or persons, living or dead, is entirely coincidental.

AVON BOOKS
An Imprint of HarperCollins*Publishers*
10 East 53rd Street
New York, New York 10022-5299

Copyright © 2011 by Margo Wider
ISBN 978-0-06-201841-0
www.avonromance.com

First Avon Books mass market printing: December 2011

Avon Trademark Reg. U.S. Pat. Off. and in Other Countries, Marca Registrada, Hecho en U.S.A.
HarperCollins® is a registered trademark of HarperCollins Publishers.

Printed in the U.S.A.

10 9 8 7 6 5 4 3 2 1

This is the second of my "sister" books, and so I decided to dedicate it to my own sisters, both in blood and in spirit. Like Christina, I have only one real sister—Fran, and so this book is for her. It's also for my very good friend, Ellen, my Jaunty Quills sisters, and my brainstorming partners, Anne Mallory, Robyn DeHart, and Shana Galen. My life is so much better with all of you in it.

Acknowledgments

My thanks to my editor, Amanda Bergeron, for her insightful editing of the plot and characters in this novel. Her sharp understanding of the conflicts in this story helped me to make it a better book.

Brazen

Chapter 1

Sweethope Cottage, Cumbria. Early Summer, 1816

My lady, do you need assistance?"
    Christina Warner, Lady Fairhaven, heard the footman's concerned voice calling to her from outside the closed door. Blast it all, she ought to have been more careful while moving the chair across the room to her late husband's armoire. "No, Alfred, all is well," she said, loud enough for the footman to hear.

"Or as well as it can be," she grumbled, climbing onto the chair. "Considering . . ."

She lost her balance and started to tip.

"My lady!"

Dash it, anyway! How did the man know? She grabbed the top of the armoire and hung on. "Naught to worry about, Alfred!"

She caught her breath and ran her hands across the top of the tall chest, finally encountering the key she sought.

She grabbed it and stepped down from the chair, wishing she didn't have Alfred hovering just outside and wondering, no doubt, what she was up to in his former master's bedchamber.

It was none of his concern.

With key in hand, Christina quickly went to the safe that her husband had hidden behind a cushioned panel in the window seat. She knelt before it and ran her hands around its edges. Her fingers caught on a latch and the panel popped open, exposing the safe. She stuck the key in the lock.

"Lady Fairhaven?"

"Go downstairs, Alfred. It's nearly time to leave."

Only one more thing to do after she took the jewels from Edward's safe, and then they needed to get back to Holywell House.

Christina had gotten over her elation at the news she'd received of her brother, especially since her entire family thought Lang was dead. But the manner in which she'd received the news had been less than stellar.

For the past three horrid months, her parents and brothers believed Lang had been killed in a dockside explosion sometime after his ship had put into port at Plymouth. It had been a few days after the fire that his body had been recovered, and his friend, Lieutenant Norris, had identified him.

But Norris had been wrong.

A few weeks ago, Christina received a blackmail note indicating that Lang was alive—and the blackmailer knew where he was and what he'd done. *What he'd done!*

She removed the box of jewels her late husband had stashed in the safe and dumped them into a small satchel. Then she opened the armoire.

Some of Edward's clothes still hung there. In the ten months since his death, Christina knew she ought to have come back to the old hunting lodge, but she hadn't wanted to leave London. Not when there was a fair chance of running into Edward's mother or his brother here in the north country.

She pulled open the drawers at the bottom of the armoire and found Edward's pistol in the last one. She took it from the drawer, then brought it, with her satchel, downstairs.

"My lady," Alfred gasped, gaping at the gun. "What are you doing with that?" He looked more than a little pale.

Just for once, Christina wished someone would take her seriously, and not assume she was a brainless chit. She clucked her tongue. "I promise not to shoot you, Alfred. Just show me how to load this thing."

He shook his head. "It has been many a year since I—"

"Nonsense, Alfred. You used to come here with my husband's hunting parties. I am reasonably certain you were required to load any number of guns for those men."

Being a woman did not make her incompetent.

Her father had coddled her all her life, and her husband had treated her as though she were a porcelain doll. It was incredibly tiresome.

Alfred swallowed audibly and took the pistol from her hand, then the ball and cloth. "Where's the gunpowder?"

Gunpowder? Oh dear. She wondered if she could really load the deadly thing and shoot the blackmailer when he turned up for his blood money.

She hoped it would not come to that, but she wanted to give every impression of being earnest when she dealt with the scoundrel. Therefore, she needed to know how to use the gun.

She rallied her resolve. "It must be upstairs, I suppose. In the bottom drawer of the armoire in my husband's bedchamber." There had been other objects near the pistol, but she had not bothered to drag them all out, unaware anything else would be needed.

Shaking his head with dismay, Alfred returned up the stairs while Christina went outside and took the opportunity to set up a target about a hundred feet away. She balanced a large rock upon a low branch near the road, and returned to the drive in front of the cottage.

Christina was not going to go on being blackmailed indefinitely. She was done with being a vulnerable young thing without the confidence or authority to carry out her own wishes. She had grown up significantly since becoming a widow.

She raised the pistol and shut one eye as she aimed

the weapon at the rock, deciding this wasn't going to be so very difficult. At least, it wouldn't be as difficult as being Edward's wife.

Her husband had been a much older man who'd gone about his married life as though he were still a bachelor. He'd kept his mistress, gone to his clubs, caroused with his old friends, and *she* had been the one to adapt. In the ten months since Edward's death, Christina had decided she preferred widowhood to being a wife. Her newfound independence suited her very well.

And now she was going to take that independence in hand and deal with the problem she faced. She was finished with being the one to adjust.

Wherever her brother Lang had got to, he was going to be in serious difficulty when she got her hands on him. How dare he disappear and leave his family to grieve so sorely?

She'd thought the first evil blackmail letter would be the end of it. *I know what Lieutenant Jameson has done and where he is.* The note had demanded that she bring one thousand pounds in official Bank of England notes—an *astronomical* sum—wrapped inside a secure package, and leave it in the reeds beside an isolated pond in Hyde Park. If she did not do so, there would be scandal, and perhaps even transportation.

Christina would not risk that. She had managed to do as instructed, thinking she'd been ever so clever in enclosing a note with the money, demanding that her blackmailer tell her where she could find her brother. She'd told him to leave her a securely wrapped note in the same location, which she would find the following day.

But when she returned, the money was gone, and there was no note in its place. Apparently, there was no honor among thieves. It was a lesson hard-learned.

She'd received the second demand for money ten days later. This time, she was to take two thousand pounds—*two thousand!*—to the church next to the Tower of London. She had barely two weeks to raise the money, hardly any time before her blackmailer exposed Lang's offense—whatever it might be. And Christina knew from Lang's past history that it might well be a serious one.

Lang had never been an easy child, and his adolescence had been even worse. If there was mischief to be made, he was always at the bottom of it. Their father, the Earl of Sunderland, had given him no choice but to go into the navy, and he had not disgraced himself. At least, not until he'd gotten himself killed in a horrific explosion at his ship's home port. Or had deserted the navy.

Christina did not know which was worse.

Alfred came out, carrying the firearm in one hand, and the other shooting accoutrements in the other. "My lady, this is all you'll need, though I highly suggest you reconsider—"

"Yes, I understand your concerns, Alfred. I cannot tell you why I need this . . . Please do not ask."

Visibly resigned, Alfred prepared the pistol to fire, showing her every step of the process. It was surprisingly complicated. She'd always thought—

Well, it did not matter what she'd thought. It was not going to be easy, but she could do it. She took the thing in hand and cocked it, and aimed toward the rock on the tree branch.

"Careful, my lady!"

She pulled the trigger and jumped at the loud noise it made.

The rock target did not move. Apparently, it was not as easy as it looked.

"We must try that again," she said to Alfred when they'd both recovered. "I didn't realize how the gun would lurch in my hand."

Alfred gave a great, disapproving sigh, and started to take the pistol from Christina. But she held on to it, insisting that she be allowed to load it and make it ready to fire. After all, she would have to do this by herself when she encountered the blackmailer.

She managed it all without making too great a mess. When the pistol was ready once again, she raised it, cocked it, and aimed, but was startled by the sound of hooves on the road. She fired reflexively, just as a man rode into sight.

He gave out a shout and pulled up on his reins as he grabbed his arm. "What are you about, woman!" he demanded, his voice angry and rough.

While Christina stood paralyzed with the pistol at her side, Alfred hastened to the gate and on toward the stranger, as though *he* might be held responsible for shooting the man. But the rider did not stop.

Christina felt numb with shock. She dropped the gun, her mind in a daze. She did not know what to do as the man she'd shot rode directly toward her.

She held her ground as he came to a stop within a foot of her and jumped down from his horse.

Gavin Briggs had known he was at the right place the second he'd seen the woman.

And then she'd shot him!

He was off his horse and standing in front of her before he really knew what he was going to do. And yet she stood fast, all color drained from her face, even more beautiful than her sister.

But haughty as hell. He refrained from rolling his eyes, but gave up a short, silent plea to be spared the snobbery of the privileged class. He'd experienced far too much of it during his recent visit to his father, Viscount Hargrove, who demanded to be apprised of Gavin's wartime assignments from Lord Castlereagh's office. Such information was not to be shared. Hargrove was a meddling, gossiping old fool, and Gavin would not risk the security of any other officers who were still engaged in clandestine pursuits on the continent.

Of course, they'd argued over it, and his father had cut him off without a farthing.

Well, Viscount Hargrove could go hang. Gavin had done well enough on his own during the decade or so that he'd served in the army and the foreign service. And he was soon to do even better.

But his upper arm burned like fire at the moment, and blood seeped from the wound. Keeping his eyes on Christina's, he tore off his gloves and pressed the palm of his hand to the injured spot, but the compression did not help.

He fought quite unsuccessfully to rein in his temper. "I don't suppose you have a clean cloth I might use to stanch this . . ."

She remained speechless.

"Well, what about your petticoat?" he growled. "Don't all intrepid heroines jump at the opportunity to tear off a strip of—"

She turned on her heel and made a dash for the house, and Gavin was unsure whether she was fleeing him or hurrying to get a cloth for his wound.

He hoped his sarcasm stung as badly as the wound she'd inflicted upon him. What in bloody hell was she doing with a pistol, anyway?

He followed her into the house, blood dripping down between his fingers. Her footman came after him. "Sir," the man said. "If you'll just come with me."

Gavin ignored him and went after Christina through the front rooms until she reached the back of the house and went into some sort of small utility room. She wore the unrelenting black of mourning, but her jacket and skirts were cut in a way that framed her figure to perfection.

Not that he noticed.

Her hair was short and quite curly—and the bounce of those soft curls was so feminine and enthralling he almost had trouble remembering to be angry with her. Almost.

He could not recall ever seeing a grown woman with hair shorn so short. It was surprisingly arousing, the way it framed her utterly feminine features.

"Lady Fairhaven."

She turned abruptly. "How do you know my name?"

"I've come here for you." But not until he'd investigated every family in Edinburgh named Jameson and found the one that had taken in a three-year-old orphan girl twenty years before. He wondered if she knew.

Once again, the color drained from her cheeks. "Who sent you? If it's about that letter—"

"Letter?"

She looked at him, as puzzled as he was.

Gavin tilted his head in a slight bow and drew out the warrants signed by her grandfather, the Duke of Windermere. "I am Captain Briggs, Lady Fairhaven. I've been charged with the task of finding you for your grandfather."

"My grandfather is dead. He died . . ." The words faded on her lips and she frowned. "My . . . do you mean *my* grandfather? Impossible."

Her tone was incredulous. But at least it was clear that she aware she was not Lord Sunderland's actual daughter.

In his search for Christina and Lily Hayes, Gavin had learned a number of things about the two sisters. First and foremost was that their grandfather had not relented in his estrangement from his daughter's family, even upon news of her death. He'd sent his steward to London to collect the girls and place them in separate homes far from Windermere Park.

And then he'd forgotten about them, until the recent death of his son and heir. Only then did the old bastard finally realize he had no one but the two granddaughters he'd abandoned years ago. Now he wanted to see them. Wanted to put them into his will.

Christina had been taken by Windermere's man to a family in Edinburgh. The Jamesons turned out to be the Earl of Sunderland and his barren wife.

Gavin discovered that Sunderland and his countess had known little about the child. But as Lady Sunderland had not been able to bear her own offspring, she welcomed the chance for a daughter of her own. They'd agreed to ask no questions about her origins, and had accepted a generous stipend for her care.

Gavin learned that the stipend had grown substantially, and had become Christina's dowry on her marriage to Edward, Viscount Fairhaven, some sixteen months earlier. Gavin also knew that Fairhaven had died suddenly—an ailment of the heart—in the arms of his mistress.

Gavin could not fathom why the man would look elsewhere for his satisfaction—unless his wife was a far colder woman than she appeared.

He doubted that was true. Fairhaven had been more than twenty years older than his wife. Perhaps she had not been able to abide the carnal attentions of a middle-aged peer. Perhaps the man had been as cold and insensitive as Viscount Hargrove, Gavin's own sire.

Or maybe he'd simply been a fool.

It was none of his concern. All Gavin needed to do was take Lady Fairhaven back to Windermere Park and present her to her grandfather in order to reap the very generous reward he'd been promised for finding the duke's twin granddaughters.

The footman finally made his presence known. "My lady—"

"Alfred, ride into Runthwait and fetch a physician."

"Stay here, Alfred," Gavin countered. "I need no physician."

With her eyes darting toward her servant, Christina lifted her chin and directed Alfred to do her bidding by her very manner. She'd learned her role well.

"But my lady, I should not leave you—"

"Do as I say, Alfred." Her voice was firm. Tough. With the slightest hint of a burr from her Scottish upbringing. Gavin was surprised she would send the man off, leaving her alone with him. He looked out the window to see if there was anyone else near the house.

He saw no one, heard no one moving about on the upper floor. But with clear orders from his employer, Alfred left to do as he'd been instructed. Fine. Let him ride the distance to Runthwait, only to return and find his mistress gone.

Once Alfred had left, Gavin focused on his goal: to get Christina to her grandfather at Windermere Park and collect his money.

"I have no grandfather, Captain Briggs," Christina said stiffly as she took a length of white linen from a shelf.

"On the contrary, you do."

"Take off your coat." She said it as though she had not heard him.

He complied, removing his greatcoat as well as his jacket. Both bore holes from the lead ball that had grazed through the flesh of his upper arm. It stung, and was bleeding profusely, but he'd suffered far worse during his years of service to the crown.

"Your wound needs to be stitched."

"This is hardly a wound, Lady Fairhaven. You barely grazed me."

She appeared dubious, but he had far more important business here. The lead ball had passed across his skin—was not lodged in his flesh—so there was nothing more to do than bandage it and control the bleeding. He'd have a nice scar for his trouble, though. To go along with a few others he'd collected over the years.

Maybe he ought to charge old Windermere a few hundred pounds more for his trouble. Get something more useful than a medal this time.

"Your grandfather is the Duke of Windermere," he said.

She stopped cold, speechless for the moment. Gavin took the thick roll of linen from her hand and pressed a wad of it to the bloody site. He had to admit it *was* bleeding fairly freely, but experience told him it would soon stop. "The old duke disowned your mother, Sarah, when she married a London barrister—a man called Daniel Hayes."

A small crease appeared between her delicate,

dark brows. "Nonsense. I-I was an orphan when my parents took me in."

"True. You *were* an orphan." He might have taken a kinder tone if only she had not been so stiff and unyielding. "Your real parents drowned in a boating accident on the Thames in 1796. You were three years old at the time. But even after the demise of your parents, your grandfather was unrelenting in his denial of you and your sister. He sent you both away to be fostered out of his sight and awareness."

Her astonished eyes flew up to meet his. "My sister! *My sister?*"

Gavin felt rather brutal, in spite of himself. "Aye. You have a sister. Her name is Lily."

Chapter 2

Fortunately, there was a chair behind Christina when she sat down hard. *A sister.*

She had never imagined . . . and yet it felt quite right. The name Lily struck a chord deep within her and she knew Captain Briggs was speaking the truth. But a grandfather who'd disowned her?

She felt a sharp pang unlike anything she'd ever known. All these years she'd had no family but the Jamesons—they were her parents and younger brothers. They'd taken her in when she'd had no one, loved and nurtured her as though she were their own. They were all she'd ever needed. And when she'd grown, her father had seen to it that she made a favorable match in marrying Edward. She'd known who she was.

"Your mother had a brother," Captain Briggs said. "He was the duke's heir, but he perished last year during a typhus outbreak."

Christina had a fleeting memory of a little girl

with black hair like her own. They'd hugged and played under the watchful eye of . . . someone. She could not remember who'd been watching, but she could feel the warmth of a loving gaze, and hear a woman's soft laughter.

Her mother. Not Lady Sunderland, but . . . Sarah. The daughter of a duke.

Christina felt her chin begin to quiver and she turned away from Captain Briggs to gaze out the small window in the servants' pantry. The backs of her eyes burned.

"Why does this grandfather want me now?" She tried to collect herself and think. "I . . . I cannot inherit, so what is the point?" Why should her life be any more disrupted than it was?

"There is more to be said about that, Lady Fairhaven. But let it suffice for the moment to say that your grandfather is in ill health. He does not expect to live much longer, and his conscience troubles him."

As well it should, Christina thought, if what Captain Briggs said was true. She could barely sort out the captain's revelations.

A deep wave of grief came over her, sorrow for the parents she could not really remember, for the woman who'd borne her and died so soon after.

"My sister. Where is she?"

"Lily married quite recently," Briggs replied. "She and her husband, the Earl of Ashby, are probably at Windermere Park now."

Christina looked back at Captain Briggs, watching as he dabbed at the blood from the wound she'd inflicted. It really did need to be stitched, whether he believed it or not. "My sister . . . Lily wanted to see him?"

"Not really. But she had her reasons for going to Windermere."

Christina composed herself and stood. She took the cloth from Briggs and cringed at the sight of what she'd done to him. She took charge and blotted his wound through the shirt, thinking it was probably the one way she might be able to regain some control. She had three brothers whom she loved. But a sister!

"This isn't going to stop bleeding," she said. "Remove your shirt so I can bandage it properly while we wait."

"I'm not quite sure I trust you to bandage anything." His tone was gruff, and Christina sensed he was unaccustomed to taking orders. Likely as unaccustomed as Christina was to *giving* them. But she was getting better.

"Point taken. But I assure you I am usually a very civilized person. Lately, though, circumstances . . ."

A muscle in his jaw flexed—involuntarily, Christina was sure—as he unfastened the few buttons at his neck. He slipped the shirt out from his trews and pulled it over his head, mussing his thick, dark hair. The disorder did not decrease his physical appeal in the least. "Under what possible circumstances would a viscountess need to wield a firearm?"

She hardly heard his question when he bared the broad expanse of his lightly furred chest. He was solidly built, his muscles thick and well-defined, and his abdomen . . .

A disturbing, foreign sensation stirred within her at the sight of his masculine physique. Her husband had been relatively hairless. And nearly as smooth as she.

Captain Briggs seemed to be a different species altogether. He was hard and rugged, his muscles seemingly chiseled from stone. He was impervious to any discomfort from the bullet wound. And there were scars—at least three, from what must have been significant injuries. She could only wonder what had happened to him.

"This will only take a moment." Gathering her wits, she took the linen and quickly tore it into strips, then folded one section into a large square and pressed it to the wound. Then she wrapped his arm with the remaining strips.

"How did you learn to do this?" he asked.

"I have three younger brothers. One or the other was always in some kind of scrape. Blood was often involved." Especially when it was Lang. He had a penchant for fighting and other mischief. She could not imagine what he'd got up to now.

Whatever it was, Christina had no intention of letting some anonymous scoundrel expose his actions, which were likely to have been scandalous. Her father could deal with Lang once she found him.

At least for now, she could not bring herself to inform her family of the blackmail letters. They'd gone away to Italy to escape some of the pain of

Lang's loss, and Christina would not raise their hopes when it was entirely possible that the letters were a cruel ruse.

A deep shudder shook her from within. Lang might actually have been killed as reported, and the blackmailer was just an opportunist taking advantage of the situation. She had to find the scoundrel, had to find out what he knew.

A sudden thought struck her. "Captain Briggs, how did you find me?"

"It was a long and complicated process. I will not bore you with the details."

"It must have been difficult . . ." A plan began to form in her mind. "Did my grandfather engage you to find my sister as well?"

He gave a nod, lifting his densely muscled arm as she wrapped the linen around it. Christina kept her focus on her questions and not on the thick musculature of his arm and the odd prickle of awareness that skittered down her back.

"Did you know where my sister had been taken when our parents died? Who had raised her?"

"No. I went to London—where Sarah and Daniel Hayes lived—and started asking questions."

Christina could not imagine what the questions had been or whom he would have asked. How did one begin to find a needle—or two—in a haystack?

"Can you locate anyone? Anyone at all?"

She found him looking at her, not at what she was doing, but at her face. He was very close, close enough that she could see flecks of silver in his light blue eyes. And his lashes—impossibly long and black as coal. A small crescent of a scar at the corner of his eye only added to the stunning appeal of his features.

He did not respond immediately to her question, holding her gaze until he blinked and turned to look at his arm. "Yes," he finally said. "Anyone."

Christina could think of no other person who showed such complete confidence. She finished the bandaging and tied the knot. "So . . . Windermere has paid you to find me?" she asked.

The brow over his right eye lowered ever so slightly. "He is not obliged to pay me until I take you to him."

"Are you one of those Bow Street men?"

"No. Apparently, your grandfather heard of my expertise at . . . finding people . . . on the continent."

"In the army?"

"Aye." A muscle in his jaw tensed.

Christina stepped away and crossed her arms, considering what to do. He seemed in no hurry to pull on his shirt, but took a quick glance at the hole in its sleeve. Leaving it on the table, he quit the room.

Christina knew he wasn't leaving Sweethope Cottage. After all, he must have come some distance for her. And he wouldn't be paid until he produced her for her grandfather. He had to stay.

She *did* want to meet her sister. It was just that the situation with Lang was so immediate.

Christina quickly made up her mind. She was going to have to delay that meeting until she found Lang.

And Captain Briggs was the key to doing so. He'd found Lily with few clues, and it couldn't have been easy to find the recently widowed Lady Fairhaven, née Christina Jameson . . . or rather, Hayes.

She followed Briggs to the drawing room at the front of the house and waited when he stepped outside and went to his horse. Half naked, he reached up and took down a leather satchel while Christina gaped at his bare back. His shoulders. His lean waist. The ripple of muscle when he moved his arms. The way his longish, dark hair brushed his neck.

She watched with interest as he came back to the house, pulling on the fresh shirt that he'd taken from his satchel. He was far more rugged than Edward, and seemed to fit into the rustic setting of Sweethope Cottage far better than her late husband ever had.

It had surprised her to learn Edward had bequeathed her the country house, for she'd visited there only a few times. But of course, he had not planned on dying so precipitously. Or in such outrageous circumstances.

"If we leave now, we can make it to Windermere the day after tomorrow," Captain Briggs said when he turned and saw her standing at the window in the drawing room.

"I'm not going to Windermere," Christina replied.

"Yes, you are."

"I need to go to London first."

He tucked the long tails of his shirt into his trews. Then he caught her gaze and spoke quietly. "I'd rather not tie you to the back of my horse, Lady Fairhaven, but I will if I—"

"Do you order your wife about this way, Captain Briggs?"

"I have no wife, Lady Fairhaven. And I assure you that if I *did* have one, she would be far more tractable—"

"I am being blackmailed, Captain. I need to go to London right away."

It wasn't what Gavin expected to hear. He thought she would simply say she had no interest in meeting the old bastard who'd abandoned her. *That*, he could understand. *This*, he was unprepared for.

Blackmail.

He'd learned nothing about Lady Fairhaven to indicate any reason for blackmail. But of course that was the point. Blackmail could only be about a secret that needed to be kept.

"I want you to help me find and stop the man who's blackmailing me."

They were wasting good time. "How do you expect me to do that?"

"You said yourself you can find anyone." She crossed the room to a heavy, mahogany writing desk and opened a drawer. Taking out a folded sheet of vellum, she handed it to him. "I received this two weeks ago at my parents' home in London."

He read the note, blanching, Christina presumed, at the outrageous sum that was demanded. "Lieutenant Jameson . . . One of Lord Sunderland's sons?"

She nodded. "My middle brother. We were told he was killed soon after he left his ship—*The Defender.*"

He avoided rolling his eyes or sighing in frustration. He had not heard this about Lady Fairhaven's family. "Where?"

"Plymouth."

"When?"

"In mid-February," Christina replied, taking a seat in a large chair by the fireplace. She seemed awfully small in the heavy leather chair. She was a pampered anomaly in this rustic country house so far from any sizable town.

She was naturally fair-skinned like her sister. And now that her color had returned, her cheeks took on the same fetching pink as her lips. She looked at him with an urgency that he was only beginning to understand. "I cannot go to Windermere until I've silenced this . . . this . . . extortionist."

"Silenced? How?"

"I intend to find him." She took the letter from Gavin's hand and looked at the outrageous contents as she spoke. "I intend to go to All Hallows Church and lie in wait for the villain who sent this."

Gavin frowned. "Lady Fairhaven . . ."

She stood abruptly, her jet-black curls springing gently as she paced in front of the fireplace. "They told us my brother was dead, but . . . I know it is possible they identified the wrong man."

Gavin knew it could happen, but only in certain circumstances. A drowning, a fire, a certain sort of gunshot wound . . .

"My brother has been known to get into trouble, though he seemed to have kept his nose clean ever since he went into the navy. It's entirely possible that—"

"Lady Fairhaven, what you propose is dangerous. And you might not—"

"I will not keep paying this man. Did you see? He wants two thousand pounds this time!"

"*This* time?"

She stopped pacing. "This is the second letter I received. I paid him the first time—one thousand pounds. And I received nothing in return."

Gavin let out a mirthless laugh. One thousand pounds was a staggering sum. Far more than the average family's yearly income. "What did you expect?"

"*What did I expect?* That the man would provide me with the information I paid for!"

"Which was . . . ?"

"Where my brother is. What horrible deed he's supposed to have done. How he escaped the explosion and fire on the Plymouth docks."

Gavin shook his head at the haughty, naïve young woman before him. He could not even imagine having so vast a sum as one thousand pounds to just *give away*. And now her blackmailer wanted two thousand. For information on a man who was likely as dead as he'd been reported.

"This character has no reason to give you any information, my lady. You've paid him and now he's got you on his hook. Like a fisherman's worm."

"But I have no intention of wriggling quite so uselessly."

The thought of Christina acting hastily in this matter—and alone—gave him pause. He needed to get her to Windermere or he wouldn't collect his reward. "What will you do when you finally come up against your blackmailer? Please do not tell me that was the reason for your exercise this morning with the pistol."

"What would you have me do? Let him get away with it?"

"Lady Fairhaven, I would have you notify your father of this letter and allow him to deal with it."

"I will not give my family any more cause to worry," she said with some force. "They've gone away to our villa in Genoa, and . . . Well, if . . ."

Her throat moved as she swallowed, and Gavin knew she'd considered the possibility that her brother was truly dead, and the blackmailer merely gulling her.

She didn't want to face it. "Lady Fairhaven, if your brother was not killed, what do you think happened to him?"

She gazed down at the letter as though she would find the answer there. "I don't know," she said in a small voice. "With Lang, anything is possible."

"Is he likely to have done something illegal?"

"Like what?"

"Murder, theft, smuggling, forgery. To name a few."

She shook her head. "No. He's not a criminal."

"There could have been circumstances . . ."

"I don't think he would kill anyone." She folded

the letter and put it on the desk. "But if he has done something scandalous, it might cause an end to Felton's engagement."

"Felton?"

"My eldest brother, our father's heir. He is engaged to marry the daughter of the Marquess of Bedlington. The marquess's family accompanied ours to Genoa."

Gavin's arm throbbed and when he glanced down, he noticed the bandage darkening with blood under his shirt. He pulled off the clean garment before it could be ruined, and tossed it over a nearby chair.

"Captain Briggs!" He'd shocked her aristocratic sensibilities, but that was little concern to him. The only thing that mattered was finding a way to get her to Windermere as soon as possible. He feared that if he could not convince her that her brother was dead, he would be trapped into assisting her.

He crossed his arms over his chest. "I have no wish to bleed all over my only remaining intact shirt, Lady Fairhaven. Who was the last person to see your brother after he left *The Defender*?"

"Lieutenant James Norris. They were good friends."

"And Norris agrees—your brother might not have been caught up in the explosion and fire that was supposed to have killed him?

She looked away. "No. Lieutenant Norris identified Lang's body."

Christina needed a moment to compose herself. She left Captain Briggs in the drawing room and returned to the pantry to retrieve his old shirt and another length of linen.

No, James Norris did not think Lang had survived. But several men had been killed in the accident. Christina had overheard the talk . . . it had been difficult to identify Lang. What if he'd already left the area when the explosion occurred? Maybe he didn't even know he was thought to have died.

It was her only hope, and now that she had news to the contrary, she did not want to consider, much less speak of, the possibility that it was untrue. She was determined to find out the truth.

She took the shirt back to Captain Briggs, then reinforced the bandage around his arm. "Please wear the shirt until Alfred returns with the doctor."

Thankfully, Briggs donned the garment, then looked down with irritation at the hole in the arm. Or more likely, irritation with her ultimatum.

"I promise to repair that for you . . . I-I mean to say I'll have one of our maids . . ." She sounded like her pretentious old mother-in-law. "Oh hang," she muttered. "It will be fixed for you. Just . . . Please, help me to deal with the blackmailer and find Lang. Then I will go with you to Windermere."

He breathed a quiet curse, a couple of words she could barely hear.

It was then that Christina knew she had him.

She returned to her seat in Edward's big leather chair and put her hands in her lap to wait.

"Let me see the letter again," he said.

She handed it to him and he read. Whether it was to remind himself of its contents or to gain some time in which to think, she did not know. But when he finally looked up at her, she saw that he had made up his mind.

"Do you have the money? The two thousand pounds?"

She shrugged. "Not yet."

"How do you propose to come up with that sum? It's an insane fortune."

"I know how much it is, Captain Briggs. All I need to do is take my jewels—"

"Your jewels?"

"My husband bequeathed me this house. I own it and all its contents." It had probably been an oversight on Edward's part, but Christina would not quibble with it. At least she had the satisfaction of knowing his mistress had received nothing more upon his death.

By all accounts, she'd caused it.

"Lord Fairhaven kept jewels here?"

"He obviously did not intend to die as he did, else he might have secreted them away somewhere else."

Briggs quirked his brow. "You suppose he did not intend for you to have them?"

She shrugged. "Some he gave to me. Others . . ." She stiffened visibly and picked at a thumbnail. "Well, I've learned in recent months that he gave at least a few pieces to his mistress."

Christina almost managed to disguise the catch

in her voice. But not quite. She could not allow Edward's unfaithfulness to bother her. After all, theirs had not been a love match. Her father had promoted the marriage because of its advantages—affection not being one of them. She knew he thought he'd done well by her. At least, until the scandal of Edward's death became public.

"I'll go with you to All Hallows Church," Briggs said, "but you have to leave the pistol behind. We won't need it. And when we're done at the church, you'll return to Windermere with me. Agreed?"

Chapter 3

Gavin could not believe she'd put his back to the wall so effectively.

Clearly, Christina Warner was a force to be reckoned with. She was not about to make a quick trip to Windermere for his benefit while there might be information to be had about her brother. It would be a wild-goose chase, but Gavin had no choice but to help her if he wanted his ten thousand pounds from Windermere.

"You realize things might be exactly as they seem," he said, getting back at her just a little. He supposed he could throw her over his shoulder and tie her to his horse, just as he'd threatened, but Windermere was more than sixty miles away. He needed her cooperation.

She refused to yield. "Or the blackmailer might have some new information."

"It's hardly likely."

She shuddered in her chair and then stood quickly,

as though she wanted to step out of her own skin for a moment. Her ties were obviously much closer to her adoptive family than Gavin's were to his own father and brother. "So you expect me to ignore the possibility that Lang is alive and . . . and could be in trouble? Or in need?"

"Why wouldn't he have contacted someone in that case?"

"Because he's Lang. He's always been . . . unpredictable."

Gavin believed she was being generous with her description, but gave her a short, resigned nod. "All right. I'll go to All Hallows Church and see what I can do."

"Thank you." She appeared relieved that she did not have to consider any dire possibilities. At least, not at the moment.

"We ought to leave now," Gavin said. If they went right away, they could make Windermere by tomorrow night. He only had to convince Lady Fairhaven that would be best.

"Not until the doctor has seen to your arm."

"My arm is not an issue," he said, approaching her. He looked dark and dangerous. "Pack what you need and . . . Do you have a carriage?"

"No, we came on horseback." She gestured to the clothes she wore, and Gavin realized she was pointing out that it was a riding habit.

"Perfect. Much faster that way."

"Captain Briggs, I—"

"I repeat." He took her arm and turned her toward

the front door. "If we start now, we can make forty miles before dark."

He started moving her along, but she stopped dead in her tracks. "But Alfred—"

"Leave him a note." He drew out a few coins and dropped them on the writing table. "This should cover his trouble and that of the doctor as well."

"Unhand me, Captain Briggs," Christina said, breaking his grasp on her and turning to face him. "You realize it is entirely improper for me to travel alone with you? We must stop at Holywell House—"

"There is no time for that. Holywell House is completely out of the way."

Not completely. It was only a slight deviation to the east. Fortunately, her mother-in-law had not been in residence when Christina had arrived the previous evening. She always felt like an undesirable child in Leticia's presence. The older woman had not been pleased with Edward's marriage, and Christina had come to realize Edward had married her only for political gain. He'd wanted her father's favor. "It will not take long—"

"Aye. It will. We can ride to Windermere first and—"

"*Windermere!*" She narrowed her eyes. "We agreed there is no time for any such diversion."

"Lady Fairhaven—"

"I will return to Windermere with you after." She swallowed. This could be it. The rendezvous in the church could provide her with crucial information about Lang. She was not going to chance missing it, even to meet her sister. "I promised to go to Windermere with you after we deal with matters in London, and I stand by my word, Captain Briggs."

She made an attempt to dismiss him from her mind, but found she could not. The thought of spending several days and nights with the man while they traveled together was all too intriguing to be strictly proper.

And altogether impossible. She sat down at the writing table and jotted a quick note to Alfred, then turned to speak to Captain Briggs. "I'm quite sorry, Captain, but we—" she said, but he'd already walked out of the house and was standing on the front drive. She rose from her chair and followed him outside, putting her note to Alfred on the top step, along with Captain Briggs's coins.

He stood waiting impatiently, and Christina reminded herself that she was a viscountess, a woman of some authority and mistress of her own fate, even though she did not feel it.

She took a moment to put on her hat, then pulled on her riding gloves, and assumed the haughtiest attitude she could muster as she approached him, carrying her satchel full of Fairhaven jewelry. She had no doubt it would bring at least two thousand pounds. Some of the pieces were absolutely breathtaking.

But she didn't want any of it. They were only reminders of the husband who had held such little respect for her.

Christina did not know what would happen in

London, but she was absolutely certain she needed to have the two thousand ready . . . just in case. There were several reputable jewelers in town, any of whom would be pleased to buy her treasure. She was sure she could get a good price for each piece.

"Captain Briggs."

He turned impatiently toward her.

"I am sure you are aware that I cannot travel with you alone, sir. As I attempted to tell you before, we must go to Holywell House and fetch my maid. And I'll need my carriage, since I'll have to bring luggage. And my footmen. For safety, of course."

Gavin stood perfectly still as Lady Fairhaven walked past him down to the gravel drive. She moved with purpose, heading toward the stable a short distance from the house.

Short of tossing her over his shoulder and carrying her all the way to Windermere, he was not going to get her to Windermere in the next couple of days. He sighed, unable to keep from feeling more than slightly irritated by the turn of events.

And he'd thought it would be simple once he'd discovered who Windermere's second granddaughter was.

He understood she had little enough reason to want to meet the grandfather who'd abandoned her. But Gavin had seen the spark of interest in her eyes at the mention of meeting her sister. He knew it was a large part of Lily's reason for going to Windermere Park.

Gavin had to give it one more try, to see if he could entice her to Windermere rather than riding all the way to Holywell to collect her maid and her carriage.

He caught up to her. "Lily is your twin, you know. You're identical in appearance, your voice, your mannerisms . . ."

It caught her off guard. Christina stood still as Gavin walked on, her hand pressed against the center of her chest. "Identical?"

He nodded. "Born the same day, only a few minutes apart. The sixth of April." He'd found himself wishing he'd located Lily a few weeks earlier, before she'd arrived at Ashby Hall and met the earl she'd married. Lily was a modest, sweet-tempered young woman, raised in humble surroundings—quite unlike her sister, the very epitome of all that Gavin despised in the aristocracy. Perhaps if he'd met Lily before Lord Ashby . . .

He brought himself up short. It was water over the dam. He'd been summoned to Windermere by the dying duke merely to find the old man's granddaughters and bring them back to Windermere Park. For that, the duke would pay him an exorbitant fee.

In retrospect, Gavin should have realized the duke's heir, Baron Chetwood, would cause trouble. Gavin recalled a chance encounter with the baron and his wife before he set out in search of Lily and Christina.

The two of them had come like carrion birds to await the old duke's death, but when it became obvious that Windermere was not quite ready to give up the ghost, Chetwood's frustrations erupted. Gavin had come upon them in a small parlor at Windermere Park while they were in the midst of a serious argument.

Gavin happened into the room just as Lady Chetwood spat, "You wouldn't dare!"

At that, Chetwood grabbed his wife's arm. "Just watch me," he growled, raising his fist. It seemed to Gavin the man was about to strike her, but stopped cold when he caught sight of Gavin, then spun away from his wife, his face red, his fury barely under control.

With considerable distress, Lady Chetwood had quit the room in haste, and Gavin followed suit. He had not realized at the time that Chetwood would become his problem. Though it had been clear the baron was capable of substantial violence, Gavin did not expect the man to go after Windermere's granddaughters. He'd only subsequently learned that Chetwood was a prominent member of the depraved Hellfire Club.

One serious attempt had been made on Lily's life, and Gavin made the logical assumption that Lord Chetwood had been responsible for it. He knew the baron was a greedy lout with extravagant tastes who had not taken well to sharing Windermere's fortune.

In order to protect Christina, Lily's husband, Lord Ashby, intended to visit Windermere and see that he changed the idiotic stipulation that required his granddaughters to come to him before they would be eligible to inherit. Ashby would convince the old duke that Chetwood ought not to inherit either Lily's or Christina's portions under any circumstances. That way, the baron would have no reason to do away with either of the two sisters.

"The ride to Holywell is an unnecessary delay, Lady Fairhaven," he said, hoping to sway her. "You could make your sister's acquaintance before we go to London . . ."

She raised her chin and continued her march toward the stable, her stride that of a self-assured viscountess. "There is no time."

"We can make the time."

"Now that I know I have a sister, Captain Briggs, I will meet her. But not until I deal with the situation at All Hallows Church. That must come first."

"If we ride to Windermere, we can leave from there—"

"I will not travel without my maid."

"Your entourage, you mean," he muttered. He'd known any discussion would be futile, but he'd had to try it.

"I beg your pardon?" she asked.

"Then let's head to Holywell, by all means." He could not keep the sarcasm from his voice.

Gavin had not spent much time in Britain during the past decade. Early in his career, he'd been recruited by Colonel Manningham to become a rifleman, and distinguished himself while an officer in the Ninety-fifth Rifle Regiment. Soon afterward, he'd been tapped by Lord Castlereagh to become a specialized agent of the crown—sometimes seeking information on enemy movements, other times eliminating threats with a well-placed bullet. This was what his father had wanted to know—details about activities Gavin intended never to share with anyone.

He'd been away when his younger sister's pregnancy had become visible—and his father had tossed her out. Gavin had heard of Eleanor's difficulties only when their cousin, Hettie Mills, had written him from London.

Eleanor had always been a quiet girl, far too meek for her own good. Their mother's death had put Eleanor squarely at the mercy of their father and their taunting elder brother, Clifford. Neither was disposed to be kind to such a docile child as Eleanor, though Gavin had done what he could to protect her from their malice.

He regretted having been unaware of her predicament and unable to be there to protect her during her most serious time of need.

Fortunately, Hettie had opened her modest home to Eleanor before the child was born. But *un*fortunately, Cousin Hettie's circumstances were nearly as dire as Eleanor's. And now that her meager income was supporting Eleanor as well as her little daughter, life had become increasingly difficult. Gavin needed to intervene. He'd sent money, of course, but he was not a wealthy man.

Not yet. But once he collected his fee for finding the Windermere granddaughters, there was a manor house and small estate in Hampshire that he intended to purchase. It was a place where he could retire in peace, where Eleanor and her child could live in comfort and free from worry.

For years, he'd thought about finding a tidy little piece of land where he could make his home with Amelia Winter, but that was not to be. The woman he'd loved since his youth had wed another while he was away. Lady Amelia had become the wife of an earl whose status was far more favorable than that of a viscount's younger son and former officer in His Majesty's army.

Her jilting had stung badly. Amelia had known Gavin would never inherit anything of significance from his tightfisted father, but she'd promised him her heart anyway, insisting it did not matter. She'd written often to say she anxiously awaited his return from the continent. But everything had changed during the last year of the war. The letters had become less frequent, their tone more distant. Something had definitely been amiss.

Gavin knew it was pointless now to reflect upon Amelia's perfidy. He supposed it was better this way, since she would eventually discover what his primary function had been while in Lord Castlereagh's service.

And she would be appalled.

What gentlewoman would want a former assassin for a husband? Especially one with few prospects beyond his army pension?

Gavin's assignment from Windermere had been an unexpected boon, one that would provide him with an income that was far more than he ever expected. He intended for Weybrook Manor in Hampshire to be a new beginning, not only for himself, but for his sister. She was unknown in Hampshire, so there was no reason that anyone would ask about her daughter's legitimacy. Their neighbors need never know that little Rachel's father had been killed while serving in France before he'd had the chance to marry her mother.

It was also an ideal place for Gavin to try to assuage his conscience and forget all that he'd been required to do during the past few years in Castlereagh's service. Best yet was that Weybrook was far removed from Durham, so neither he nor his sister would be subject to the disdain of their arrogant father and brother.

Gavin considered his current mission and vowed it would be his last. He could not begrudge Lady Fairhaven wanting to know the truth about her brother, much as he wanted to. Because if Gavin had learned of Eleanor's death, and then the possibility that she was alive, he would do all he could to pursue the matter. So he would help Christina determine what had happened to Lang, and then drag the woman back to Windermere by her hair—by those fascinating curls—if need be.

Then he could buy his property and spend his hours poring over the agricultural journals he'd acquired in anticipation of becoming a gentleman farmer.

Gavin followed Christina into the stable. She

stood awash in light from one of the high windows as she reached up to slide the bridle over the horse's head. She looked like some kind of ethereal being— an angel or a—

Gavin gave a quick shake of his head to force a return to sanity. Christina was naught but the high-and-mighty daughter of a man who had inherited his power and influence. She was naught to Gavin but a very troublesome means to a ten-thousand-pound prize.

For that kind of money, Gavin should have known the quest would not be an easy one.

Christina fastened the buckles, then reached for her saddle, surprising him with her initiative. He let her lift the saddle, but took it from her before she had to carry it to the horse. In all fairness, he would not have made his sister do this herself, either. There were certain things a lady should not be required to do.

He secured her saddle and the satchel containing her valuables, then turned to her. "Allow me," he said, offering to lift her onto the horse.

"But your arm—"

"Is hardly worth noting." Although he did not mind letting her feel some guilt over it.

She moved to the horse's near side and when Gavin stepped close and placed his hands at her waist, he caught her scent. It reminded him of a rich delicacy—something he could sink his teeth into and savor. A tempting morsel. Small wisps of her silken hair curled about her ears, and her lashes were spikes of coal black, framing expressive eyes as green as spring grass.

Gavin blew out a breath of air and lifted her easily, then stepped away as she settled herself on her saddle.

It was just as well that they would take her carriage to London. It would prevent him from having to wrap his hands about her waist every time she mounted and dismounted. With Christina inside her carriage, Gavin might be able to lose the imprint of her appealing, feminine body from his hands.

Now that his return to Windermere was so effectively thwarted, he was in no real hurry. It was unlikely that Lang was still alive, no matter what the blackmail note said. Gavin thought it might actually be better if they didn't make it on time for her appointment at All Hallows Church. It would save them all a lot of trouble.

Christina could not imagine what had caused her to shiver as Captain Briggs lifted her onto her mare. She was not cold in her snug riding habit. On the contrary, she felt quite warm. She just hoped she was not coming down with something. She had no time for illness, not now, when she actually had a plan for dealing with her blackmailer.

She waited as Captain Briggs walked out of the stable, pulling on his jacket and greatcoat as he moved. With a tight agility that gave her pause, he swung himself up onto his horse and started down the drive, quite obviously expecting her to follow.

Which she did.

He rode without talking to her, annoyed, she supposed, at being forced to help her in London. But what else was she to do? He was a godsend—help that she had never expected.

"How do you think we should handle the situation at All Hallows Church?" she asked her companion. Not that they were companions, exactly. He was her unwilling escort.

Well, it was no matter. She refused to be intimidated by him.

"I have no idea."

"What do you mean? Surely you have dealt with . . . with . . ."

"Blackmailers?"

"Well, perhaps not exactly blackmailers, but possibly in the army, you—"

"Is that what you think of our British military, Lady Fairhaven? That we're all rogues and scoundrels?"

"Of course not. I just—"

"You just thought I would know the workings of a blackmailer's mind."

"Do not put words into my mouth, Captain Briggs." How he managed to anger her. "I only meant that . . . Well, you have the look of someone who can . . . someone who has . . . You've probably dealt with disreputable characters in the past." He looked rather disreputable himself. She'd seen the scars on his body, any of which could have been the result of a serious wound.

His right brow lowered. "Disreputable?"

"Please do not take offense, Captain Briggs," Christina said, exasperated. "I merely meant to say that the army . . . well, you are an officer—"

"*Was* an officer."

She moistened her lips. "Did you never have to deal with any reprobates under your command?"

Briggs gave a nearly imperceptible shake of his head. "No," he said—with distaste, if she was not mistaken. "Tell me, Lady Fairhaven, what you expect me to do."

She plucked a bit of lint from her sleeve as they trotted along, and tried not to feel self-conscious. Of course, she had no right to ask him to help her. But neither had he any right to take her to the man who admitted abandoning her as a young child. "I am not quite sure."

"The blackmailer's letter instructed you to leave the money in a packet inside the lectern at the back of All Hallows Church. Were you planning to do so?"

"My first thought was to put the money in the lectern and then lie in wait."

"With the pistol, I presume." His tone was slightly condescending, and beyond annoying. It was not *his* brother who was in jeopardy.

"Yes." Clearly, taking the pistol had not been a very good idea. *And* she had shot him. But still . . .

"Are you familiar with the area around All Hallows Church?" he asked.

She let her gaze drop just below his shoulder. The bullet had created a small, frayed hole. She cringed inwardly, recognizing, not for the first time, that he had ample reason to be put out with her. "No," she replied. "I've only been to the Tower once, and we did not spend any time nearby."

She'd gone with Edward while they were courting. Her mother had accompanied them, of course, along with her youngest brother, Colin. The family had all been in favor of her marriage to Edward. He'd been a wealthy peer, with a reputation as a responsible, fair man. A woman who was merely the adopted daughter of an earl could have done far worse.

But Christina wondered if her father would have been quite so favorable toward the marriage if he'd known about Mrs. Shilton—Edward's mistress. Apparently, Edward's arrangement with Mrs. Shilton had not been altered by his marriage—much to his detriment. Her parents had not been able to hide from Christina the circumstances of his death, distressing as they were.

"Then you are likely unaware that there are several entrances to the church, as well as an undercroft," Captain Briggs said, interrupting her thoughts.

"Undercroft?"

"Aye. A lower level beneath the church—a cellar."

"Then I am very glad of your assistance, Captain . . . or shall I call you Mr. Briggs?"

He turned to face forward. "Whatever you prefer."

She found she could not think of him as anything but "Captain" Briggs, not when he carried such an air of command.

"Given the geography of the church," she said, "what do you think we ought to do?"

"If we are to cover every entrance, then we'll need assistance."

She shook her head. "No. The fewer people who are involved, the better." She did not know what they were going to learn about Lang, and she wanted to keep his affairs private. It would not do to jeopardize Lang's and the family's reputations, not when Felton was about to make a brilliant marriage to the Marquess of Bedlington's daughter.

Captain Briggs's brow darkened slightly in disagreement, but Christina was undeterred.

"If we keep to a schedule, we can arrive in London at least a day or two in advance of the date I am to leave the money at the church, can we not?" Christina asked. "Which should give us ample opportunity to explore the possibilities at All Hallows, after I sell the jewels."

He made no reply, beyond a nearly inaudible sigh.

Chapter 4

Holywell House was a large manor, similar in design and size to Gavin's house—or rather, the house he hoped would be his when he finally had the funds to purchase it. He could hardly believe he was being thwarted when he was so close.

He could write Eleanor to let her know of the delay, but since he was going to London himself, he decided to tell her in person. He had some money now . . . Eleanor and Hettie were welcome to all of it, for there would soon be more. He only had to get Christina back to Windermere to collect it.

A groom ran from the stable to the front of the house and assisted Lady Fairhaven to dismount, relieving Gavin of that task. He was grateful, he had nearly forgotten her scent and the sensation of her body so close to his during their long ride.

Gavin did not care to refresh his memory. He was looking for peace—not for a liaison with a woman who had known wealth and prestige all her life and would have extravagant expectations. As Amelia obviously did.

He took his travel bag from his saddle and walked into the house behind Christina, far too aware of her removing her hat and gloves, freeing those shining curls and baring her delicate hands.

She spoke in quiet tones to the housekeeper, requesting that a guest room be prepared for him. Gavin knew it was pointless to protest, to try once again to convince her to take a side trip to Windermere with him before leaving for London.

Gavin took his leave of the obstinate woman, and followed a footman to a well-appointed guest bedroom. It was more comfortable than any of the rooms he'd let during his travels to find Windermere's granddaughters, and far grander than any place he'd stayed on the continent. He was never opposed to sleeping in comfort, for he knew their journey to London was not likely to be quite so easy. They would have to make better than thirty miles a day in order to make it to Town in time to deal with Christina's blackmailer.

Not that he shared her urgency to do so.

He went to the window and looked out at the rolling hills surrounding the Holywell estate, all covered with the new growth of spring. The various shades of green brought Lady Fairhaven's eyes to mind, and Gavin turned away from the window, quite unwilling to reflect on anything to do with the viscountess.

Her remark about her husband's mistress—not to mention her cautious manner with Holywell's housekeeper—gave him pause. There'd been a vague catch in her voice when speaking of the jewels her husband had given away, and her tone with the housekeeper was not at all in keeping with that of an arrogant, pampered noblewoman.

He shook his head. No conjecture about her mattered in the least. Whatever else she might be, Christina, Lady Fairhaven, was the key to his ten thousand pounds, which he had every intention of collecting.

He wondered if he would be able to convince her during their journey to London that there was no point in trying to trap the blackmailer. Because he seriously doubted it could be done.

Christina congratulated herself. She had not wrung her hands or betrayed any other sign of nervousness when dealing with Mrs. Fields, her mother-in-law's housekeeper. "Steadfast Guardian of the House" was more like it. During Christina's rare visits to Holywell, she tried not to allow Mrs. Fields to intimidate her, but rarely succeeded.

If Christina had kept ownership of the house and refuted Leticia's claim to it, she would certainly have dismissed Mrs. Fields and brought in someone more suitable.

But Christina had not wanted to keep the house where she had never felt comfortable, even with Edward. More importantly, she hadn't cared to scrap with Edward's mother over the provisions of his will. Edward had clearly left the house to his wife, but since Leticia wanted it, Christina had capitulated.

The whole affair had required numerous meet-
ings with solicitors and seemingly countless signatures, which kept Christina from going to Italy with
her family. But it had seemed the right thing to do.

Holywell had been Leticia's home far longer than
Christina had had any claim to it, and Mrs. Fields
was the dowager's faithful minion, full of disdainful
airs. Quite obviously, she had disapproved of Christina's marriage to Edward as much as his mother.

Of course, as she was Edward's widow and the
rightful beneficiary of Holywell House, no one
would challenge Christina's right to use the house on
occasion, and it suited her now. She had been pleased
to find none of her in-laws in residence on her arrival the night before. Not that she minded Edward's
brother and his wife so much . . . but her mother-in-
law was the most daunting woman Christina had
ever met. She felt quite fortunate that their paths
had crossed only two or three times since Edward's
death.

Christina had made the long trip from London
already, and ridden all the way from Conistone the
day before. Since she had arrived too late to go on
to Sweethope for the jewels, she'd spent the night at
Holywell House and ridden to the cottage that morning. She and Captain Briggs had made good time on
their return to Holywell, but it was too late to begin
their journey to London. She had to spend one more
night at Leticia's house.

But at least now she had Captain Briggs, who
provided her with some hope of catching the black-

mailer. They would be on their way in the morning, one step closer to discovering where Lang was and what he had supposedly done.

She waited for Briggs to be taken to his room before starting up the stairs toward her own, but was stopped by the housekeeper before she'd climbed one step. "My lady," Mrs. Fields said. "Lady Fairhaven is in residence. She arrived soon after your departure this morning."

Christina tried not to show her chagrin. All those signatures at the solicitor's office meant that her mother-in-law had every right to be there. But Christina would have preferred not to see the woman anytime soon.

She raised her chin and spoke with a confidence she did not feel. As her mother had always told her, attitude meant everything. "Did my mother-in-law order supper?"

"Yes. We told her you were expected back."

"Thank you, Mrs. Fields. Whatever Lady Fairhaven ordered will be acceptable."

As much as she preferred to keep her business to herself, Christina could not keep Captain Briggs's presence from Leticia. She supposed she could ask that he take his meals alone in his room, but one of the servants would undoubtedly mention that a strange man had come back from Sweethope Cottage with her. Without Alfred.

She started for her bedchamber, unbuttoning her pelisse as she climbed the stairs. Lady Fairhaven need not learn anything about the blackmailer's demands for money. As far as her mother-in-law and everyone else knew, Lang had perished three months ago in the explosion at Plymouth.

Perhaps Lady Fairhaven would make an attempt to treat her with some unaccustomed gentility. How novel that would be. She had not even thanked Christina for ceding Holywell to her. Clearly, the woman believed it had been hers in spite of Edward's will.

Christina still wondered if her mother-in-law had known of her husband's liaison with Mrs. Shilton. The death of her son in his mistress's arms was an awkward subject, one of which they had never spoken. But the circumstances of Edward's death had not been kept secret, and all of society had learned of her husband's incredibly bad taste to have been caught dead in such a situation.

Christina had turned to her mother in her grief and shame. All at once, she and the rest of society had discovered she was an inadequate wife. Everyone knew her husband had found it necessary to turn to another woman for his satisfaction.

Her mother had tried to soothe her by saying that many gentlemen of society kept mistresses. But Christina had challenged that notion, offering her own father as an example. Lord Sunderland had never kept a ladybird, not when he was so openly affectionate and devoted to his wife. Her parents enjoyed a lusty marriage, and were not shy about demonstrating their devotion to each other.

Clearly, not all men of society were unfaithful pigs.

Christina did not care to share any more personal information with society—or with her late husband's mother. She had little connection with the woman anymore, anyway. Her second son had become viscount, and now Leticia pinned all her hopes on him and his wife—a woman who had already borne two children, a boy and a girl.

She proceeded to the top of the stairs and turned in the opposite direction of her own bedchamber. No one was in the corridor, so there was no one to note her direction toward the guest bedroom at the opposite end of the staircase from her own.

She tapped lightly at the door, and Captain Briggs pulled it open, standing half dressed once again, his hair and chest moist from a recent washing. Her mouth went dry and the ability for rational thought escaped her.

He'd shaved and combed back his hair, making him appear civilized, and yet somehow more dis-reputable than before.

She pushed into the room and closed the door behind her.

"My lady, is there something . . . I can do for you?" His arm was still wrapped in the bandage she'd put on him earlier, but blood had seeped through it. No doubt someone in the house would have some salve and a fresh bandage for him. She would make a point of asking one of the footmen to see to it.

She clasped her hands together and averted her eyes from his naked form. "I don't want anyone to know I've come to your room."

"Yes, I can see that."

She bristled. "Pray, do not think of entertaining any untoward ideas, Captain Briggs. I've come to tell you . . . My m-mother-in-law is in residence. And she knows nothing of this business with Lang."

He lowered his dark brow. "Of course not. That *is* the point of blackmail."

"Well, yes, but I thought . . ." He wiped a bit of shaving soap from his neck, and her eyes seemed to lock onto the spot. "I-I thought we ought to agree on an explanation for why you are here."

"What about the truth?"

She raised her eyes abruptly. "No! I don't want her thinking any—"

"The truth about you being Windermere's grand-daughter," he said. "That is no secret. Your sister will have already made her visit to the duke by now, and you will do so soon."

Christina felt her heart pounding in her throat. Of course. She had hardly given any thought to Windermere, the situation with Lang being foremost on her mind.

And catching Captain Briggs in the intimate act of shaving had disconcerted her, scattering any coherent thoughts from her mind. She really ought to go.

"Yes. Right," she said.

"As far as I know, you are mourning your brother as well as your late husband."

She put her hand over her heart. "Thank you, Captain Briggs. I appreciate your discretion."

"Anything to get you to Windermere," he said,

pulling his clean shirt over his head, "and the sooner the better."

"Supper will be served soon," she said. "But I'll send someone up to see to your arm."

"Not necessary."

"If you're afraid to be stitched—"

"No, Lady Fairhaven, I—"

"All right then, there must be some healing liniment or salve and some bandaging cloth about the house." She saw his ruined shirt draped over a chair.

"No one need bother."

She picked up the shirt. "I'll have someone mend this for you before we leave in the morning."

Gavin watched the door close behind Lady Fairhaven. She was a whirlwind of agitation and worry.

Not that she need have any concerns on his account. She might be the most novel female he'd ever seen, with her cropped hair and flashing green eyes, but he had no use for her, beyond getting her to Windermere in order to collect his money.

He supposed Christina had good reason to be worried. He would not enjoy being in her position—being the victim of a blackmailer. She clearly cared for her brother and was hopeful for proof that he was alive. And to find out what kind of trouble he'd gotten into.

If he'd gotten into anything at all. Sadly, Gavin did not believe Christina would ever glean the information she sought from the blackmailer.

He wondered who it might be. A shipmate, perhaps. But why extort money from his sister? The earl was likely deeper in the pockets than his daughter.

It must be that by the time the blackmail plot was hatched, the earl and his family had decamped to Italy. It would be much more difficult, if not impossible, to extort money from him at this juncture, and Christina didn't have the option of putting off her blackmailer's demands while she awaited her father's assistance.

It gave rise to a number of questions. Gavin decided to find a moment alone with Christina after supper to ask them.

It was just dark when Gavin descended the staircase to join Christina in the dining room. He assumed the elder Lady Fairhaven would be present as well, and did not look forward to spending an evening in idle chitchat. He met no one as he made his way to the dining room, but heard voices as he approached.

"—unseemly to be seen gallivanting about, Christina. Though I don't suppose I should have expected any better of you."

"Mother, I have barely left Sunderland House since Edward died. And now, with Lang—"

"And that hair. Whatever possessed you to chop it all off?"

The old woman did not give Christina the opportunity to answer, and Gavin found himself feeling some sympathy for her.

"I told Edward he erred in choosing you. But his word was good as gold, and he would not renege on his promise to your father."

"Some would say I was the one who erred in marrying your philandering son, Lady Fairhaven," Christina retorted, but in a deceptively civil tone. Gavin nearly applauded her brass.

"Well! I'm sure I nev—"

"Mother, please. Might we eat our meal in peace this evening?" Her voice turned far more respectful than the old lady deserved, and Gavin would not have blamed Christina if she spit in the old lady's eye and left the table. "Besides, I have some news."

"The only news of interest would have been that you had borne Edward's child. But of course that is im—"

"We will have a guest for dinner."

"You dare invite a guest to my house?"

Gavin's vague annoyance turned into something darker and a bit more dangerous.

There was a long, charged silence before Christina spoke, and Gavin felt the same as he had before a kill, tense and focused.

The old lady spoke again. "You might consider tempering your—"

Gavin strode into the room. "Good evening, ladies."

Christina's mother-in-law looked up at him in surprise, with more than a little disdain. Gavin spared barely a glance to Christina, but could not help but note that she had changed out of her riding clothes and into a charcoal-gray gown with black trim. Its scooped neck gave only a hint of the swells of her breasts and showed her delicate collarbones to perfection.

"Mother, here is the guest to whom I—"

"Yes, yes, I can see that." Lady Fairhaven held up a quizzing glass, studying him in as imperious a manner as Gavin's pompous father would have done. His already formidable dislike of her grew. "Who is he?"

Gavin gave a bow and smiled, though he did not feel the least bit friendly toward the old harpy. "Captain Gavin Briggs, at your service, my lady."

"Briggs." Frowning, she glanced over his form, from the top of his head to the floor.

Gavin had learned long ago never to allow himself to feel intimidated by those who believed themselves superior. He had lived for many years with his father and brother at Seaholm Hall, therefore, he knew better.

"You were a friend of my son's?" she asked.

"No, my lady, much to my regret, I'm sure. I've come to—"

"I know of a family called Briggs, from Durham." She gave him a sidelong glance. "You have the look of them. Tall and dark."

"My father is Oscar Briggs, Viscount Hargrove."

"Hmm," was all she said. She did not smile or give any other indication of recognition. "Be seated, Briggs. You are giving me a cramp from looking up at you."

The old lady was nothing to him. Less than nothing, but her attitude—so much like his father's—rankled. Lady Fairhaven was a woman who'd known wealth and privilege all her life, who felt justified in casting judgment upon others. From his introduction, she had gleaned correctly that he was a younger son, hardly worthy of her notice. No doubt she also would have tossed Eleanor out to fend for herself, even if she did carry her grandchild.

And he found he did not care for her treatment of Christina.

"If you were not one of Edward's friends, what are you doing here?" She cast a suspicious eye toward her daughter-in-law as servants entered the dining chamber and began serving the meal.

"My mission involves Lady Christina Fairhaven." He stated it as though it were an official military assignment, just to put the old woman off her high horse.

He knew he'd succeeded when her hand fluttered to her chest. "What mission?"

"Your daughter-in-law is the long-lost granddaughter of the Duke of Windermere. The duke wishes to see her."

The old woman frowned fiercely. "Nonsense."

"On the contrary, I assure you it is quite true."

The woman turned to Christina. "What say you, young lady?"

"I'm afraid I hardly know what to say. My parents, the Earl and Countess of Sunderland, took me in as a young child . . ."

"Then they are not your parents, are they?" Lady Fairhaven said acerbically.

Christina's head tipped slightly to one side, but her gaze fell unwaveringly upon her mother-in-law. "For all intents and purposes, they are."

Gavin somehow managed to speak civilly to the old lady. "Christina's parents were estranged from the duke at the time of their deaths. And when Windermere learned of the accident, he had his granddaughters given away to families who would care for them."

Lady Fairhaven pursed her lips. "Windermere's son and heir died not long before I lost my Edward."

Gavin gave a slight nod. "That is correct. And that loss, in addition to the duke's poor health, has prompted him to seek out his granddaughters."

"A bit tardy, I would say."

"Be that as it may, I've come to take your daughter-in-law to Windermere."

"When?"

He caught Christina's eye. "As soon as possible. Tomorrow, I hope."

Christina returned her gaze to her plate, but Gavin detected the sudden flush of color on her cheeks.

He had intentionally kept her secret from the old lady and given a legitimate reason for her to leave Holywell House right away. Unfortunately, he did not believe he'd changed her mind about making a detour to Windermere first.

As soon as Christina learned that her mother-in-law had come to Holywell, she'd instructed her maid, Jenny, to pack her things. Whether or not Captain Briggs truly intended to leave on the morrow, she had no intention of staying under the same roof with Lady Fairhaven any longer than absolutely necessary.

How dare Leticia act as though Holywell House had been hers all along? She had not even acknowledged Christina's generosity in transferring the property.

Edward's mother had never cared for her. She'd made it clear she favored a cousin—her brother's daughter—for her son's wife, though Edward would not hear of it. He'd called Viola a horse-faced birdwit.

Christina had been appalled at the insult of his own cousin, but she'd been secretly pleased that he'd chosen her. He'd been handsome and erudite, and the fact that he'd preferred her when he could have had any other young lady had been heady, indeed.

But the weeks after their union had shown her the error of her maidenly expectations. Edward had not given their marriage a chance to thrive, not even visiting her bed frequently enough to give her a child. Little had she known he would not convey his entire allegiance to his wife, but exclude her from all but the most mundane aspects of wifehood.

What she shared with Edward had been so very different from her own parents' marriage, she could not help but be disappointed. Her mother's advice had been to give it time. Surely, the marriage would succeed if Christina could be patient. After all, Edward had been a bachelor for a very long time.

Jenny helped Christina to undress, and she

donned the chemise she'd had made specifically for her marriage bed.

What a jest that had been. Edward had not noticed it, not even once, in spite of the fact that it was nearly transparent. Christina had not considered the possibility that he was not as anxious to share marital intimacies as she was. She'd worn the pretty chemise thinking to entice him, to seduce him.

Her wedding night had been very different from the impression Christina's mother had given her during their private talk before the wedding. Clearly, her parents enjoyed something very special, else her mother would not have filled Christina's head with tales of sweet seduction and gentle lovemaking. Christina had experienced neither during the six months she'd been married.

She sat down at her dressing table and picked up Captain Briggs's torn shirt. "That will be all, Jenny."

"You should let me do that, my lady," Jenny said, reaching for it.

Christina shook her head. "You know you're terrible with needle and thread."

"Aye, I am," Jenny replied. "Your mother should have sacked me when she found out."

"You make up for it in other ways," Christina said, for it was true. Jenny was a few years younger than Christina, and a far better companion than most of the young ladies Christina had met during her seasons in London. The young maid was always cheerful, and she had excellent taste in colors and styles. Christina was certain she was the only person on earth who had the ability to put Christina's shorn locks into an arrangement that did not look too ridiculous.

"Go on to bed, Jenny. Sleep well, for tomorrow will be a long day."

Jenny left the room and Christina began to sew by the light of the two sconces in the room. After being scandalized by Christina's recounting of how she'd injured Captain Briggs, the maid had laundered the shirt and placed it by the fire to dry, but it was still slightly damp. At least the gash in the sleeve was clean.

Sewing soothed Christina. Rhythmically slipping the needle and thread through the fabric of the shirt quieted her nerves after the taxing interlude with Leticia. She had not seen the old woman in months, during which she'd been free of her barbed remarks and blatant insults.

She was surprised the woman had not asked about Sweethope Cottage or the jewelry that now lay carefully spread out on Christina's bed. Some of it looked new, and Christina guessed Edward had purchased it in recent years—whether for her or his mistress, she did not know. But she assumed there must be heirlooms among the older pieces.

She guessed Edward's mother had not known of the safe hidden in the master's bedchamber at Sweethope Cottage, or she'd have demanded its contents along with Holywell House. Christina was not supposed to have known about it, either. But shortly after they'd wed, she'd happened upon Edward taking the key from the top of the armoire and opening it.

She'd felt embarrassed coming upon him in a private moment, and had withdrawn before he noticed her. Now she knew better. It was Edward who had been wrong in keeping secrets from her.

But Christina did not want to dwell on past events. The only point in thinking about them was to avoid making the same mistakes. When she married again, she would know her husband far better than she'd known Edward. She would settle for nothing less than a man who cared for her and wanted her to share his life. Perhaps that was love . . . She did not know.

What she *did* know was that she would not abide another husband who thought more often of his horses and his London diversions than he did of his wife. Next time, her marriage would be a love match. Perhaps one of her former suitors would still want her. Lords Marsham and Everhart had courted her avidly, though both had been rejected for various reasons by her father. And there had been others, such as Marquess Gerville and Viscount Brundle—not as pleasing to her, but perhaps she had changed. Or *they* had.

She caught sight of her reflection in the glass and managed to refrain from touching her hair.

Her shorn tresses were more than a slight embarrassment. Christina had cut her hair in a burst of pique after her sister-in-law had remarked on how much Edward had loved it.

Christina had known that was patently untrue.

Edward had not loved her in the least, but had married her for her dowry and her connection to the Earl of Sunderland. To Christina's knowledge, Edward had not loved anything about her, besides her status.

How he would have enjoyed learning she was the granddaughter of a duke, she thought bitterly.

She finished mending the shirt and set it aside, then rose from the cushioned bench, only to stifle a startled squeal. Captain Briggs stood just inside her room with the door closed behind him.

Chapter 5

"What are you doing here!" she hissed. She could not fathom how he'd gotten inside without making any sound.

"Lower your voice, my lady, unless you want everyone to know your secrets."

"My secr—"

"If we leave here at first light, we can make it to Windermere by dusk."

How was she supposed to think when his large, imposing presence dominated everything about the room? When she stood quite exposed before him in her flimsy chemise?

She stood hesitating for a moment, then took the few steps to the bed where her banyan lay on the coverlet beside her cache of jewels. Her revealing chemise had been meant for a husband's eyes, and not those of Gavin Briggs, although Christina found herself surprisingly aware of the masculine appreciation in his eyes. She felt thoroughly brazen as she stood there pulling on her banyan, unable to bring herself to toss him out.

"I must give you credit for your persistence, but as I already said, I have very little interest in meeting the duke."

He stepped closer and Christina felt the shiver of gooseflesh rising on her skin. "Windermere is only a day's ride. We can go to London from there."

From somewhere deep inside, she found the will to give a slow shake of her head. "You know there could be delays under the best of circumstances. And I have little enough time as it is to get to London on the appointed date."

Besides, when Christina met her sister, she would not be hurried. She wanted to have adequate time to spend with her, to get to know her.

A muscle in Captain Briggs's jaw tightened, then relaxed. She hoped it was a sign he was resigned to her decision.

"Then I must know more about your brother."

She took a deep breath. "You should have asked me about him on our ride to Holywell." It was a verbal gibe, for she was quite aware he had been in no mood to talk during their ride from Sweethope Cottage.

His expression darkened, but he made no retort. Nor did his eyes dip below her neck this time. Most improperly, she found herself wishing he would take notice of her again.

But he was a perfect gentleman. Well, she amended, as perfect as a gentleman could be who'd broached a lady's bedchamber when the house was all abed. And perhaps he was not as affected by her appearance as she'd been by his.

He wore the same clean clothes he'd had on at supper, a white shirt, dark green waistcoat, and black jacket. He looked altogether too dashing—and too dangerous—for her peace of mind.

Christina noticed his hands, sun-darkened and large, relaxed at his sides, and could not help but wonder about their touch. Would he be a skilled lover—unlike Edward, who'd never taken any care with her, leaving her feeling frustrated and wishing for something more?

"You realize you should not be here."

"You do not seem overly troubled by my presence." He took a few steps forward, closing the distance between them. He didn't even take notice of the glittering jewels lying on the bed.

Christina forced herself to stay perfectly still, but she had to tip her head back to meet his eyes. "What do you want to know about my brother?"

"Where was he last seen?"

"In a public house with his friend, Lieutenant James Norris."

"Someone questioned Norris?"

Briggs smelled of shaving soap—crisp and clean. And there was the hint of a cleft in his angular chin. "Lieutenant Norris and Lang were good friends. He was given leave to come and see my father when Lang . . . after the explosion."

"It was Norris who identified Lang's body?"

She nodded and noticed his gaze flash to her hair. How she wished she'd kept her long, wavy locks. Perhaps then it would have been a more admiring glance.

But he lifted one hand and touched a wayward curl at the side of her face, and she lost track of his question.

Apparently, so did he. "Whatever possessed you to do this?"

She felt a wave of defeat, aware that she looked absurd. "I know I shouldn't have—"

"On the contrary, Lady Fairhaven. It's outstanding."

Christina's hair was far more than outstanding. Gavin's fingers itched to do more than just touch one of those audacious curls, and her nearness trumped his frustration at not being able to take her to Windermere right away.

He knew it had been a mistake to come into her bedchamber, especially after he saw her wearing the thin, gossamer gown. It was like a second skin, baring just enough feminine flesh to whet his appetite, its shadows hinting at the lush curves beneath.

He should have turned right around and left her bedroom, except that he could not help but touch one of the shining black locks that curled at her temple. It was incredibly soft, its scent teasing him to bury his face in it.

And more.

God, he was a fool.

"Was Norris caught in the explosion, too?" He

lowered his hand and turned his attention from the sweet line of her jaw in order to focus on his questions.

She took a breath that sounded shaky to his ears. He had to give her credit for not screeching and summoning a footman to toss him out.

"No. The lieutenant said he and Lang went together to pick up their mail," she said as she returned to her dressing table and sat down. The pale green banyan did not afford him the same alluring view as before, but he appreciated the elegant line of her back and the sweet spot just below her short curls. He thought it would taste just as—

"Then they stopped in a dockside tavern to celebrate passing their lieutenant's examinations. Lang seemed disturbed by a letter he received but would say nothing about it. He left soon afterward to . . . to answer the call of nature, Lieutenant Norris thought. He never saw Lang again."

Gavin took a seat on the boudoir chair next to the incredible glittering treasure laid out on the bed, resulting in a surprised flaring of Christina's expressive green eyes. He'd shocked her again, and still she did not protest his presence. She was not quite the stiff and reserved viscountess his mother had been. And she was nothing at all like her mother-in-law.

He was not sure exactly what to make of her. She had more audacity than any society wench he'd ever known—taking her husband's pistol with the intention of dealing with her blackmailer alone . . .

And yet she'd allowed old Lady Fairhaven to belittle her mercilessly before Gavin's arrival in the dining room.

He'd have told the old battle-ax to go hang.

"Sailors don't generally stop for one drink," he said, ridding himself of the unexpected wave of empathy for the woman who was impeding his plans. "How long were they together in the tavern?"

"I don't know," she replied with a small frown. Her voice was rich and smooth, like his father's best brandy, which was a timely reminder that she belonged to his father's class—she was the widow of a viscount.

"They were joined at the tavern by another man . . . an acquaintance of mine . . . a former suitor, actually."

It probably meant nothing. "Who was this suitor? Your father questioned him, of course?"

"It was Viscount Brundle," she said, and Gavin noticed a little shudder of distaste at the mention of his name. "His estate is near Plymouth. And yes, my father questioned him, but Brundle left before Lang, so learned nothing new."

Of course not. They'd probably gotten soused, and when Lang Jameson left the tavern, he'd obviously gotten caught up in the mishap at the warehouse. And paid for it with his life. "How long after your brother left the tavern did the explosion occur?"

"Lieutenant Norris was not sure . . ." Her eyes shimmered slightly, and Gavin realized she was holding back tears of distress. "They . . . I believe they'd been drinking quite a bit."

"As sailors are wont to do," Gavin said to himself.

There wasn't any point in prolonging her anguish, because it was hardly likely that Lang had survived and gone on to commit some kind of offense for which his family could be blackmailed.

But he'd promised to escort her to London and see what they could learn. Unfortunately, he knew the news was not going to be good.

"*The Defender* is at sea once again." Her voice quivered. "Would it help if you spoke to Lieutenant Norris yourself? Or perhaps Lord Brundle?"

Gavin hardened his heart against any feelings of sympathy. The woman had shot him! And now she wanted him to travel with a treasure that most men would kill for. His task for Windermere had become absurd.

"We could detour to Plymouth first. Before London," Christina suggested.

That was all he needed. One more bloody destination, carrying a cache of valuable jewelry with them.

"But no, there won't be time to do both," she said, frowning in thought, answering her own question.

"No. One destination or the other, but not both." Gavin stood. It was time to get out of there, before his urge to touch more than her springy curls overcame his better judgment. "We'll go to All Hallows by the Tower on the appointed day and see if we can find your extortionist."

"And if we don't see him?"

"I agreed to go to the church with you, Lady Fairhaven. Not solve your problems for you."

Captain Briggs barely greeted Christina the following morning, but she approached him before he mounted his horse. "Captain Briggs."

He removed his hat and tipped his head slightly.

"Your shirt." She handed him the shirt she had mended and Jenny had folded neatly, hoping he had not noticed it on her dressing table the night before. She did not care to make it known—especially to Leticia—that she had completed the task herself. What would her mother-in-law say to that?

Captain Briggs took the garment from her, not once taking his eyes from hers. "My thanks, Lady Fairhaven. It would have been an inconvenience to do without it."

He slipped his shirt into the satchel behind his saddle, then took the reins from a waiting groom. Christina stepped back, but found herself entirely too distracted by the sight of his powerful thighs flexing as he mounted his horse. She took in a deep breath as he rode up to speak quietly to Hancock, the driver of her carriage.

She wasn't quite sure how to interpret his visit to her bedchamber the night before. At times, his glance had smoldered with sensual promise. But then his expression changed, and held such disdain, she had to wonder if she'd said or done something—besides shooting him, of course—to earn his scorn.

In the end, it was clear she was mistaken about the smolder. He had barely looked at her after taking a seat beside her bed, and she realized he had not found her particularly appealing.

She blushed at the thought of standing so brazenly before him in her bedroom, pulling on her banyan so very casually, as though fascinating gentlemen regularly visited her bedchamber.

What could she have been thinking? She should have turned him out of her room immediately.

He was far too rough and dangerous for her, and too gruff by half. But something about him touched a deep, completely inappropriate craving inside her.

Such foolishness. Christina intended to spend her remaining months of mourning in respectable widowhood, and then perhaps look for a suitable husband of her own choosing. He would be someone who would do more than provide her a home and security, as Edward had done. She wanted children, and most of all, she wanted a spouse who would share his affections with her.

With only her.

She left a note for Edward's mother—being far more gracious and grateful than was really necessary. Or deserved.

In truth, Christina was even more grateful to be leaving, which, of course, she had not added. She had not forgotten how tiresome it was to live under Leticia's disapproving eye, and would not have come to Holywell if she'd known her mother-in-law would be there.

That was another requirement of her next husband. In future, she would have no unpleasant mother-in-law to deal with.

Trevor, her footman, handed her into the carriage and she caught sight of Captain Briggs circling around to ride ahead. Her driver, Hancock, carried a rifle on the seat beside him, and Trevor was armed as well. "Trevor, didn't Alfred return from Sweethope last night?"

"Aye, but Captain Briggs said he was not to come, my lady."

"I beg your pardon?"

"Just saying what the captain told—"

Christina stepped down from the carriage. "Captain Briggs—"

He turned and caught her gaze with his piercing blue eyes. "A problem already, my lady?" His manner was too condescending by half.

She could play at the same game. "Why did you dismiss my footman?"

"We need to be as inconspicuous as possible. An extra footman will only raise questions about your person. And the goods you carry."

She did not like to admit that he was right. Even though the jewels were locked inside a strongbox and stored beneath the cushioned bench inside the carriage, it was best if they did not call attention to themselves in any way.

She gave him a slight nod and returned to the carriage, with Jenny right behind her.

Their destination was the small town of Middleton, where Captain Briggs would secure overnight lodgings for them. Christina spent the day's ride deliberately thinking of everything but him.

She turned her thoughts to her sister—*Lily*. Christina had no real memories of anything before the birth of her brother, Felton. She knew he was not really her brother, but she had been welcomed into the Jameson family as though she truly belonged there.

Felton had been a joy, and Christina now knew it was because her parents had feared they would never have children of their own. They'd been married for several years before Felton's birth, which was why they'd taken in Christina when she was a small child.

They were a close family, and neither she nor her brothers had ever felt any distinction between them. It was as though they were all the same in their parents' eyes. She had never given it a second thought.

With Captain Briggs's news about her true parents, Christina knew that she'd once been a child in dire need, a child whose cold, uncaring grandparent had wanted nothing to do with her or her sister. She had no use for such a man.

She had asked Captain Briggs about Lily, but he'd said little. Only that Lily had been raised by a vicar and his wife, and had recently married an earl. Her sister had done well, considering her modest upbringing.

Christina could not fathom why she had been

taken to the Earl of Sunderland instead of a family like the one that had taken her sister. Captain Briggs could offer no explanation, either.

Perhaps she could discover the answer one day, after she met Lily. But as much as she wanted to meet her sister, her priority had to be Lang. If he was still alive . . . She needed to uncover the identity of her blackmailer and learn what he knew about her brother.

Then she could meet Lily, wherever she was. Christina wanted sufficient time to spend with her sister, for them to become friends without any distractions. She didn't care one whit about the duke—he could go hang, the old curmudgeon. How could he deny his own daughter? His orphaned granddaughters?

She did not doubt his sudden pang of conscience was due to the death of his son. Now that he had no direct heir, he felt some belated urge to know his other kin. *How very kind of him!*

Christina could not help but be intrigued by thoughts of her sister—her twin. She doubted Lily had shorn her hair as Christina had done, but according to Captain Briggs, they were otherwise the same.

It was unimaginable. She'd heard of twins, of course, but had never known any others. She wondered how it would feel to meet a mirror image of herself. As much as she loved her brothers, Christina had always wished for a sister, and now, as improbable as it was, she had one.

Christina dozed as she thought about the issues

that faced her, but she soon slipped into dreams of the
man who'd invaded her bedchamber the night before.

It was going to take all Gavin's considerable patience to get through this journey to London and
back north to the Lake District. He did not appreciate being given no choice in the matter, but if he did
not take Christina to London and help her with her
bloody blackmailer, she was not going to cooperate
with him later.

He spent most of the day riding ahead of her entourage, feeling irritated as he kept an eye out for
unsavory travelers who might threaten her and her
valuable cargo. He should have told her to leave it
at Sweethope Cottage, and find some other means
of raising the money she needed once they arrived
in London.

But she was no fool. She would have considered
every other possibility before traveling all the way
to Cumbria to collect the jewelry from the safe at
Sweethope Cottage.

At least her carriage was nondescript, and her
driver and footman were armed. Gavin didn't know
if either man could shoot, but they were both young
and fit. And they were being paid to see to Christina's safety.

Gavin was uninterested in riding on or in Christina's carriage and being jostled along on its stiff
springs. He was even less willing to spend any more
time than necessary in close quarters with her. He'd
been far too tempted by her last night.

Slipping into her bedroom had been a grievous error. He'd found her attractive when fully dressed, but she was beyond tempting in the shimmering white gown she'd worn in her bedchamber. He had to admire the way she'd stood up to him without cowering in the least. She was a woman to be reckoned with.

But not by him.

It was late afternoon when Gavin arrived at the Middleton Arms. He'd ridden ahead since the road had been devoid of travelers all afternoon, and he felt certain Christina and her party would be safe.

He had never been to the small village before, having spent little time in England since his school days. It seemed ironic that he barely knew the countryside in his own land, while he was more than familiar with every little hamlet and village in France.

He did not care to reminisce. The war was over, and he would never again be called upon to commit any of the vile deeds that had been required of him in France.

The Middleton Arms was a decent inn, and Gavin decided it would be sufficient, as long as the beds were not too hard or too lumpy.

Taking his saddle pack with him, he left his horse with a lad at the stable and crossed the road to the lodging house. It was not difficult to secure rooms, for there were only a few other lodgers at the inn. He ordered a meal to be prepared for Lady Fairhaven and her party, then went into the taproom to take his ease.

He had to admit some small part of him did not object to the challenge of dealing with Christina's blackmailer. As much as he wanted to put an end to his roving days and settle down in his own house in Hampshire, he had a niggling fear that it would not suit him. He could not quite imagine waking up in the same bedchamber every morning, eating his meals in the same room every day, or looking out at the same landscape all through the seasons.

What if he did not like it? Worse, what if he could not stand it?

He thought of the agricultural journals he'd stashed in his pack and took a swallow of the scorching whiskey the barkeep put before him. He rather liked the thought of running his own farm. Of producing, rather than destroying.

When he'd been promoted from the Ninety-fifth Rifle Regiment, he had not considered the toll his new position would take. He'd sought out the most dangerous of Britain's enemies and eliminated these men in cold blood. Problem solved. No battle involved.

His missions had taken him all over the continent. There were times when he'd been able to merely thwart an enemy strategist or information gatherer, but it was usually more expedient to simply remove the problem. Gavin had done his part to ensure England's victory over Napoleon, following orders and answering personally to Lords Castlereagh and Wellington.

He felt much more than relief that it was over. His duty, while clear, had not been as uncomplicated as he'd thought it would be.

Luckily, it was only a matter of time before he could purchase his farm and retire there in peace. As soon as he collected his money from Windermere, he intended to send for his sister and niece, and they could move into Weybrook Manor. He only had to be patient and handle Christina's situation in exactly the same way that he'd have dealt with an assignment in France. With careful planning.

He turned his thoughts to the task before him and considered everything Christina had told him about the last time Lang had been seen.

It was hardly enough to make anyone think the young lieutenant might have survived the blast. And yet there was at least one gaping hole . . .

Bloody hell. He did not want to get caught up in an investigation of Lang Jameson's death. Surely his father and the dockside authorities had already done a sufficient job of it. But if Lang's companions were not sure how long before the explosion he'd left the tavern . . .

Gavin downed another swallow of whiskey. Christina's limited information was not enough to go on. If they did not make contact with the blackmailer and find out what he knew, Gavin feared she would want to travel to Plymouth and retrace Lang's steps.

It was the last thing Gavin wanted to do.

He drank again, the liquor helping to dull the uncertainty of his mission. Of finding out what a blackmailer could possibly say about Lieutenant Jameson, of moving into Weybrook Manor and farming his land for the rest of his days . . .

He told himself he could leave Hampshire if life as a gentleman farmer did not suit him. He could hire an estate agent to manage things while Eleanor stayed and ran the house. His payment from Windermere would give him plenty of money to live on until the estate produced an income, so his sister and her daughter would be well provided for.

Luckily, Gavin had insisted on being paid whether or not the duke was still alive when his granddaughters came to Windermere Park. He'd had it put down in writing, and duly witnessed.

All he had to do was get Christina back to the Lake District. But he'd learned—with some difficulty—that she was not an easily manipulated woman.

Contrary to what Christina believed, Gavin had no experience with blackmailers. Of course, he had dealt with any number of villainous men, but Gavin himself was the most dangerous one he knew. Christina had no idea whom she was dealing with, and it was far better that way. He hoped no one ever learned of his wartime missions.

He shuddered at the thought of Christina trying to deal with the blackmailer herself. The situation could quickly become hazardous, especially if she confronted the man with that pistol she'd found at Sweethope. She could easily find herself in Newgate, awaiting trial for murder. Of an innocent bystander.

Gavin finished his last swallow of whiskey and put down his glass for more. The barkeep accommodated him.

He did not believe events at All Hallows Church

would play out well. Christina's expectations were naïve and unrealistic. She was mad even to have considered taking a gun into London and threatening the blackmailer with it. And Gavin doubted they would learn anything of her brother from him. The blighter had to be lying about what he knew.

In Gavin's opinion, this was a wasted trip. Christina should just ignore the blackmailer and let the dice fall as they may. Lang Jameson was a grown man and an officer in His Majesty's navy. If he was not already dead, then the consequences of his actions should be his own to deal with.

But Gavin would never convince Christina of that, no more than he could leave Eleanor to her own devices after she'd been tossed out by their bastard of a father. Gavin had to do what he could for her, just as Christina was doing for Lang.

Of course she hoped her brother was still alive, in spite of the fact that his actions might jeopardize another brother's betrothal. Which meant Gavin was stuck on his present course, and there was nothing he could do about it.

Though he was not usually much of a drinking man, he decided his present situation warranted it.

He gestured for the barkeep to refill his glass a third time.

Immediately upon her arrival at the inn, Christina started for her room, but caught sight of Captain Briggs through the doorway of the adjacent taproom. He remained silent, tossing her a solemn glance while saluting her with a glass that held a small amount of rich amber liquid. Then he turned away and downed it in one long gulp.

Christina swallowed hard, too, as she watched his throat move. But she turned away quickly and followed Jenny to the staircase. She did not care to speak to Captain Briggs anyway, as his behavior that morning had bordered upon rude. Besides, there was nothing further to say.

Christina was not a seasoned traveler. She'd spent most of her youth at the Sunderland home in Edinburgh, only going to London for the season when she turned twenty. In spite of her excitement at experiencing her first season, she'd missed her younger brothers, who'd stayed home. She'd missed riding out to the country with them, missed playing cards, missed laughing at all their antics.

Life had become sedate and dull after her marriage, as Christina had tried to become the wife Edward wanted.

They'd taken a few short trips together, but rarely had they needed to stay in an inn. Not when friends and family expected their traveling acquaintances to come and stay.

Christina followed the innkeeper up the stairs to her room and stopped at the threshold to survey it. The chamber was clean, the fire warm, and the bed appeared to be adequate. It would do.

"I would dearly love a bath," she said to Jenny after the man had left.

"I'm sure that can be arranged, my lady. I'll see

about it," the maid replied. "Do you want to go down for supper or shall I have it sent up?"

Christina thought about the probability of encountering Captain Briggs again, and made her decision. "I'll have it here."

It was decided that the strongbox with her jewels would stay with Hancock and Trevor. One of them would always have it under his guard while the other left the room to go out for a meal or any other necessities.

Christina decided the small bedroom suited her. She was tired and irritable from her long ride inside the carriage, and envied Captain Briggs his day outside on horseback. There was a time when she'd have insisted upon riding alongside him, all the way to London. Rain or shine.

She went to the window and opened the shutters, and saw that night was quickly falling. Visible on the left was the road they'd traveled from Holywell House, and there was a small village to the right. No one was about, and Christina assumed the townspeople had all gone home for their suppers.

She lit the candles in her room, then opened her traveling case and took out her sleeping gown and banyan. She intended to have her meal, then take a long, hot soak, and retire for the night. She had no intention of thinking about Captain Briggs and the dour look he'd given her from the tavern room.

She supposed it was unfair for her to drag him into her troubles, but what was she to do? Pay the blackmailer again and abandon any possibility of gathering some information about Lang? The Sunderland family had never forsaken her, and she was not about do any such thing to Lang. If he was in need of help, she was determined to provide it.

Jenny returned with her supper, a simple but hot meal. Afterward, servants brought in a large copper tub and filled it with steaming, hot water. Christina undressed with her maid's assistance, then stepped into the tub. She sank down into its soothing heat and closed her eyes with pleasure.

"Here now, my lady, let me wash your back."

Christina allowed Jenny to help her for a few minutes, then dismissed the girl. "We've all had a long day, Jenny," she said when the young maid protested. "Go and have your own supper and get some rest. I'll finish my bath and get myself to bed. I won't need you until morning."

Jenny did not protest. "If you're sure, my lady."

"Of course I'm sure." She would relax in the tub for a few more minutes, then go to bed. She was tired, but anxious—about the trip, about Lang . . . and about Captain Briggs. But the hot water was having the soothing effect she'd hoped for. The heat seeped in and her jostled muscles began to relax. She closed her eyes and leaned back. "Go on with you," she said to Jenny. "I'm sure the kitchen is warm and the staff more than happy to gossip."

Jenny left the room and Christina tried to make her mind a blank. But now that all was quiet, she found it impossible. She pictured Captain Briggs's hands, large and capable. His fingers were long and blunt-tipped, and thick blue veins tracked across their backs.

She could not keep herself from imagining their touch.

The room shifted slightly when Gavin stood. He was not accustomed to quite so much drink, but the occasion had warranted it. He was doing what he must to ensure the income he needed. He did not have to like it, and he could appreciate that at least this time, he didn't have to do anything too abhorrent to earn his pay.

He had to believe Weybrook Manor was perfect for his needs, that it would be a good home for Eleanor. Far from Durham and their father, they need never have any contact with the rest of the Briggs family again.

But the property could easily slip through his fingers. Going to London with Christina would set him back a month. Ten days to Town and ten days back, minimum. There would be a day or two—maybe more—to deal with the blackmailer and follow up on what might transpire at All Hallows Church. And then back to Windermere.

He should have followed his instinct at Sweethope Cottage and abducted her. He could have just tossed her onto his horse and taken her to Windermere and been done with it. Collected his ten thousand pounds and gone down to Hampshire to haggle over the price of the property with the owner, old Mr. Wickford.

But then he would not have seen Christina in her
bedroom, wearing the revealing chemise. He would
not have touched the curls near her ear and known
the silky texture of her hair.

He wouldn't have spent the day's ride thinking
about touching her again.

He made his way to the staircase, more than ready
for a night's sleep. Clearly, he should not have imbibed quite so heavily, for his footsteps were unsteady as he climbed the steps, and his head was
full of folly. He just wanted a good night's rest and
to be ready to ride at least forty miles on the morrow.

The candles in the sconces cast flickering shadows across the corridor. Gavin had not yet visited
his room, but the innkeeper had said it was the one
before the last on the right. He switched his traveling
pack to his other hand and opened the door to find a
fire burning steadily, and candles already lit.

"Jenny?"

The sound of Christina's voice stopped him in his
tracks. And when he glanced to his left, he saw her,
stepping out of her bath, naked and so stunning, he
dropped his pack to the floor.

He didn't know if he would ever recover from the
sight she presented. Somehow, he managed to pick
up his pack and walk to the bed, if a bit unsteadily.
He dropped the pack on the bed and turned to look
at her again.

Chapter 6

Christina let out a little scream and reached for the linen towel Jenny had left for her. She covered herself quickly, but it did not stop a ripple of shock—and an acute awareness of his heated masculine gaze—from coursing through her.

His sudden appearance in her room and her ridiculously improper reaction to his presence astonished her.

But not so much that she forgot what she needed to do. Holding the towel in front of her, she extended her arm and pointed to the door. "Get out!"

But he did not move.

Christina felt the cool air of the room at her back, and when his gaze slid down the length of her body, so poorly concealed by the linen, she shivered. Arousal hit like a fist unfurling in the deepest recesses of her body. She felt her nipples tighten as the wave of lusty awareness spread. No one had ever looked at her as Captain Briggs was looking at her now, and her body responded with a will of its own.

"You're in my room," he said. He stood far too close, his feet separated and braced upon the floor as though planted on the deck of a rocky ship.

"You are mistaken, Captain Briggs." Her voice sounded breathless. "This is *my* room."

He shook his head, and some of his disheveled hair fell forward onto his forehead.

He was so tall and rugged, his face all masculine planes and angles with the dark hint of beard on his jaw. Christina knew his hands would be strong and abrasive against her skin, unlike Edward's soft, smooth ones. Some perverse part of her hoped he would ignore her demand to leave.

Such a thought was beyond shocking. He had to go.

"Captain Briggs." She attempted to wrap the linen around her body without revealing any more than she already had.

"Would y'like some help?" He walked toward her.

"No!" She said in a panic, pulling the sheet tight against her. She did not know what she would do if he touched her.

Allow it, no doubt. Right after she melted.

She took a deep breath. "You must go, Captain Briggs."

He stared at her a moment, then took a quick glance around the room. If she was not mistaken, he lost his balance slightly. "This looksh pervect t' me."

"You're drunk!"

"The hell y' say." His mirthful tone grated on her

nerves. How dare he come into her private quarters in this condition. *In any condition!*

"Your words are slurred," she said, stalking toward him, "and you're weaving."

"Weaving?"

"Swaying."

"Bluddy hell. I'm not drunk. I never drink."

Christina took hold of his arm, keeping a death grip on the towel. "I saw you drinking in the taproom when I arrived."

"Not yushed to it."

He started to sit down on the bed, but Christina did not allow it. She pulled his arm and dragged him away from the bed, moving him toward the door. "Go and find your own bed."

"I'd rather sleep in yours."

Christina swallowed. "You cannot, Captain Briggs. Not now or ever. Go away." Anywhere but there.

She pushed him out the door and closed it after him, turning the key in the lock, something she had sadly neglected to do after Jenny's earlier departure.

When morning came, Gavin's head felt as though it were filled with cotton batting. It throbbed without mercy, but fortunately, the innkeeper had a cure for it. He gave Gavin a bitter concoction of tea and herbs that helped take away the worst of the ache.

But not the memory of telling Christina he'd like to sleep in her bed. Or something on that order.

Hell's bells.

He took his leave just before dawn, torn between feasting his eyes upon Christina when she came down, and getting far ahead of her carriage so she would not have an opportunity to see him in his current rough state.

He did not generally consider himself a coward, but an early departure won the day.

He might have imbibed too much whiskey the night before, but he remembered everything in perfect detail. Climbing—well, staggering—up the stairs, entering Christina's bedchamber. Her glance of surprise. Her smooth, soft curves. His glimpse of her small, pink nipples and full breasts before she covered herself with the thin linen toweling. Her long, shapely legs . . .

He hardened at the thought of her shining green eyes and the way they'd flashed with anger. He realized she had passion to spare underneath her prim mourning clothes and haughty temperament.

He found himself envying her husband.

For a man who'd had little enough reason to care what any woman thought of him, Gavin was surprisingly sensitive to the way Christina might judge him. And he could not help but wonder how her body would feel beneath his.

She elicited a hunger in him like some wild animal just coming out of hibernation—his senses more acute, his need more real than he could ever recall.

Tamping down such ridiculous, irrational musings, he found Hancock in the stable, preparing for their departure. When Trevor joined them, they agreed they would fire one shot in case of any trouble. Even so, Gavin did not intend to ride too far ahead. He would stay well within hearing of a gunshot, as he made sure the road ahead was safe.

Christina awoke several times during the night, feeling certain someone had entered her bedchamber. Each time, she discovered she had only imagined it, or dreamed it.

And each time, she felt an acute disappointment that Captain Briggs had not returned to her.

Such a fantasy was beyond absurd. She had no business thinking of the man in any terms beyond his function as her escort to London and the man who would help her deal with her blackmailer. Whatever sensations he'd aroused when he'd barged in on her were inappropriate and unwanted.

Well, perhaps not unwanted, if she were honest. The frank admiration she'd seen in his eyes had been exhilarating.

She longed for a man's attentions. A man's touch.

But not just any man. Certainly not a mercenary who collected bounties on the people he sought.

She dressed before Jenny came up, and ran a brush through her hair. Then she marched down to the dining room to speak to Captain Briggs before they left the inn. She wasn't sure whether she was more annoyed with herself or Briggs, but she intended to chastise him for his drunkenness the night before. And more importantly, for invading the privacy of her room, unannounced and uninvited. *Sleep in her bed*, indeed!

She ignored the shiver that skittered up her spine when she recalled the moment he saw her, and the blatant admiration in his gaze. What Captain Briggs thought of her was inconsequential. No doubt the sight of any nearly naked female would arouse the same reaction in most men. And her unruly body had merely reacted the way any woman would when placed in such an intimate situation.

Or perhaps only a woman who craved the knowing touch of an attractive man.

She banished such thoughts from her mind and walked into the dining room. There were several travelers there, some of whom were drinking cups of hot tea, and others preparing to depart. Christina did not see Hancock or Trevor, but as she looked about, Jenny came from one of the back rooms, carrying a tray with a cup and a steaming teapot on it.

She moved in the direction of the staircase, but stopped when she saw Christina. "My lady. You're already . . . I thought I would wake you with a nice hot cup of tea."

"Thank you, Jenny. Where are the others?"

"Hitching the horses," she said, placing the tray on a nearby table.

"Did you see Captain Briggs this morning?"

"No, my lady," Jenny replied. "Do you want me to try to find him?"

"No, that won't be necessary. Perhaps he's in the stable with Hancock."

" 'Tis likely, my lady." Jenny poured tea into the cup. "Shall I go get your bag so we can leave right away?"

"Yes, please." Christina sat down and looked out the window as Jenny left the room. She felt oddly let down when she did not catch even a glimpse of her escort.

She sipped her tea and turned her thoughts to what she was going to do when they arrived in London. Her plan was to take her valuables to a few discreet, reputable jewelers and sell them for the banknotes she needed. Then she would place the money inside the lectern at All Hallows Church and hope they caught sight of the scoundrel before he took the packet and slipped away.

Christina had never visited the church, and had only been to the Tower area once. Captain Briggs seemed to know it, which would be very helpful— she hoped. Perhaps there was a concealed place where they might lie in wait and watch for the rascal who knew Lang's whereabouts.

And then, Captain Briggs could apprehend him.

Briggs was a daunting figure. He was obviously stronger than most men, and clever enough to have found her and her sister. Surely, he would be able to get the information she needed from the blackmailer without too much difficulty. He would retrieve her money from the scoundrel and demand answers. And when they knew where Lang was . . .

Then it became complicated. Whatever they learned about Lang, Christina would want to go to her brother. He must be in some sort of difficulty, and Christina intended to help him out of it.

But that would interfere with her promise to return to Windermere with Briggs if he helped her in London.

She gazed out the window, considering what to do, when he came out of the stable, leading his horse. He smiled broadly at one of the young grooms and flipped him a coin. Then he mounted his horse with the muscular mastery of a seasoned horseman, and rode out of the stable yard without looking back.

And then Christina remembered to breathe.

It was a long ride to their next stop, a roadside inn not far from North Riding. This one was smaller than the Middleton Arms, located in a nearly isolated spot at a crossroads.

Gavin would have preferred a more populous site, but the day's ride had been closer to fifty miles than forty. He was sure Lady Fairhaven and her maid would be more than ready to stop by the time they arrived.

He took rooms for their party and made a point of checking on the exact location of the chamber where Christina would be lodged. He had no intention of repeating his mistake of the night before. And he would not drink, either. He had no interest in muddling his mind as he had done the previous night, even if it did help him forget his concerns.

It had only raised a few new ones that were just as disturbing to his body and soul.

Christina was unlikely to arrive for a while, so

Gavin followed the innkeeper to his own room and settled in alone, the way he'd done through most of his adult life, following orders and completing assignments. Tracking the enemies of the crown had occupied far too many years, and his deeds weighed heavily upon his conscience. He'd obeyed his orders without question, as any good soldier would do.

But now that he saw so many English soldiers home from the war, he knew any one of them might have been the target of an enemy assassin's bullet. An assassin like him.

Gavin suppressed the wave of disgust that came over him and thought about the nights he'd gone without a roof over his head, following his prey until the right moment, and then . . .

Perhaps he wasn't civilized enough to live a quiet life in the country. Maybe he ought not to live with Eleanor and her child. After all he'd done during the war years, his presence might poison the household, poison his niece.

It seemed Amelia had made the right choice, after all, though her abandonment still stung.

Gavin made an attempt at civility and took the time to shave, removing his shirt for the task. He washed, and took a moment to examine the wound in his arm. It was healing well, probably due to the attention given it by Christina at Sweethope. Satisfied with its progress, he took the mended shirt out of his pack and pulled it over his head. Christina had been the one to repair it, he was quite sure. But she seemed not to want it known.

Because a viscountess ought to be above such menial tasks? No doubt that was true. But he'd seen it on her dressing table the night he'd broached her room at Holywell, and he could smell her sweet fragrance when he pulled it over his head. He could almost imagine her soft hands—

Appalled that such mawkish tripe even entered his mind, Gavin pulled on his waistcoat and jacket. What difference did it make, who'd mended the shirt? She'd damaged it—it was only right that she fix it.

Just as she'd fixed his arm.

There was still some time before dark, and Gavin felt restless. He went down to the public room of the inn and ordered an innocent glass of ale while he waited for Christina's party to arrive. Turning as a large group of travelers came inside, Gavin nearly choked at the sight of a thickset man with sandy brown hair, wearing a monocle.

Chetwood!

No, Gavin realized with limited relief, it was not Baron Chetwood, but a man who looked so much like him, the sight of him gave Gavin a start.

He put down his glass, his mind suddenly racing. He had discounted the possibility that Chetwood would have any reason to want to do harm to Christina. But what if the baron had not learned of the change in Windermere's will? What if Lily and her husband had not yet managed to travel to Windermere Park and demand the changes?

Feeling something akin to panic, Gavin realized it

was possible there was some reason they hadn't yet left Ashby Hall. Which meant Christina could still be a target of her grandfather's wrathful heir.

He should have thought of it sooner. He never should have gone up to Edinburgh on his search for Christina before making sure *himself* that the old duke had made the changes to his will and informed Chetwood of them.

He muttered a low curse under his breath and quickly stormed out of the inn. Returning to the stable, he did not wait for a groom to saddle his horse again, but quickly did it himself, and then mounted up.

If Chetwood didn't know about the change in the will, he might have hired some more ruffians to do his dirty work as he'd tried with Lily. And even if he did know, Gavin suspected the baron was petty and vicious enough to demonstrate his displeasure at losing a large portion of Windermere's possessions.

By the vilest means possible.

"You did not sleep well last night, my lady?"

Christina crossed her arms. "Of course I did. Why?"

"Oh, no reason," Jenny said quickly.

But Christina had to admit she had not been very good company all day. Not that Jenny had any grand expectations, but they'd always been quite compatible. Christina knew everything about Jenny's parents and siblings, and had given various members of her family generous gifts on different occasions—Christmas, christenings, feast days.

Jenny had become Christina's maid three years before, when Christina had come out in society. She'd gone with Christina to Edward's house after her marriage, and been a great comfort when the circumstances of her husband's death had become known.

She had not understood it any better than Christina.

"I do hope we're almost there," Jenny remarked.

Christina looked out the window, but saw no sign of a town. She shook her head. "We must still have some distance to go," she said.

She was weary, too, for it had been a long ride in the enclosed carriage, and in truth, she had *not* slept well. But she could hardly admit the reason for her insomnia to Jenny, as close as they were.

"The miles would clip along faster if Captain Briggs were to ride inside with us, don't you think, my lady?"

Jenny's sentiment was far too close to what Christina had been thinking most of the day. "It would be far too crowded, Jenny. Did you not notice the man's height?"

"Oh aye." She sighed. "He has a horseman's long, strong legs. And those shoulders. Aye, you're right. We'd surely be crowded. But oh . . . what a lovely crowd."

Christina remembered quite well the powerful lines of the captain's legs. And the breadth of his shoulders.

And she would never forget the way he'd looked at her when he walked in on her as she exited her bath.

In spite of his intoxication—or perhaps because of it—lust had burned in his eyes.

Edward had never looked at her with such abject desire. During the months of their marriage, he'd bedded her weekly at most, and without much enthusiasm. She'd thought perhaps she was odd, since she'd felt a great deal more desire. But Christina had been too embarrassed to seek her mother's counsel. And then Edward had died.

The circumstances of his death explained his indifference, and crumbled Christina's wifely confidence. She had failed at capturing her own husband's passions.

"Where do you suppose he got that little scar at the corner of his eye?"

Christina had wondered not only about that small scar, but the ones she'd seen on his torso, too. He'd been wounded several times but somehow managed to survive. "In the war, I suppose."

"It makes him look . . . I don't know . . . dangerous."

Christina made no reply. He *was* dangerous, if only to her peace of mind. Her thoughts became unclear when he looked at her as he'd done the previous night, and her body burned in that utterly frustrating way she'd experienced whenever Edward came to her bed.

Just the thought of Captain Briggs's beautiful, strong hands was enough to make something melt inside her.

"But he's a handsome sot in spite of it, don't you think?"

Christina did not want to think of Captain Briggs or the impossible sensations he made her feel. "I'm hungry," she said. The man occupied far too many of her thoughts as it was, without Jenny going on about him, too.

"Aye," said Jenny. "I hope the next inn has better fare than what we had at the Middleton Arms. The mutton stew had more turnips than mutton."

Christina nodded absently and turned her thoughts in the complete opposite direction of Captain Briggs and considered her sister, and the Duke of Windermere.

Her grandfather had to be a cold, uncaring fish to have turned out his own daughter, and then *her* daughters when they were so deeply in need.

Christina wondered about her parents, about her mother who'd married against her father's wishes and borne two children. Where had they lived? Had they been happy? Had her mother ever regretted her decision to wed Daniel Hayes?

She hoped not. She found herself exceedingly glad her mother had chosen her own husband, and trusted that Sarah had found the love and compatibility that had been lacking in Christina's own marriage.

"The carriage is slowing, my lady."

Christina glanced out the window and felt a moment of alarm when she realized Jenny was right. But they were still some distance from their destination.

She'd worried about carrying so much valuable jewelry, but there had been no other option for obtaining the kind of money her blackmailer demanded. They had taken the precaution of traveling as inconspicuously as possible, and both Hancock and Trevor were armed.

Still, every sensational story Christina had ever heard of highwaymen came to her, and she scrambled to try to think what she would do if they were stopped by villains.

She heard her driver's voice, but could not make out his words. Suddenly the carriage lurched forward, moving even faster than before and jamming Christina's heart into her throat.

Chapter 7

Gavin was surprised by the degree of relief he felt when he saw Hancock's calm, sedate expression. Clearly, nothing untoward had happened since Gavin had ridden ahead. And the carriage had only a few miles to travel before they reached the safety of the inn where he'd come to his ominous realization.

"Captain Briggs, sir—is there trouble ahead?" the driver called out to him as he started to slow the horses.

Gavin shook his head. "No, but keep moving, Hancock!"

The driver touched the brim of his hat and spurred the horses to a gallop while Gavin fell back to flank the carriage. There was a gap in the curtain, and he saw Christina's questioning expression.

An explanation was in order. She needed to know about Baron Chetwood and the danger he'd posed to Lily only a few weeks before. What a fool he'd been to assume the man was no longer a danger to Christina.

He tipped his hat, breathed slightly easier, and sped up to ride alongside Hancock at the front of the carriage. As soon as the carriage arrived at the inn, he was going to speak to Christina and warn her of the possibility that Chetwood had her in his sights.

Jenny sat back and sighed with relief. "I wonder what that was about. Could you hear what they said?"

Christina gave a small shake of her head. "I hope there's no trouble ahead."

"Wouldn't Captain Briggs have said so? To warn Trevor and Mr. Hancock to watch for it?"

"Hmm. Likely so," Christina replied, though she worried that there might actually be some difficulty ahead, but they were driving on in spite of it.

She sat tensely, feeling worried, as well as hungry, tired, and uncomfortable. She would be on edge until the last stretch of the day's journey was over. When the carriage stopped in front of a large inn, Christina did not wait for Trevor to come and open the door.

She unlatched the handle and looked out, only to encounter Captain Briggs reaching for the door handle. If she was not mistaken, he was glowering at her. It was quite a different look from the blatantly lustful gaze that had burned through her the night before.

"Go ahead, Jenny. I'll be right there."

Without breaking his gaze on her, Captain Briggs

assisted Jenny down the step first, then stuck in his hand for Christina. She made a process of gathering her small traveling bag and reticule, then descending the steps as regally as possible.

She did not know why he seemed so angry—unless he suddenly remembered to be annoyed at having to travel to London with her. Whatever it was, she intended to demand an explanation after they were settled in their rooms.

She took his hand and his touch caused a hot pulse of awareness to shudder through her. Never before had she considered that one man might be more "manly" than another, but she could not help but think so now. From his voice to the way he looked at her, she felt the tug of his virility deep in her womb.

And there seemed to be nothing she could do about her reaction to him.

"I'd like a word with you, Lady Fairhaven," he growled. The harshness of his voice matched his dark visage.

"Perhaps later, Captain Briggs." She took as haughty a tone as possible. She would not succumb to the absurd attraction she felt. He was just a man.

And he needed to understand who was in charge of this venture.

"No. *Not* later. I'll see you in your room in five minutes."

Christina clenched her teeth and raised her chin, then walked away, unwilling to argue with him in front of the servants in the stable yard. Clearly, he was not about to bestow on her one of those brilliant smiles she'd seen that morning in Middleton.

She could not imagine the reason for his anger, or what he wanted to say to her. Nor would she meet with him in her bedchamber. That had happened twice already, and each time, she'd found herself at a severe disadvantage.

She entered the inn after Jenny, who was already starting up the stairs behind the innkeeper, a man named Palmer. Jenny stepped aside to allow Christina to walk ahead of her, and the man took them down a long corridor, not unlike the one at the Middleton Arms. He pushed open the door to a small guest room with barely enough space for the bed and Christina's bag.

Unwilling to make the mistake she'd made the previous night, she put her hand out for the key. The innkeeper gave it to her.

"Captain Briggs already ordered a meal for your party," he said, "and it will be ready soon. I'll send one of the girls up to fetch you when we're ready to serve."

"Thank you," Christina said as she removed her hat and set it on the bed. "Is Captain Briggs's room nearby?"

"Aye, my lady," Mr. Palmer replied, indicating a room not far from Christina's, "just there. But you'll be safe enough up here with your maid. I keep a respectable house."

"I'm sure you do. Thank you." Christina removed her pelisse and set it on the bed as the innkeeper turned to leave. "Is his room locked?"

The innkeeper frowned at what Christina seemed to be suggesting. "My lady—"

"These rooms have all been let in my name, on my account, have they not?" she asked in a puffed-up tone.

"Er, yes they are, my lady."

"Well, perhaps you would unlock it for me," she said. "There is something I need to leave for him."

The innkeeper looked unsure, but did as he was told after only a moment's hesitation, and Christina made a point to remember this in future. Taking on the imperious tone her mother used during certain circumstances truly worked. Christina had been remiss in not following her example.

Jenny cast Christina a doubtful glance as Mr. Palmer left them, and whispered to her. "What are you going to do, my lady?"

"Only give him a dose of his own medicine." Even if she had stepped into his room at Holywell, it was nothing like what he'd done to her. *Twice!*

"Lady Fairhaven—"

"Do not worry, Jenny. Nothing untoward will happen. Now, go downstairs and get me some water for washing."

The maid looked dubious, but knew she was not to argue with her mistress. "A bath?"

"Not tonight. A basin will do."

It would be a long time before she could step into or out of a tub without remembering the expression in Gavin Briggs's eyes when he'd caught her naked. She did not think she wanted to recall it now.

* * *

Gavin searched the inn for the blasted woman, but she was nowhere to be found. Her bedchamber was empty, and she was not in the common rooms, or anywhere else on the main floor.

Damnation. He had told her he would see her in her room in five minutes.

She was not there, and her maid was not in sight, either. He checked with her footman and driver, who said they'd last seen her going up to her room.

He was in a severe temper when he went to his own room for his greatcoat. Clearly, something had happened to the bloody woman, and he was going to have to search the grounds for her. He pushed open the door to his room and stood stock-still at the sight of her, sitting on a chair next to the fire. Calmly waiting for him.

"What is it, Captain Briggs? You appear surprised."

Bloody hell. "I told you—"

"But you do not give me orders, Captain." She smoothed her skirts. "And now you know how it feels to have someone breach your chamber without your permission. You can be grateful you have your clothes on."

Chapter 8

He was not grateful for it in the least.

The most sensitive parts of his body roused at the thought of pulling her unclothed body against his. Of slipping his fingers through her shining curls.

With her chin raised in defiance, those same parts demanded that he kiss the audacious, self-satisfied expression right from her blushing face. Somehow, his better sense prevailed.

"I am more than aware that I am not the one giving orders, else you would be safely ensconced at Windermere, visiting with your sister and collecting your inheritance."

"We have been over this, Captain Briggs," she said, then frowned. "And what do you mean—*safely*?"

Gavin clasped his hands behind him and reminded himself that it was *he* who had been remiss. He should have considered Chetwood. If he'd explained about the bastard—perhaps even exaggerated the threat—Christina might have agreed to go directly to Windermere. Except that would mean abandoning her purpose in London.

And Gavin had come to understand she had the same kind of bond with her brothers that he shared with Eleanor. None of them would let the others down.

"Besides the fact that you are traveling with an enormous fortune in your carriage?" he asked.

"I have to bait the blackmailer with something, don't I?" She turned away to the fireplace and the flickering light seemed to shimmer in her short curls. Her ordinary black traveling gown hugged her curves in a way he'd never appreciated on any other woman.

She could have baited the blackmailer with that— her backside—and left her jewels at Sweethope Cottage.

Gavin scrubbed a hand across his face with irritation and frustration. Just because he'd had one tantalizing glimpse of her delectable attributes was no good reason for him to keep ruminating on what he'd seen. Much as he would enjoy another foray into her private chambers, she'd made her point.

"We need to come to an understanding, Lady Fair—"

"No," she said, whirling to face him, her cheeks reddened by anger, "*you* need to come to an understanding, Captain. This trip to London is undertaken by my authority. You are here to support me . . . and my decisions."

Gavin had never realized how entertaining—or

how arousing—it could be to witness a woman in full pique pacing the floor. He took a seat, crossed his arms over his chest, and watched as she strode from one end of the room to the other, lecturing him.

"Mind, I do not say I will not accept your guidance when we arrive in London," she said. "But I will make the decisions regarding the blackmailer. And my brother."

Gavin stretched out his legs and watched, when every inch of his body begged him to stand and face her. Touch her. Taste her.

"Of course I would never have actually shot the man, but I might have threatened him . . . a little . . . into telling me what he knows about Lang."

Still, Gavin did not say anything. He was not sure he even could—she stirred his blood as no other female he could imagine. Even Amelia.

"And I would gladly pay the two thousand pounds, just for news of my brother. Do you understand what it would mean to me to find him alive?"

She clutched her hands against her chest, almost in the same way she'd held the towel against her breasts the night before. Gavin could almost feel the softness of those feminine mounds in his hands, and how she would react to his touch.

"Have you nothing to say, Captain Briggs? Are you listening, or am I wasting my breath talking to you?"

He took note of her full lips and knew exactly how they would feel upon his heated skin. Like a ripe fruit, sweet and tangy on his tongue. Or even more probably, like the explosion of a fiery cannon.

He knew better than to allow his fantasies to flourish this way. He stood. "Lady Fairhaven, this is not a one-sided proposition."

"Of course not. You don't want to go to London, and I don't want to go to Windermere. And here we are. An agreement was made."

Gavin took a deep breath. She was safe, at least for the night, and he'd seen no signs of danger since their departure from Holywell. That didn't mean Chetwood had given up.

She frowned. "What is it? What haven't you told me?"

She was far too perceptive for his peace of mind. "There is another factor that might interfere with our journey to London."

"What could possibly—"

"Your grandfather's heir is a man named Randall Vaughn, Baron Chetwood."

"A distant relative, I assume, since my mother's brother is dead."

He gave her a quick nod. "And an unsavory one."

"Exactly *how* unsavory, Captain Briggs? And what has he to do with anything?"

"Chetwood attempted to eliminate your sister from inheriting anything from your grandfather."

She lowered her brows. "What do you mean?"

"He hired two scoundrels to find her and do away with her before she could go to Windermere and meet her grandfather. Meeting him was a condition of her inheritance. And yours."

She gave him a fierce look, her face flushed with color. "*Do away* with her? Wh-where are these men now?" she demanded with indignation, and Gavin could not help but admire her spirit. With the kind of devoted determination she showed toward Lang, it was no surprise that she would feel the same about her sister, in spite of never having met her.

He answered her bluntly, although he did not specify exactly what he'd done. "I've dealt with them."

She met his eyes, then folded her arms as she shuddered visibly.

Gavin refused to feel like a monster, at least not over this. Chetwood's men had ambushed him and attempted to kill him to prevent him from finding Lily and taking her to her grandfather. And then they would have done the same to her. Gavin could feel no guilt for doing exactly what they had intended to do to Lily.

"And you think this baron will try to . . . to do away with *me* now?"

"No. At least, I don't think so."

"You're not making sense, Captain Briggs." She resumed her pacing. "If you . . . *dealt* with the men sent by—"

"Lady Fairhaven, your grandfather initially wrote his will stipulating that you and your sister would inherit all his unentailed wealth, but only if you both went to Windermere to meet him, and to claim it."

She stopped in her tracks. "I take it to mean that if

we do not go to Windermere, Baron Chetwood will inherit it?"

Gavin nodded. "Yes. As heir to your grandfather's title, Chetwood will inherit the entailed properties. But there was a provision that the duke's unentailed wealth—which I gather is substantial—is to be divided equally between you and Lily. *But only if you could be found and brought to him."*

"You said there was a provision. *Was?"*

"When I set out on my search for you, Lily and her husband were planning to travel to Windermere and speak to the duke about that untenable—and dangerous—condition of his will."

"But . . ." She chewed her lower lip for a moment. "Baron Chetwood? He was not informed of the change?"

Gavin hesitated. That was the sticky point. "If the changes were made—"

"If?"

"If Lily and Ashby arrived at Windermere. If your grandfather was still alive when they got there . . . If they were able to find Chetwood . . . and if Chetwood was willing to let it go . . ."

Christina was frowning again, and Gavin could almost see the thoughts and questions churning through her mind. They were questions he should have asked before they set out for London.

"If all went as planned, then your grandfather has at least attempted to make Chetwood aware of the changes."

"Attempted."

Gavin could only give a brusque nod. He didn't know if he was overreacting to seeing Chetwood's look-alike, or if there was good reason to worry. But then he recalled the viciousness of the man's verbal—and almost physical—attack on his own wife in the parlor at Windermere Park.

"Baron Chetwood is a mean rogue of a man. It's possible that when he learns of the changes to your grandfather's will, he will harbor even more animosity toward you and your sister."

"Because we will inherit some of the duke's wealth?" She swallowed, the movement of her throat inviting his touch, perhaps even his kiss.

"And because the man has expensive . . . interests." There was no need to mention that Chetwood was rumored to be one of the Hellfire Club's most outrageous members.

"Do you think Lily is still in danger?"

"She has her husband to protect her."

Christina looked straight at him with those striking green eyes. "And I have you, haven't I, Captain Briggs?"

Christina hoped Lily's earl was as formidable as Captain Briggs. She could not imagine a tougher adversary. One thing bothered her, though.

"Captain Briggs, this is the first you've mentioned Baron Chetwood to me. In three days."

"Because I assumed the man was no longer a threat."

"But now you think he is? Has he . . ." Oh dear. "Have you seen him?"

He shook his head slightly, noticeably disturbed by his oversight. "No."

"Then what?"

"I remembered what a greedy reprobate he is reputed to be, and what he tried to do to your sister. The man has no conscience whatsoever, and would certainly view your grandfather's will as unfair. He is . . ."

Captain Briggs paused for a moment, considering his words.

"The baron is utterly foul. He is as far from trustworthy as a man can be. And I was wrong to assume he was no longer a threat."

"What interests? You mentioned they are expensive."

"Not suitable for a lady's ears," he growled.

She tried to imagine some vice she had not heard of in recent months. "Well, I've learned since my husband's death that there is gambling, drinking, and womanizing . . . What else can there possibly be?"

"Lady Fairhaven, you do not want to know."

She took him at his word and did not pursue it, not when he stood so close, with his magnificent hands on his hips, and one powerful leg slightly bent. Christina did not believe she'd ever known anyone quite so elemental.

Perhaps she ought to abort their trip to London and hurry back to Windermere with him. But that would mean abandoning her brother, which she would never do. And besides, if Captain Briggs was correct, Baron Chetwood was likely to be angry still, even after she and Lily collected whatever inheritance the duke bequeathed them. Going to Windermere would not make her any safer.

She could not concern herself with Baron Chetwood now.

"Then I can assume you intend to stay nearer to my carriage as we travel?" If not actually inside . . .

He nodded and moved even closer to her. "Aye. Or at least, I will not be far from you. I'll be able to hear a shout, or a shot if one of your men fires his gun."

He was so large and imposing, and Christina felt an achingly strong need to trace the crescent scar beside his eye. Or put her finger to the slight cleft in his chin and feel the rasp of his whiskers.

She took an unsteady breath. Perhaps she'd erred in breaching his room alone. "Wh-what if something happens and my men aren't able to fire a shot?"

"They're capable lads." He took another step forward. "They'll manage it."

"I sincerely hope you are correct, Captain Briggs."

"All I know is the sooner we get to London, the better."

She pressed her back against the door, facing him. "Captain Briggs . . . When we get there . . ."

He pivoted slightly and placed his hand against the doorjamb, quite near her head. A dangerous gleam came into his eyes and she felt an expectant thrill shudder through her.

He spoke quietly, his voice deep and rich. "I have no idea what will happen, Lady Fairhaven."

"I was thinking . . ."

He touched her hair with his free hand, his eyes roving the contours of her face. She felt speechless as he dipped his head toward hers. His breath feathered against her cheek, sending spears of heat through her.

"Do you h-have any sort of plan?"

"Aye." He cupped her jaw with his hand and ran his thumb across her lower lip just before he kissed her.

Christina seemed to melt against him, her body touching Gavin's in all the right places.

He'd been right. She tasted like an explosive, just before detonation.

He angled his head and opened his mouth, eliciting a sound of arousal from deep within her breast. He coaxed her lips open, and slid his tongue in. She met it tentatively, growing bolder as he sparred with her.

He felt her hands on his shoulders, resting passively at first, then squeezing tightly, skimming into the hair at his nape, drawing him in. She trembled and he slid his arms around her, pulling her tight.

Gavin wanted naught but to take her to the bed and lie her upon it. To open the buttons of her bodice and bare her body, to slip his hands under her skirts and find heaven.

He knew he had to stop. She was not some treasure to plunder. It was her return to Windermere that would gain him the treasure he sought. Not an illicit liaison.

He broke the kiss.

But he did not immediately release her. Touching Christina was far more intoxicating than he had imagined, and he doubted he could ever get enough of her.

"Christina," he whispered.

Her eyes were unfocused.

Gavin relished the last few moments he would feel her fingers in his hair, her breasts against his chest, her thighs against his own.

He clenched his teeth and gave her a moment to realize what was happening. What she must do.

Awareness came to her gradually, and her eyes widened. She lowered her hands as Gavin pulled away, and he wondered if she would slap him—as she had every right to do.

But she merely stood looking at him with confusion in her eyes, then swallowed and turned to open the door. She fumbled with the latch and Gavin had to reach past her to release it.

Once it was open, she fled without a word.

Christina ought to have felt mortified, but she did not. She was somewhat embarrassed, for what proper lady allowed herself to be so thoroughly kissed in such a wholly *im*proper setting—a man's bedroom? It was entirely too wicked. She'd let herself in for it, of course. She had not observed respectable decorum, and thus, she paid the price.

But what a price it had been.

She pressed her hand against her breast and could still feel her heart racing. No one had ever kissed her with such incredible fervor. Another moment more and she would have burst into a blazing beacon of desire. Or rather, lust. She had not wanted it to end.

Even now, she felt let down, frustrated. She'd wondered about Gavin Briggs's hands, and now she knew. They were gentle yet demanding, sensual and knowing. She could only imagine how skilled he would be if he actually bedded her.

Oh God, she could not possibly be thinking such a thing. Captain Briggs was only her escort. He was not a man she would ever consider as a husband . . . and yet he made her blood sing. His kiss had been astonishing. Drugging.

If Edward had seduced her with such skill, she'd have tied him to her bed and never allowed him to leave. She just hadn't known . . .

Jenny came into the room and caught sight of Christina's face. "Oh my, is aught amiss, my lady?"

"Not at all," Christina replied a bit too quickly.

"Well, you're as pink as you were when you had too much sun last summer. Remember?"

"Yes, I remember quite well." Although this flush was entirely different.

Jenny touched the back of her hand to Christina's forehead and cheek. "You might be a bit feverish, my lady," she said, frowning. "Perhaps you ought to lie down and I'll see about getting you some tea and toast. It would not do for you to become—"

"No, thank you, Jenny," Christina retorted. She was not about to sit in her room, afraid to face the man whose tongue had worked some kind of unexpected magic on her, whose hands had pulled her hips against his, pressing that amazingly hard, hot part of him against her just minutes ago. "If you'll just open a window—it's a little too warm in here."

Jenny turned a dubious look toward her mistress as she did so, and Christina started unfastening her bodice. She changed out of her traveling gown and into more suitable attire for supper, a simple round dress of black cambric with pale gray trim at the cuffs and collar.

"Are you sure you wouldn't like me to—"

"Thank you, but no. I'll go down to the dining room and sup with the other travelers." She hoped Captain Briggs would be there. She wanted to know if her throat would go dry and her heart shudder in her chest at the sight of him.

Heaven help her, but she had begun to crave those astonishing feelings he'd awakened in her. She wanted more.

Gavin wasn't sure how he was going to survive the rest of their journey to London and back. He wanted Christina with an intensity that was unequaled in his experience.

He noticed everything about her, from the soft blush of her cheeks to the delicate veins of her hands. Her neck was elegant, made impossibly more so by the fringe of curls that caressed it so softly. She'd tasted like the smoothest brandy he could imagine, and she was as soft as the petals of a flower.

And she was a duke's granddaughter. A viscount's widow. She was essentially an earl's daughter, too.

Gavin was estranged from his own father, and the highest rank he could hope to achieve was that of gentleman farmer. Hardly a life she would expect.

Dwelling on the beautiful bounty that lay beneath her clothes was not productive in the least. Nor was it prudent.

But he didn't seem to be able to help himself. He wasn't even sure how he'd managed to break it off earlier, going against every instinct he possessed.

He dug out one of his agricultural journals in an attempt to distract himself from the incredible lust she'd stirred in him, but to no avail. He was still aroused and not likely to find satisfaction any time in the near future.

Especially not with Lady Christina Fairhaven.

Gavin hoped she would not go down to the dining room for the supper he'd ordered, but remain in her own chamber as she'd done the night before. In the morning, he would have some distance, and when he saw her for those few minutes before she entered her carriage, he would be able to keep his mind on the day's journey.

He passed the time gazing at—but not absorbing—articles about fertilizers and crop rotation, and when he judged it time for supper, went downstairs. Trevor was sitting at one of the long tables in the dining room taking his turn at the meal while Hancock was presumably staying in the room they shared, guarding Christina's jewels. The lady herself was nowhere in sight.

Gavin let out a long breath of relief and glanced around the room. It was crowded, so he took a seat beside Trevor as a comely young serving maid brought him a plate. She stayed overlong at the table, smiling and making eyes at him. Much to his dismay, her flirting did not rouse him, in spite of the fact that her fair skin and hair reminded him vaguely of Amelia.

He found himself quite unmoved. Dark, shining curls preoccupied him these days, and the lithe figure of the serving maid could not compare to the soft womanly curves that had been pressed against him only a short while before.

"You've got that one's eye, Captain," Trevor said quietly, out of the side of his mouth.

" 'Tis you she's watching, Trevor."

The young man blushed and bent his head over his plate, finishing his meal as a new voice saved him from further embarrassment.

"Might we join you gents?" The man was tall and brawny, and dressed in sturdy, good quality clothes for travel. His plain but pleasant-looking wife stood just behind him.

Gavin nodded his assent and the couple sat down across from him as Trevor stood and took his leave. " 'Tis time for me to take Mr. Hancock's place."

"Aye, Trevor. See you in the morning," Gavin said.

The newcomer put out his hand for Gavin to shake,

his sharp eyes friendly and confident. "Charles Crocker, from Crocker Farm in Derbyshire."

"Gavin Briggs."

"Where are ye bound, if ye don't mind my asking, Mr. Briggs?"

"To London," Gavin replied, though it felt strange to answer directly, without deception. After his years in Castlereagh's service, he was quite unaccustomed to traveling openly, without pretext. "And you?"

"We're on our way home from a buying expedition in Yorkshire," he said.

"Crocker Farm?" Gavin asked, welcoming the distraction from the dark-haired lady who occupied far too many of his thoughts these days. "What do you raise at Crocker Farm?"

Christina went down to the crowded dining room, where she saw Captain Briggs sharing a table with a prosperous-looking gentleman and a lady who appeared to be his wife. Briggs was smiling and engaged in a very lively conversation.

Christina could not help but notice that he reserved his smiles for everyone but her.

He glanced up, and an arc of awareness sizzled between them, scorching all the nerves in her body with a purely pleasurable burn. If she had to choose, she decided she could live without smiles.

She stood still for a moment, stunned by her reaction to the sight of him, then managed to compose herself and approach his table. He and his companions came to their feet as she took a seat.

"Lady Fairhaven, allow me to present Mr. Charles Crocker and his wife."

"Please, resume your meal," she said as the two made their bows and spoke of their pleasure at meeting a viscountess. "And don't let me interrupt. You were speaking of . . . ?"

"The growing season in Hampshire, my lady," said Mr. Crocker.

"Ah . . . you're from Hampshire, then? Traveling far from home, aren't you?"

"No, my lady," said Mr. Crocker. "'Twas Mr. Briggs who was asking. Seems he plans to buy a farm and settle in Hampshire."

Christina cast a surprised glance at Captain Briggs. She had not known that about him . . . but why should she? They hardly knew each other.

And yet she knew how he tasted and the rasp of his whiskers against her cheek. She knew his scent and the strength of his arms around her.

But the Crockers had learned more about his life during the course of one supper in his company than she had throughout their several days together.

Christina realized she'd taken much for granted when all she really knew was that Captain Gavin Briggs was the son of a nobleman, and a former army officer who had been commissioned by a duke to locate his granddaughters and return them to him. She also knew he was nearly impervious to pain—if his reaction to the wound in his arm was any indication—and that he'd been wounded more than once before that.

A logical conclusion was that he planned to use his reward from the Duke of Windermere to buy his Hampshire farm. And it caused her no small amount of guilt for having delayed their journey to Windermere and his ability to collect his payment from her grandfather.

Another troublesome thought came to her, and Christina felt more than a little bothered by the possibility that he might have someone—a young lady— waiting for him to establish himself in Hampshire. No doubt a man as handsome as Gavin Briggs had admirers. But he would not have kissed her as he had if he were betrothed, or promised in any way.

Would he?

Christina's husband had not been faithful, but she knew not all men were like Edward. Her father was a good example of a loyal and committed husband. Lord Sunderland had never strayed from his wife's bed, Christina was sure. She wanted to think that Captain Briggs was the same kind of man.

Not that it made any difference to her.

"Mr. Briggs," said Mr. Crocker, drawing Christina from her ruminations. He looked guardedly to his left, toward the front of the building. "I believe we might be in for some trouble."

Chapter 9

Christina looked up sharply, shaken from her musings by the quiet alarm she heard in Mr. Crocker's tone. The voices in the room quieted as three men in long dark coats and broad-brimmed hats came into the inn and stood just outside the dining room. The innkeeper demanded to know what they wanted, but the largest of the men shoved him aside and walked into the dining room.

She felt Captain Briggs's body stiffen beside her, and for the first time in her life, Christina felt serious fear. Clearly, he believed they were about to be accosted. But were they Baron Chetwood's men?

He spoke under his breath to the Crockers. "Whatever you do—do not mention Lady Fairhaven's name."

She saw the couple's cautious nods of acknowledgment, and then Briggs spoke quietly to her. "As soon as you're able to leave without notice, go up to your room and bar the door. Keep your maid with you if she's up there."

She took a deep breath, more than willing to do as he instructed. But as the rogues came into the room, they blocked her path of escape. She could not leave, so she remained beside Gavin and prayed that Trevor or Hancock would hear something amiss and come into the room with their guns loaded and ready.

The three intruders were brawny and ominous-looking with heavy beards over their rawboned faces. It was quite clear they were not merely travelers looking for food and lodgings. They had come to do mischief.

"Ladies and gents," said the tallest one as he stepped inside the dining room. "Put yer money on the tables. And yer jewels . . . aye, whatever ye've got. We're not particular," he added with a toothless grin.

Christina swallowed a wave of panic. What if they rummaged through all the rooms after they finished here and found her jewels? What if she lost the means to trap her blackmailer? *Where were Hancock and Trevor?*

"Now see here!" cried Mr. Palmer from somewhere behind the men, though Christina did not hear a shred of authority in his voice. "Leave this establishment immediately. You are not welcome here!"

She cast a furtive glance at Captain Briggs, who sat in his chair, unmoving. His jaw was clenched tight, and he was not looking at the men. He was doing *nothing*!

Christina could not allow them to ransack the inn. She had to act. But how? The innkeeper was futilely trying to get the men to leave his guests alone, but the leader turned on him, viciously. He spread his hand over Palmer's face and shoved him hard, sending him sprawling on his back across a nearby table.

Women cried out with alarm, and several of the guests stood and made halfhearted protests. But the intruders did not relent. They started pushing and shoving everyone who stood in their way as they moved through the dining room, throwing punches, ripping jewelry from hands and necks, and tearing purses from belts.

They seemed invincible.

Christina was terrified. She felt an overpowering urge to hide behind Gavin Briggs, or even get up and flee the room, to somehow get past the villains and run upstairs to the safety of her room.

But Captain Briggs reached over and placed his hand on hers as he spoke quietly to Mr. and Mrs. Crocker. "When they get to us, be ready to stand quickly and move back. Play along with them if need be."

Mr. Crocker gave a small nod of acknowledgment.

Christina wanted to ask what he was going to do, but was too afraid of calling attention to them. She had not doubted that he could protect her as they traveled, but the situation in the dining room was impossible. There were three of the intruders, and none of the guests in the dining room had seemed capable of thwarting them. What could Captain Briggs possibly do?

The tall robber's gaze was suddenly upon her, but

Christina refused to look at him when he came to her table, even when he spoke. "Lor, what've we got 'ere? A nice piece of fluff, eh, lads?"

The other two came to his side and eyed her in a manner that made her skin crawl.

"Look a' that hair. What's it, d'ye think?"

"Is it a lad or a lass?" They all eyed her, guffawing like fools at the stupid joke.

"And you!" one of them shouted at Captain Briggs. "Big feller like you. Can't do naught fer yer woman now, eh?"

Christina felt a scream rising in the back of her throat as the leader reached for her. But Mrs. Crocker stood suddenly. Her husband did the same, tossing his money pouch on the table. "Here now. Leave the lady alone."

The intruders ignored them, but Christina felt Captain Briggs's body tighten beside her.

"We'll just have a taste o' this fine litt—"

Gavin suddenly came to his feet, jerking up the table as he moved. Christina jumped away as he hauled the heavy wooden plank by its two legs and heaved it at the villains, catching them by surprise and knocking them to the floor.

Bedlam ensued.

"Leave, Christina!" Gavin commanded as he and Crocker held the table in place on top of their assailants, momentarily incapacitating them. "Get out of here. Now!" He wanted her as far away from danger as possible.

Fortunately, she did as he ordered and hastened away from the skirmish. He hoped she would hurry up to her room and lock herself in, for he did not know if these reprobates were alone, or if there were more accomplices outside.

Once she was gone, he summoned some of the other men to help him and Crocker secure the criminals for the authorities. He told the innkeeper to check outside and see if there were more of them, and to send someone for the nearest magistrate.

A couple of the men collected the stolen money and valuables and returned them to their proper owners, while Gavin and Crocker hauled the villains to a windowless pantry outside the kitchen. There the scoundrels would remain until the magistrate and a constable or two arrived to take them away for trial.

When all was settled, Gavin made for the stairway, anxious to check on Christina. But he found himself surrounded by the crowd of people who had been accosted in the dining room.

Gavin wanted no accolades, for he had only done what he'd been trained to do: to think on his feet and act quickly. And he'd accomplished his primary goal, which was to assure Christina's safety. He wanted to get upstairs and see that she was all right, and finally managed to extricate himself from the congratulations and offers of drinks.

Slipping up the stairs, he made his way down the narrow corridor to her bedchamber. He knocked on the door and heard movement within.

"Who is it?"

He smiled at her response and some of the tension in his body dissipated. She wasn't about to open the door to just anyone. "Me. Briggs."

He heard the key work in the lock and when she opened the door, she threw herself into his arms.

He held her close, for she was shaking violently. He slid his hands across her back, pressed her gently against him.

"You . . . I was so afraid. And you didn't move. I thought you weren't going to do anything." Her voice was soft, unsteady.

"Timing is everything." His cavalier remark was intended to lighten the moment, but he felt her breath catch. He pulled away slightly and looked down at her face. She was far too pale. "Are you all right?"

She nodded. "Yes. Just frightened. I've never . . ." She pressed her face against his chest and his arms tightened around her.

He wanted her intensely, but he knew she was only holding on to him now because of shock and fear. She wasn't thinking about lying with him, or letting him undress her slowly . . . sensuously . . . baring every inch of her lush skin to his view, to his touch . . . to his lips.

He stifled a groan.

"Are they gone?"

"Not gone, but locked up and waiting for the constables."

"Were they . . . Did they have anything to do with Baron Chetwood?"

He didn't want to talk, but she clearly needed reassurance. "No. Just your ordinary burglars."

Gavin still didn't know if Chetwood would attempt to harm or interfere with Christina, but their intruders didn't seem to have targeted Christina. They were after everyone's valuables.

Her shuddering subsided and he dropped his arms away from her body and took a step back, clearly needing to put some space between them. "Where is your maid?"

"I don't know," she said, wrapping her arms tightly around herself. She looked small and vulnerable, and Gavin wanted to ignore his instincts and gather her close once again. He wanted to taste her. To feel all those soft curves fitting against the hard planes of his body.

But he knew better. He needed to keep his perspective and remember she was a mission to him, a task to complete.

He forced himself to look away from her and surveyed the bedchamber. It was small, with only one narrow bed, a small armoire and a chair beside the fireplace. It was almost identical to his own. "Your maid has another room?"

Christina nodded. "I don't usually require her to sleep close by."

Gavin nodded, unduly pleased to know she was not the demanding kind of woman his mother had been. Lady Hargrove had needed servants at her beck and call day and night. His mother had been ridiculously spoiled.

"I'll be back in a few minutes."

"Wait!" she cried, taking a step toward him. "Where are you going?"

"To check on your maid." And to regain some sanity. He'd felt like a madman from the moment Christina had been threatened, and had not yet taken a moment to calm himself.

But all was well. Christina had not been harmed, just as he'd known. But he'd had to reassure himself.

He found Christina's maid in a small room near the one shared by Trevor and Hancock.

"Do you think we'll have any more trouble, Captain?" Hancock asked.

Gavin shook his head. "No way of knowing. Just because no one saw any other accomplices does not mean there aren't any."

Hancock nodded.

"Is Lady Fairhaven all right?" her maid asked. "Does she need me to stay with her?"

"No," Gavin said. "I'll guard her room until morning."

He hadn't realized his intention until he said it, and the servants seemed to think nothing of it. They bid each other good night, and Gavin returned to the staircase. He had a feeling it was going to be a long night.

Christina had never been more frightened. Or more impressed. Gavin Briggs was even more formidable than she'd imagined. She'd made her escape from the dining room and gone partway up the stairs, but stopped to turn and watch him subdue the thieves from a safe distance.

She'd mistaken his inaction at first, but he'd been calm and poised throughout the confrontation with the villains. He'd waited, and then moved against them at exactly the right moment. Then he'd given her the opportunity to get away to safety, and managed to spoil the intruders' evil plans. He'd protected everyone in the inn.

And all he could say was *timing was everything*.

Things might have gone quite differently had Captain Briggs not acted as he'd done, and Christina could not help but wonder if Lang had gotten himself involved in similar difficulties in Plymouth.

She hoped Lieutenant Norris had misidentified Lang's body, but if he was not dead . . .

Where was he? What did the blackmailer know?

She had to believe Lang was alive. He was just . . . Well, Lang was her most unpredictable brother. Felton used to call him a loose cannon. But Christina knew better. Lang was sweet and true in his own way, even though he did not always follow a conventional path. He would have moved mountains to help her, and she would do no less for him.

Even if it meant racing down to London with a small fortune in jewelry and dangerous situations on the road. The incident in the dining room left her feeling as wobbly as a newborn kitten, and a little bit giddy. She knew she should not have thrown herself into Captain Briggs's arms, but she'd done it without thinking. She'd needed the warmth and strength of his arms around her.

And perhaps she wanted to see if he would kiss her again.

Christina knew it was not right. Any further intimacy with Gavin Briggs would be thoroughly improper. She had been a faithful wife, and a pure widow. She had not been tempted to wantonness in any way.

But her chastity had never been tested. Until now.

Her husband's intimate touch had not roused her desires the way Captain Briggs's slightest glance did. Gavin's kiss had caused a burning heat in her, and Christina could not imagine how she would respond if he actually made love to her.

Her knees weakened and she sat down on her bed, only to jump at the sound of a knock at her door. She guessed it was Gavin, bringing Jenny to her, but she knew enough to ask before opening her door.

But it was Gavin, answering the same as before, and a ripple of pure lust skittered down Christina's back at the sound of his voice.

She opened the door but did not see Jenny.

He did not come into the room, but tipped his head toward it. "I'm staying in here tonight. Make yourself ready for bed while I'm gone."

"Wh-what?" Her heart pummeled the inside of her chest.

"I'm going to sleep here. . . ."

Christina's breath caught when she thought of

lying beside him, of feeling his arms around her.

And more.

But then he pointed to the floor by the fireplace, not far from her bed. "I'll make a bed for myself there."

"Is that . . ." Oh God. "Is that necessary, Captain Briggs?"

He took a few steps across the hall to his own room, then turned and pinned her with an intense look before opening his door. "I hope it proves unnecessary, Lady Fairhaven. But it would be best if you were in your bed by the time I return."

Leaving his door open in order to keep watch over the hall outside their rooms, Gavin refused to consider what she might be doing behind that closed door. Removing her clothes and slipping into the bed? It was far too unsettling a thought.

And yet he would be spending the night lying within inches of her bed. That was far more unsettling than his lascivious fancies. Worse, perhaps, than actually taking her in his arms and exploring every inch of her.

It was going to be pure torture.

He loaded his pistol, then gathered up the blankets from his bed and hoped he was not making a huge mistake. Spending the night with Christina was temptation personified. Knowing that she would be lying warm and soft and vulnerable in the bed only a few feet away from him, wearing naught but something feminine and delicate, could very well be his undoing.

He jabbed his fingers through his hair and reconsidered. Perhaps he ought to get Hancock up here with his muzzle loader and make him stand guard over her.

Dismissing the idea as soon as it came into his head, Gavin returned to Christina's bedchamber. She unlocked the door and stepped aside, but not before he caught sight of the fragile chemise he'd imagined, lightly draping her incredibly feminine form.

His throat went dry and his hands ached to touch her. But he set down his blankets and the pistol, then went to the window that overlooked the front of the inn.

He tried not to think about the woman who stood behind him in the flickering light of the fireplace, or her willingness to share a room with him while barely dressed.

It had grown dark outside, so Gavin could not see any interlopers lurking about. If anyone was out there, they would want to remain hidden until all the lamps in the inn had been put out. That's when trouble would begin, if the prisoners had any other accomplices.

He'd checked to be sure the inn's doors were barred and the windows were all locked. Still, it was doubtful that he would get much sleep that night, concerned as he was about the possibility of more trouble.

And extremely aware of the woman who would be lying in the nearby bed.

"Is anyone out there?" Christina asked.

She was still standing near the door and Gavin knew it would be a very bad idea to turn and look at her. He wasn't sure he could keep his hands off her.

"Lady Fair—"

She moved, and he felt her beside him.

"What are you doing?" he asked.

"Just wondering if you would kiss me again."

Chapter 10

Christina could hardly credit that she'd actually asked him to kiss her. While she'd been yearning for his touch ever since he'd kissed her in his room, he would not even look at her.

She knew it was foolhardy. Possibly a little bit mad. It was what she wanted.

"Will you not even look at me?" She did not know how she had the brass to speak so boldly to him.

"This is a very bad idea, Lady Fairhaven." He turned toward her as he said the words, and she saw a flicker of appreciation as well as desire in his eyes.

"I know," she whispered. "But you made me feel . . . I was never kissed in such a way and I . . ."

His hands were tight fists at his sides and his jaw flexed once. He was going to refuse her, and Christina felt like an awkward, foolish goose even for thinking she could seduce him.

"Such an absurd idea. Please forget I ever mentioned it." She swallowed and took a step back, blushing madly as she crossed her arms over her chest. She knew she ought to say something else, something about the incident with the thieves or perhaps a remark about the Crockers. Anything to cover the clumsiness of the moment.

But she was tongue-tied and her throat felt as though it was closing up with a thick, burning sensation. It was mortification.

Dear Lord. She would not succumb to tears.

She turned away quickly, before he could see the moisture welling in her eyes. As soon as she composed herself she would tell him he did not need to stay with her, that she would—

He grabbed her suddenly and pulled her back, turning her as she fell against him. "Aye, it's the most foolish idea you've had yet."

He crushed his mouth to hers, as though *he'd* been the one who'd hungered for her kiss, her touch. His hands spread the heat of his body across her back, and when they slid down to cup her bottom, she was lost. She wanted it. She wanted everything.

She opened her mouth under his and felt the incursion of his tongue. He mastered her so easily, pulling her close, thoroughly rousing her senses. She felt the hard evidence of his arousal as he moved against her, and heard a gruff growl deep in his chest.

All at once, he lifted her into his arms and took her to the bed, lowering her to the mattress as he came down half on top of her. As he kissed her again,

Christina heard the dull thud of his boots hitting the floor. He shoved his jacket away, then pulled back to look at her.

"You had better be damned sure this is what you want, Lady Fairhaven."

She almost winced at his rough tone, and the formality of her title. But there was a burning need inside her, a need only he could assuage. She wanted him desperately.

Without breaking the contact of her eyes on his, she answered by untying her chemise and slipping the sleeves from her shoulders.

He lowered his head and pressed his lips to her neck, then moved to her collarbones as he worked her chemise down. His lips and teeth teased her sensitive flesh, and every coherent thought skittered from Christina's mind. He cupped her breasts and swirled his tongue around one nipple, and she almost forgot to breathe.

Pleasure shot straight to her womb at his sensual touch and Christina felt herself melting. His whiskers rasped against her skin, and his breath was the only sound breaking the silence of the room. He slid his hands down to her waist, pulling her chemise lower as he went, feasting on her as though she were a banquet of something he found . . . irresistible.

A tremor ran through her, not from being cold, but from the heat they generated together. His big hands were hard and calloused, but every bit as gentle—and knowing—as she'd imagined. He was so exquisitely male—his scent and texture and the deep timbre of his voice—and Christina felt wholly enveloped by his taut body.

She pulled at his shirt, desperate to feel his bare skin against hers. He interrupted his ministrations for a moment and ripped his shirt over his head, baring that superbly sculpted chest she'd so admired.

He was big, strong, and invincible.

He tugged at her chemise, and Christina lifted her hips to allow him to dispense with it. She felt brazen and debauched and thoroughly shameless when he came back to her, shifting his hands beneath her hips, looking at her more intimately than she'd ever imagined anyone would do.

His bold gaze was unspeakably arousing, and Christina basked in the frank sensuality of his expression. He looked into her eyes as he descended on her, lowering his mouth to her feminine mound.

He found an incredibly sensitive spot where he kissed her, then used his tongue, swirling and licking until she was writhing with need. Suddenly there was pressure, and she felt him slip a finger inside her. He used his mouth and tongue, building her pleasure until it became unbearable. Her nerves clenched tightly, pulsing as her muscles quickened and contracted in wave after wave of pure sensation.

Gavin needed to be inside her.

Watching her climax had nearly brought on his own, like an untried lad still in school. The next time she came, he wanted to feel her sheath tightening around his cock.

It was madness, he knew. But he would not stop now. He tore off his trews and inched back up her body, kissing a path to her magnificent breasts, and then taking her mouth. He covered her with his body, slipping between her legs and positioning himself at the threshold of her body.

His arms were trembling, and he was going to be a raving disaster if he did not take the plunge now.

She cried out as he entered her and he stilled, his brain in a fog of arousal, yet aware that it had been some time for her. His heart pounded heavily in his chest, and after his moment of stillness, he could not help but move. She wrapped her legs around his waist and pulled him in.

And then he was lost.

She gazed up at him, her expression one of astonishment. Gavin was barely aware of his thoughts, but something drove him to satisfy her far better than her husband had ever done, to displace his memory from her mind.

Using one hand to tilt her hips, he sank into her, intensifying their contact. He began slowly, then increased his rhythm. She writhed against him, tightening her legs around him. Her breathing became more rapid than before, and the blacks of her eyes widened as he pushed her over the edge once again.

Two more thrusts and he went along with her, lowering his chest to her breasts. A deep rasp shuddered from his lungs as her nails scraped his back and her body trembled and tightened around him.

Spasms of intense sensation pulsed through him from the point where they were joined to the farthest reaches of his body. He quaked against her, every inch a repository of pure pleasure and utter satisfaction.

Her arms and legs slid away and she became boneless beneath him, but he was not yet ready to withdraw from her.

He propped up on his elbows and looked down at her, feeling shaken and not a little confused. He'd bedded a number of beautiful, willing women, but could not recall any who'd been so frankly responsive. Christina was made for a man's touch, and if he was not mistaken, she possessed far less experience than he'd have expected from a widow.

And yet she had thoroughly seduced him.

He had an impossibly strong urge to clasp her body tightly to his, to press light kisses to her shoulders as she slept and hold her against him all night.

What an idiot he was. Men such as he did not entertain such mawkish inclinations. She was naught but a few moments' diversion, a release that she'd wanted as badly as he. Now that they'd had their tumble—

The sound of a crash somewhere below shook him from his pathetic musings and he reacted instantly.

Jumping from the bed, he pulled on his trews and shirt, then picked up his pistol. He went to the door and finally turned to Christina. "Lock this after I go."

* * *

Christina climbed out of bed and went to the door, quickly turning the key in the lock. Her heart pounded nearly as hard as it had while Gavin was making love to her, and she prayed desperately that he would return unharmed.

She took her banyan from her traveling bag and pulled it on before going to the window to look down at the entrance of the inn. She could not imagine what had caused the noise that had driven Gavin from the bed, but knew it could not be good.

Still, it could hardly be as astonishing as what had transpired in this room only a few moments ago. If anyone ever learned of it, she would be chastised. Thoroughly rebuked.

And yet she could not regret what had happened. She'd never experienced the kind of passion Gavin Briggs had brought to her bed, never known love-making could be so exciting, so incredibly *intimate*.

He'd touched every part of her body with his mouth and hands, and he'd looked into her eyes so knowingly as he'd done it. He'd brought her to completion twice—*twice!*—when she had not experienced it even once with Edward.

The connection she'd felt with Gavin was astonishing. He'd seen to her pleasure before his own, and though he was a far larger man than Edward, had taken exquisite care not to hurt her.

She crossed her arms against her chest and banished the unwelcome thoughts of Edward. Her selfish husband had barely given her a thought while he

was alive, so why should she spare him the slightest
thought now?

Other doors opened and curious faces peered out.
"Stay in your rooms. Keep your doors locked,"
Gavin said. By the light of the sconces in the upper
hall, he flew down the stairs and rushed to the back
of the inn where they'd locked up the prisoners. He
found Christina's driver already out of the room he
shared with Trevor, holding his rifle at the ready.

Palmer rushed in just seconds after Gavin. "What
was that noise?" he asked, fastening his trews as he
spoke. It was clear the man had been jarred from his
bed, just like Gavin.

Or perhaps not quite like Gavin. He could think
of nothing that compared to what had just happened
in Christina's bed.

"It came from in here," said Hancock, tipping his
head toward the pantry.

Gavin glanced at the pantry door, which was still
securely locked. The prisoners were inside. Even if
they managed to untie one another's wrists, they
could not get out. Or, at least, he didn't think so.

They heard a loud rap coming from inside. "Ye've
got te let us out o' here, mate," one of the men shouted.

"Not bloody likely," Gavin muttered, feeling an-
grier than he ought for being so suddenly routed
from Christina's bed. As much as he might want to
deny his romantic sentiments, he had not yet had his
fill of Lady Fairhaven.

He wanted a great deal more.

"They're secure," he said to the men. "Everyone can go back to bed."

He withdrew, making a quick check of every window and door on the main floor . . . thinking it might be wise to delay his return to Christina. He should not go back into her room, but the woman had managed to beguile him as no other had ever done.

But Gavin did not harbor any delusions about his place in society, nor would Christina. She knew he was a younger son, with no fortune and few prospects, except what he could reap from her grandfather. She had to know unsuitable he was. Even Amelia had realized it before he'd had a chance to ruin both their lives.

He finally returned to Christina's room and found her wearing naught but the silky banyan that matched her eyes. It was cinched tightly at her waist and covered her from neck to ankles, but did little to conceal the shape of her breasts or their tips, puckering the fabric.

He was overwhelmed by the desire to take her back to bed and repeat their earlier experience. She reached up to cup his chin and her banyan gaped open, giving him a view of one luscious breast.

He could not resist sliding his hand inside as he lowered his mouth to hers. She let the banyan fall to the floor just before skimming her hands up his chest and into the hair at his nape.

Chapter 11

Christina had never been so forward in her life. And it felt wonderful.

Now she had some understanding of what Edward had sought when he visited Mrs. Shilton. It was no wonder his heart had given out while in the throes of passion. She could almost believe her own would do the same.

Gavin showed no signs of collapsing, though. His body seemed utterly invincible.

She looked into his eyes as he reached his peak and saw a quick second of something raw and uninhibited before he closed them and held her while shuddering with pleasure.

Her body quaked as he withdrew, and he slipped down alongside her in the narrow bed, pulling her against him, her back to his chest. He draped his hand over her waist, pulling her close as he caressed the sensitive skin of her abdomen.

"I've never shared a bed with anyone," she whispered.

His hand stilled and she realized he might take it

as a request to leave. She clasped her hand over his in a silent plea for him to stay. She had not appreciated the intimacy that could be shared with a lover in the moments after joining. Edward had never cared to try it. He'd always made haste to leave her bed after their couplings. There'd been no real intimacy then, and now she realized he'd had no skill in the bedchamber, either.

Unlike Gavin Briggs.

He'd made their lovemaking special, taking care to rouse her until she climaxed before taking his own pleasure. She hadn't known such fervor—or such tenderness—existed.

Perhaps she was better off without a husband, and just keep a paramour instead.

Gavin gathered Christina close and turned her in his arms in order to avoid having to look in her eyes. Clearly, what they'd done was unlike anything she'd experienced with her husband, and she might well misinterpret its significance.

It was sex. Nothing more.

The fire crackled and flickered, casting long shadows across the room. It was peaceful and quiet, and Gavin hoped Christina didn't want to talk, didn't want to examine their coupling. What it meant for the future.

He closed his eyes, then bent his knees and cupped Christina's body against his own, keeping his hand at her waist, and not on her breast as he was wont to do.

She was relaxed, but not asleep, and he could almost hear her questions. As he predicted, she turned her head and spoke in a whisper.

"You were so . . . I've never seen anything to compare with what happened in the dining room tonight. Thank you for what you did." Her voice was soft and slightly hoarse, her words unexpected.

She did not speak of the future or how he fit into hers . . . she did not mention how their bed play might have changed things between them.

"Anything to get you safely to London and back to Windermere." His voice sounded gruff and colder than he intended. Or perhaps he *had* intended it. To remind them both what his motives were.

"Would you use that pistol if someone came in?"

"Aye." It was on a table beside the bed, exactly where he'd put it.

"Have you ever shot anyone?"

"I was in the army." He prevaricated, wondering how she'd wandered to this subject. "It's what I was paid to do."

She turned her entire body and faced him. A slight dip in her brow indicated some puzzlement. "I do not know how you can do it. Soldiers, I mean. When you look at the enemy and see that he's . . . well, he's just a man."

Aye. That was one of the differences between them. He could kill, but she could not fathom it.

"The enemy might be just a man, but he would kill me first if he had a chance."

Gavin didn't want to speak of his disreputable

past any longer, so he slipped his hand down to her smooth bottom and brought her hips close while pressing kisses to her neck. He felt fully sated, but that would not stop him from enjoying her again. His arousal grew slowly but steadily when he thought of her uninhibited response to his touch.

He heard her low hum of pleasure. "I did not know you had an interest in agriculture," she said, and Gavin realized he would have to do more than nip at her neck.

"Are you not tired?" he said.

"No." She yawned. "You were talking to Mr. Crocker about wheat and turnips. About land use. Will you live on your farm in Hampshire?"

"We have a long day ahead of us," he said, putting a little space between them. "Best if we both try to get some sleep."

She took the hint, skipping her fingers down his chest to find his nipples. Gavin's breath caught. "Perhaps. But not yet, Captain Briggs."

It was a few minutes before dawn when Christina awoke. Gavin had slipped out of bed quite soundlessly and was crouched near the fireplace, building up the fire in the chilly room. Then he quietly pulled on his trews. Still shirtless, he sat down and pulled on his boots. Then he slid his fingers through his hair, and Christina's breath caught at the sight of the powerful muscles in his chest and sides.

She would never have been so bold if he hadn't kissed her in his room. His touch, his kiss, had awak-

ened something in her, something intense and for-
bidden—something she could not ignore.

He stood and pulled on his shirt, then picked up
his waistcoat, jacket, and pistol. Then he came to her,
and crouched beside the bed. "You need to get up
and lock the door behind me," he said quietly.

Christina sat up, holding the linen sheet to her
breasts. Not that there was any part of her body he
had not seen, touched, or kissed . . . But morning
brought trepidations. "I will."

He stayed for a moment, looking at her without
speaking, without touching her . . . then he turned
and left the room. Christina followed him to the door
and locked it, then returned to the bed for a little
more sleep. She had not had much of it during the
night.

He'd been quite considerate in building up the
fire for her, and staying as quiet as possible as he
dressed. He'd had no choice but to wake her to lock
the door, else Christina believed he would have
slipped silently out of the room, allowing her to rest
a while longer.

She should have expected such thoughtfulness
from him, after the gentle consideration he'd demonstrated throughout the night. In the past few days,
he'd shown her in a hundred different ways that he
was a hard man, yet she'd bent him to her will. He
could have resisted her advances the night before,
but he'd allowed her to seduce him.

She was frightfully glad he had.

Before meeting Gavin Briggs, it had not occurred

to her to take a lover; only to consider taking another husband when her mourning period was done. Now that she realized exactly how Edward had deprived her, she was going to be a great deal more selective when suitors came to call. She did not want another one like Edward.

She lay back in the bed and pictured Gavin in her mind. He and Edward were both the sons of viscounts, but they seemed a different breed altogether.

Christina could not imagine Edward doing anything to thwart the criminals who'd come into the dining room, not even if their leader had dragged her away to commit some unspeakable evil against her. Gavin had known how to overpower the three men. He'd protected her.

She owed him her life. And she could not help but feel she was being a little unfair for coercing him into accompanying her to London for her own purpose. She did not know why he hadn't simply overpowered her at Sweethope Cottage and taken her to Windermere. Clearly, he had the prowess to accomplish any feat, but here he was, at an out-of-the-way inn where they might have been seriously harmed . . . or worse. And now she demanded that he assist her at All Hallows Church.

The thought of dealing with her blackmailer brought Christina back to reality. Of course, she would do whatever she could to help Lang. He must be in some serious trouble, else he would certainly have contacted someone in the family. But since he could not, she would do whatever she could for him, even if it caused a delay in her journey to Windermere.

Besides, she was not quite sure about going there. She didn't care anything for the grandfather who'd abandoned her and her sister, and their mother before them. What did it matter if the old man was dying and regretted what he'd done all those years ago? He *ought* to regret it. No one—not even a duke—should be able to interfere with or penalize two people who cared so deeply for each other that they defied all to be together.

She curled up under the soft down blanket and realized that both sets of her parents had shared something special. Sarah and her barrister had defied her father to marry, and had not looked back. Sarah had remained estranged from her father even after her death.

Lord and Lady Sunderland remained true to one another all through the years of their marriage, even before Felton's birth, when it seemed Rowena was barren. The earl had not tried to discard her for a more fertile wife. He'd loved and cared for her in spite of their lack of heirs.

Christina tried to recall something of her life before the Sunderlands took her in, but could not, her earliest memories beginning when Felton was born. She could not even remember Lily, her twin. And yet she felt that Lily had always been there, somehow. In the back of her mind.

Christina could feel her there, and wondered if Lily felt the same.

She wanted to meet her sister, but it was not necessary to travel all the way to Windermere to do so. If Lily was now Lady Ashby, it should not be too difficult to find her. Christina could go directly to her home after London . . . after she found Lang.

But that would mean betraying Gavin.

Gavin saw Charles Crocker standing in the inn's entryway when he went downstairs. Together, they went to the back kitchen and saw that Palmer the innkeeper was already starting to work. Christina's two menservants came out of their room and glanced toward the pantry door. "Should we open it, Captain?"

"The magistrate will be here soon," Palmer said, looking over his shoulder.

Gavin decided to let each of the felons out separately to use the privy, so Christina's men unlocked the door and allowed one man out at a time.

To avoid any untoward actions from the prisoners, Gavin and Hancock kept their firearms trained on the ones who remained inside. None of them appeared half as threatening as they had the night before, but Gavin would not trust them, not even if they looked like kindly old grandfathers. He was quite clear on what they were capable of.

Standing guard as each man came out of the pantry and outside to the privy was a cumbersome process, but it kept Gavin from thinking too much about the night he'd spent in Christina's bed. It had been a long time since he'd enjoyed a woman's touch, and he told himself last night was merely a few hours' diversion with a willing woman. A beautiful, willing woman who had been insatiable.

But she was not some nameless serving wench who shared her favors in exchange for a few centimes.

Gavin did not think it had happened just because she was a widow, missing her conjugal relations with her husband. There'd been too much wonder in her eyes, too much surprise in her face for that. He suspected her husband had not been exactly attentive to her needs. Not when the bastard was so busy pleasing his mistress.

Once the three prisoners were back in their temporary gaol, Gavin and some of the other men performed a thorough search of the area surrounding the inn. They found no sign of any other interlopers, which meant it had been wholly unnecessary for him to have spent the night in Christina's room . . . in her bed.

He could not say he'd taken leave of his senses, for each of his senses had been all too acute. He'd felt every caress, and heard every sigh. He'd tasted and smelled her womanly scent, and seen the passion in her eyes. Every kiss had done more than arouse his body.

He muttered a vague curse at such an absurd notion and went outside with Bob Palmer to meet the magistrate and his men when they pulled up in front of the inn. They'd brought a cart in which to carry the criminals back to town, and were grateful to have them finally apprehended. Apparently, the rogues had been plaguing the district for weeks, and never been caught.

Gavin was relieved the villains had not been sent by Chetwood. Any man who'd been commissioned by a member of the Hellfire Club would be quick, professional, and vicious. He would never have taken the chances the robbers had attempted the night before.

The men Chetwood would send would be like the two rogues he'd used before to find and kill Lily. They might attack in a dark, narrow street, or some deserted alleyway in a town where Christina's party stopped for the night. The kind of men working for Chetwood would think nothing of striking them on the open road.

He could not believe he'd overlooked the possibility that Chetwood might still be after Christina. He would not be so lax again.

Gavin quickly finished with the magistrate, and went to join Christina's driver and footman, who'd already hitched the horses to the carriage and were leading it out of the stable.

"After last night, we'll all need to be doubly watchful," he told them. "We don't know if there are any other brigands about, so be ready for trouble."

"Aye, Captain." Hancock touched the rifle at his side, demonstrating that he was prepared.

"If highwaymen approach us, they'll come on fast," Gavin continued as Christina and her maid came out of the inn. He did not know how she managed to look so alluring in her dull black gown. Her glossy black curls teased his eyes, and the thick, dark spikes of her lashes framed her gorgeous eyes. They'd sparked so vividly with passion . . .

He forced his attention toward her men. Bedding Christina had not been the most prudent decision he'd ever made, not that he'd had any control over their mad coupling. He'd wanted her intensely.

"If anyone suspicious comes for us, I'll want you to race the horses, Hancock. Drive as fast as you can, and I'll draw off the villains by riding in another direction."

The driver nodded.

"If they overtake you, do what you can to stall them until I can get back, but if push comes to shove, give them whatever they ask for."

Christina gasped. "No! I cannot afford to lose the only—"

"Lady Fairhaven, I intend to draw them off so that you can get away to safety."

"But what if they don't follow you? What if—"

"Sometimes, my lady, you have to choose between your money and your life."

"But I—"

"Of course we'll all do everything in our power to keep your treasure safe."

Gavin observed a myriad of expressions crossing her face as she stood looking at him, but she turned suddenly and climbed into the carriage without saying another word.

He stayed close to her carriage as they continued on their journey south. He had not enjoyed those few moments the previous evening when Christina had been in danger. And he didn't care to go through any such thing again.

He hoped to reach Mansfield by nightfall, but after consulting with Bob Palmer, realized it would be an awfully long stretch. A short ride in an enclosed carriage was challenging enough. He did not know if Christina and her maid could tolerate the extra hour or two it would take to make it all the way there.

They traveled all morning without stopping until a small village came into sight. Gavin detected no threats on the road, so he decided it would be safe for him to ride a short distance ahead of the carriage. In truth, it was better if he stayed as far from Christina as possible. The intimacy of their night together had given him cravings a man like him had no business entertaining.

He rode into the village and noted two small inns where they might take a few minutes' respite. He chose the better-looking one and went inside to the taproom. After ordering a meal to be prepared for their party, he took a table in a corner with his back to the wall. It was an old habit that had served him well in the past, and after last night, he knew better than to relax his guard.

The incident at Palmer's Inn could have gone badly. Fortunately, Crocker had kept his wits about him, and helped Gavin do what had to be done.

He scrubbed a hand across the lower half of his face. Those highwaymen would have had to kill him

before he let them get to Christina. It was hard to
believe he'd allowed her to become anything more
than a complicated assignment. But over the past
few days, she'd roused a deeply buried protective
instinct. He did not quite like it.

It was one thing to take care of his sister. This was
something altogether different.

Until now, he'd always been able to keep his emotions far removed from his missions, and it had
worked well. He accomplished whatever he'd set
out to do with a minimum of trouble, and without
conscience. This task for Windermere had become
far too personal.

There could be no more notice of Christina's
smiles, or her pretty curls, or her enticing figure in
her unrelenting black. He could not dwell upon her
luscious scent or those plush lips that had tasted so
very—

Damnation. He needed to regain some objectivity
in order to get the job done in London, regardless
of what he knew the outcome was likely to be, and
somehow get her to back to her grandfather at Windermere Park in spite of it.

Hancock and Trevor sat down at Gavin's small
table, leaving no room for Christina and Jenny to
join them.

Which was just as well. Christina needed to stop
thinking about the sculpted muscles of the man's
shoulders and arms, and the taut power of his hips;

she had to divert herself from reliving the moment that he'd . . .

She felt her face heat at the thought of it—of Gavin joining his body to hers, of moving within her and building an incredible tumult in her body. She had not known such bliss was possible.

Christina had been raised a proper lady, but the rules were entirely different for widows. She would not allow herself to feel guilty for seeking out and enjoying the pleasures of a man who appealed to her.

Captain Briggs was just such a man, in spite of his heavy-handedness . . . And yet he was more than a bit intimidating.

The man in question rose from his table and stood talking for a moment with Hancock and Trevor. But when the other men went outside, Gavin stopped beside Christina. "We should go as soon as possible, Lady Fairhaven."

So formal with her now.

She clasped her hands together in her lap, disturbed that she could not keep her thoughts from dwelling upon all that had transpired during the night with him.

All that she hoped to share again.

They resumed their journey and Christina could not help but feel the tension in every member of her party as they traveled southward. They were all on edge after last night's encounter with the robbers, even lighthearted Jenny.

Christina kept the carriage's curtains open in

order to see what was happening outside, but she would have preferred to ride horseback. She was a good rider, and if highwaymen came after them, she knew she would be able to outrun them.

Riding horseback would also give her the opportunity to spend time with Gavin. But they had not brought another riding horse, so she contented herself with catching sight of her handsome lover as he rode alongside the carriage, keeping watch, protecting her . . . protecting all of them.

Christina finally turned her thoughts to practical matters. She didn't know what she would do if her jewels were stolen, for then she would have nothing to put into the lectern at All Hallows Church. No way to find out where Lang was and what had happened to him.

She had to trust that Gavin would make sure the jewels did not fall into the hands of thieves. She had to believe he would know how to capture the black-mailer when he attempted to take the money at the church.

It was absolutely vital that she find out whatever the blackguard knew. Lang was the least predictable of her brothers, although his escapades had been far fewer since he'd gone into the navy. Their father had made his expectations clear—there was not to be any more trouble from Lang Jameson. And Lang had complied, at least, to Christina's knowledge.

At the end of the day they arrived at a little town north of Mansfield. Christina was weary after her long day in the carriage, and found herself anxious to retreat into her room at the inn Gavin chose near the center of town.

She was not a very practiced flirt, and though she'd managed to entice him to her bed once, she did not know what to expect tonight. Would he come to her of his own volition or would she have to craft some excuse?

They came to a stop in a stable yard, and Christina heard the men talking with one another. She unlatched the door to listen, but Gavin made a sudden dismount and ran at a trot toward the blacksmith's shop not far from the inn.

Trevor let down the carriage steps and Christina followed Gavin. He dashed into the smithy's shop, and though Christina stayed back a short distance, she heard him shout at someone inside. "You there!"

She had not noticed the slapping noise until it stopped, but as she moved closer to the wide entryway, she saw a man with a whip standing in the center of the forge. He was a beefy fellow, his face and arms moist with sweat, his fists the size of hams.

A small boy cowered on the floor in the corner.

Christina winced at the sight of the child's thin back, crisscrossed with red welts.

"What d'ye want," growled the blacksmith at Gavin's words.

"I want you to put down that whip."

In spite of Gavin's demand, the smithy crossed his arms over his massive chest, swaying slightly. He looked drunk. And meaner than a rabid dog. "Oh right. And who'll it be who sees that I do?"

Christina had a very bad feeling about what was about to happen, especially when Gavin took a step toward the man who still held the evil-looking whip.

"Go along, boy," Gavin said to the child, who appeared too frightened to move.

"Stay where ye are," the blacksmith snarled at him.

As Gavin took another few steps forward, Christina's worry turned to panic and she wondered what she could do to intercede. Then she remembered how calm Gavin had looked last night, just before crashing the heavy dining table into the robbers.

He looked the same now. Angry and fierce, but completely in control.

"You don't want to cross me, man," he said, his voice low and lethal. "Let the boy go."

"The hell I will."

Chapter 12

The blacksmith lunged toward Gavin, who feinted to the side, then grabbed the bigger man by the arm, twisting it behind him. Before the smithy could do anything at all, Gavin had him bent over his anvil, trapping his hands behind him. He quickly wrapped the big man's wrists with the whip.

Christina rushed to the child and raised him from his trembling crouch, in spite of the blacksmith's blustering demands to be let loose.

"What's your name?" she asked the boy over the man's drunken shouts.

The child, who couldn't have been more than about five years old, was trembling violently, his tear-streaked face devoid of color, and absolutely pitiful. His white-blond hair was overlong and tangled, and his meager clothes were threadbare.

"Th-Theo," he said between quiet sobs.

"Theo, where do you live?"

"Here."

Christina looked around and saw no evidence of any living quarters. "Where?"

He pointed to a ladder that led to nowhere but a straw-strewn loft, but then shrank down when the blacksmith roared an obscenity at Gavin.

"You live up there?" she asked the boy.

Theo nodded.

Christina could not believe it. The place was not suitable even for an animal. "Does he whip you often?"

Theo slipped his thumb into his mouth.

"Where is your mother?"

"Dead, miss." He managed to speak around his thumb.

"Is this your father?" She tipped her head in the blacksmith's direction.

"My uncle."

"You have no father?"

He shook his pitiful head. "He went to war."

His simple statement tugged at her heart. Lord and Lady Sunderland had taken her in and loved her as one of their own from the day she'd arrived on their doorstep. This poor boy had not been so lucky.

But Christina could make a difference for him.

"Come with me." She put out her hand, and Theo put his small, filthy one into it. Then she walked away, feeling exceedingly moved by Gavin's compassion and his deft handling of the blacksmith.

She collected Jenny on her way to the nearby inn and sent Trevor to help Gavin while Hancock saw to the horses and carriage. And her jewels. Because no matter what else happened, she had to keep her valuables safe.

Gavin shouldn't have interfered. He knew he'd only asked for trouble by stepping in to protect the boy, but he remembered only too well the thrashings he'd suffered at his own father's hands. And nothing would make him forget the times he'd been unable to protect his sister from him.

But what in hell had he gotten himself into?

Now he felt responsible for the boy, and had to figure out what he was going to do with the bloody drunkard who'd beaten him. There was no gaol that would take the blacksmith, for it was not against the law for a father to beat his son. But Gavin would be damned if he'd let the lad within reach of the over-sized sot who'd whipped him.

He was glad he'd been able to subdue the bastard so quickly and Christina had not had to witness any more violence. Although the smithy deserved nothing less.

But Christina had been undaunted, her actions surprising him. She'd gotten the boy to safety without hesitation.

"Need some help, Captain?" Trevor asked.

Gavin pulled the smithy upright and turned him. The man's eyes were bloodshot, but he looked as though he would kill someone with his bare hands if given the opportunity. He hadn't stopped grousing about being accosted in his own shop, but Gavin ignored it.

"What's the boy to you?" Gavin demanded of him, keeping the whip wrapped tightly around the man's wrists. He had no interest in getting bashed with one of the blacksmith's heavy iron tools.

The man spat on the ground in front of him. "Ain't none o' yer concern."

"I'm making it my concern." Even though it was against his better judgment. "He's young for an apprentice. Your son?"

The smithy made a low growl. " 'E's a bloody bastard, is what."

"Yours?"

" 'Ell no."

"Come on," Gavin said as he shoved the smithy forward.

"Where we goin'?"

"To whatever hovel you crawled out of this morning."

"What will you do with him?" Jenny whispered as she and Christina looked down at the little boy who'd fallen asleep under a blanket in Jenny's room at the inn.

"He can't go back to the monster that beat him," Christina said, determined to do what she could to help the boy.

There was no reason she could not take him to London with her. Sunderland House was large and well equipped to deal with children—after all, her parents had raised her and their three sons there.

And Mrs. Wilder, the housekeeper, would welcome having a child in the house.

Theo reminded Christina of Lang. Not that they looked at all alike, but Lang was always the one in some sort of trouble. She wanted to gather the boy into her arms and protect him as she hoped to protect Lang.

But this complicated matters immeasurably. She needed Gavin to get her to London and deal with the blackmailer, and not be rescuing little country boys from their—

No. She could not fault Gavin for helping Theo. Any man who possessed an ounce of decency would have done the same.

"Did you ever see such a man?"

Christina rubbed her arms as a sudden chill came over her. "No. He was horrible."

"I meant Captain Briggs," Jenny said with a sigh. "He has such a masterful way. I was so afraid when he took himself up against that nasty old smithy."

Christina kept her eyes down, trained on Theo. Jenny knew her very well and Christina had worried that she might divulge some little clue about her liaison with Gavin. But she would not dispute that Gavin had disabled the blacksmith with amazing competence—which should not have surprised anyone, not after the way he'd handled the intruders at the inn the night before. "Oh. Er . . . yes . . . But all is well now, is it not?"

"I wonder what the captain will do with that nasty

old baggage. I hope he doesn't think he can come in here and take the boy."

"I'm sure Captain Briggs will make it clear that he's not to come anywhere near," Christina said. "We should wake him and see to the cuts on his back, and then . . ."

"Then . . . ?"

"He will be under my protection. I'll take him to Sunderland House," she said firmly. The boy was an orphan, left alone, just as Christina had been. She did not care what anyone thought of it, she would not leave him to the mercy—or lack thereof—of his uncle.

They roused the boy enough to bathe him and explain that he did not have to go back to the forge. Then they tucked him into a small cot the innkeeper had brought into Jenny's room.

"He's exhausted," the maid said.

And so beaten down. He had not even questioned where he was or what would happen to him next. "You would be, too, if you had to live in a rough loft with only a coating of straw to keep you warm at night." Christina shook her head. "He's so thin."

Jenny stepped back from the sleeping boy. "I'll wash his clothes so he'll have something to wear when he wakes."

"They're hardly more than rags. Maybe we can find something to buy for him. Surely there is a mother nearby who would part with some clothes for a price."

"Oh, no doubt," Jenny said. "I'll talk to the chambermaids. Maybe they know of someone."

Christina left that task to Jenny and went outside to the front drive to see if she could find out what was going on in the blacksmith's shop. She felt a shiver of appreciation for what Gavin had done even as she wondered why he'd done it.

She could not think of any other man who would have interfered with the blacksmith in the situation they'd just encountered. Even her father, Lord Sunderland, was loath to meddle in anyone else's affairs, though he might have in this instance.

The blacksmith was clearly a violent, cruel man, and Christina might have taken matters into her own hands if Gavin had not done something. Even now, she felt outrage burning in her throat when she pictured little Theo cowering in the corner of the filthy forge.

Several men had gathered at the open door of the smithy. Christina felt more than a little intimidated as she approached, but she remembered her mother's words. *Attitude is everything. Show them who you are.*

Raising her chin as her mother would have done, Christina pushed past the men and saw that the burly blacksmith sat on the floor with his hands still bound behind him. Trevor stood guarding him, while a man of some consequence stood aside, speaking with Gavin.

When Gavin saw her, he gave her a bow. "Lady Fairhaven, may I introduce Magistrate Thorpe, who was called to see what we strangers have done with Mr. Berry's nephew. Mr. Thorpe, Viscountess Fairhaven."

The magistrate's eyes widened when he heard her title, quite obviously unaccustomed to dealings with nobility. Christina took that as a signal to pretend to be her mother.

"If you refer to the boy, Theo, he is with my maid at the inn," Christina said imperiously. "And there he will remain."

Gavin cast a glance at the magistrate, as though waiting for him to protest.

"My lady," he said with an obsequious bow. "I'm sure we can come to some arrangement."

"Arrangement?" she asked.

Thorpe cast a glance in the smithy's direction. The man was muttering drunkenly.

"Samuel Berry has never had any use for the bastard. His ma died giving him life, and his da went and got himself killed in France."

Christina could almost feel Gavin stiffen, even though he was not standing that close to her. She merely sensed the subtle change in his demeanor.

"I will take him," Gavin said. "To my sister."

Christina shot him a look of surprise. She had not known anything about a sister, nor had she ever thought Gavin would make such an extraordinary offer to take the boy himself. Which reminded her that she knew practically nothing about him at all.

"There will need to be some . . . remuneration, of course."

Gavin appeared nonplussed for a moment, but then nodded. "I'll take care of it before we leave."

"Very good, Captain Briggs," said the magistrate. "I'll talk to Mr. Berry when he's in a more reasonable frame of mind."

Christina had covered his flank quite capably during the little skirmish with Berry and the magistrate. She'd stepped right in to rescue the boy, and later had known exactly how to manage the magistrate. She'd taken on the haughty expression and bearing of any noblewoman he'd ever met.

He'd almost laughed at the difference from her usual demeanor. But he'd been dead serious about never returning the boy to the contemptible blacksmith. He would kill the man first.

Gavin was sure his sister would not object to taking the boy and keeping him with her in London until he had secured their manor house. In any event, he had planned to give Eleanor what money he had, and it would be sufficient for the care of the boy as well as for Eleanor and her little daughter.

After he collected his reward from Windermere, he would take the boy to the manor in Hampshire. Then he would figure out what to do with him.

"You might want to consider locking Mr. Berry inside somewhere secure until he sobers up," Gavin said to the magistrate.

Thorpe gave a quick nod and gestured for two of the townsmen to come and assist. "We've got a strong room where we can keep him. When are you leaving?"

"Soon after first light," Gavin said.

"Then Mr. Berry will remain in custody until noon."

Gavin thanked the man. Satisfied that he'd done all he could to assure the safety of the boy, he left the forge with Christina, and walked to the inn with her.

"I will leave some money with the magistrate," she said. "Then the boy's uncle will have no—"

"No need," he replied, bristling. He was no pauper, and could deal with the situation he caused. "I have funds. And the boy is my responsibility. I'm the one who interfered."

She said nothing more and they went into the inn, where the proprietor met them. He took them up to their rooms, one across from the other, and Gavin wondered if he'd be able to resist joining Christina when darkness fell. Or if she'd want him.

He'd tried not to think about her during the day's ride, or dwell on the possibility of repeating the pleasures of the night before. But his efforts had failed miserably. Christina had been wildly receptive to every kiss, every caress, and he'd been thoroughly seduced by her. It was only the possible dangers they faced on the road that had kept him from being completely aroused all day.

"Supper will be served in the common room in half an hour, my lady," said the innkeeper. "Unless you'd like your meal brought to the sitting room up here."

"The sitting room will suit," she said. "And you may send up Captain Briggs's meal as well. We have matters to discuss."

The innkeeper bowed slightly before leaving the upper hallway.

"Matters?" he asked, gratified that she apparently wanted exactly the same thing as he.

Her blush charmed him completely. "Yes. What we're going to do with Theo."

"Theo . . ."

"The boy you rescued," she said, opening the door to her room. "You are to be commended for stepping in as you did."

Gavin followed her inside. "There are some who would not agree."

"No one has the right to brutalize a poor innocent the way that man did."

"Outrage becomes you, my lady." He reached behind her head and touched one of the incredibly silky curls at her nape.

Her body drifted toward his with an undeniable affinity, and Gavin could not resist pulling her to him. He touched his lips to hers in a feather-light kiss, teasing, sensing her growing arousal as well as his own.

He reached behind him and turned the key in the lock, then devoured her mouth. "I want you now."

Chapter 13

Their kiss intensified as Gavin drew her to the bed and Christina had no chance to think . . . even if she had wanted to.

He turned her and she suddenly found herself lying on the bed. Gavin's mouth and hands seemed to be everywhere, kissing, kneading, caressing, building an impossible tension with every touch. In a haze of feverish longing, she pushed his jacket off his shoulders, even as he slid her skirts up to her waist. She grabbed fistfuls of his shirt when he touched her where she was most desperate to feel him.

Somewhere deep inside, she knew she ought to feel profoundly embarrassed at being so thoroughly exposed. But his fingers were doing such amazingly wicked things to her, she could not think. She only knew there was a delicious heaviness between her legs, and Christina wanted more.

She pulled at his trews and heard his growl when she slipped her hand inside and encircled his hard length. She slid her hand all the way down, torturing him only for a moment before guiding him to the heat of her body. She was beyond ready, well on the road to *needy.*

"Please, Gavin. Now!"

She heard his deep groan of masculine pleasure as he pushed inside her, and he did not hesitate to move. The rhythm was anything but evenly paced. It was hot, fevered, and frantic. Exactly the way Christina felt.

In spite of wearing too many clothes, she somehow managed to lift her hips and meet every thrust with her own. Nothing was in her mind but his ice-blue gaze on hers, his complete attention on bringing her to climax.

Tension coiled tightly inside her, and suddenly her muscles stretched and pulled, then constricted around him. She shuddered her release and felt his own spasm of pleasure right afterward.

Hovering over her, Gavin supported himself on his powerful arms and lowered his head to take her mouth in yet another kiss that singed every nerve she possessed. He tangled his tongue with hers as though they had not just come to completion.

Then he pulled back and grinned down at her. "Until supper, my lady."

And then he was gone.

Gavin could easily make a habit of Lady Fairhaven. He ought to feel sated, but he wanted her still, in spite of their quick, wildly satisfying coupling. The scent of her soft skin stayed with him as he crossed to his own room. He would have to behave himself when they dined in the private sitting room, but it was going to be sheer hell keeping his hands off her.

He checked to see that his traveling bag had been brought into his room, then went down to the common areas of the inn, looking for Hancock or Trevor. He wondered where the blacksmith's nephew had been taken. He ought to have asked Christina, but the boy was the last thing he could think of when he was alone with her in a bedroom.

He saw the innkeeper in the taproom, who informed him that the boy had been taken to the room given to Lady Fairhaven's maid. Gavin asked to be shown to the room.

It was in the back hall where rooms were reserved for servants of the inn's guests. Gavin knocked quietly, and when Jenny opened the door, he looked past her and saw that the boy was asleep on a makeshift pallet. He guessed it was probably better quarters than the boy had ever known.

"Did you give him any food?" The child was painfully thin. Gavin did not know much about children, but he'd been on the war-torn continent long enough to know what starvation looked like. The boy's pitiful state tugged at something deep within Gavin.

"No, sir. Lady Fairhaven and I cleaned him up, saw to his wounds, and put him to bed," Jenny replied. "The poor little mite was all done in."

As anyone would be. But at least this one had Christina to tend him. The healing nick in his own arm was a testament to her care, not to mention her audacity. He might have smiled at the recollection of Christina firing her pistol if he hadn't just complicated his life beyond recognition.

"Let him rest awhile longer," he told the maid. "Then bring him up to the sitting room near Lady Fairhaven's bedchamber. I want to talk to him."

Jenny made a quick curtsy. "Of course, Captain Briggs. I'll do just that."

Gavin supposed he had no choice but to take the boy to Hampshire with him. But he was certainly not going to try to be a father to the lad, no more than he had any intention of being a father to his niece. Or any other child. A jaded old assassin was no proper example for anyone, young or old.

But now his house was becoming more of a nursery than the haven he'd intended it to be. Eleanor and Rachel would be there, and now Theo. How his simple plan had become so complicated boggled the mind.

For the first time in months, Christina wished she had something pretty to wear. But her entire traveling wardrobe consisted of dull blacks and grays and one lavender gown. While they'd been adequate only a week ago, Christina no longer felt like the proper widow she'd been before receiving the blackmail notices.

Or perhaps it was meeting Gavin Briggs. In the past few days, she'd discovered a sense of freedom she had not known before. She'd always intended to be a faithful wife, just like her mother. But then

Christina had not met many men like her father. The earl had shown his devotion to his wife and family in many small ways.

And if Christina could not have a marriage like theirs, why should she marry again?

For now, she was content in her unmarried state. Gavin was a considerate, skilled lover, and she had no intention of giving him up. At least not yet.

A shiver of anticipation went through her at the prospect of dining with him alone. Though it was not like the public dining room on the main floor, anyone might come in. She could not slip her fingers into his hair or slide her hand up his thigh. She could not breathe in his ear, nip at his neck, or try any other brazenly seductive wiles on him.

That would come later.

It was all so new, this business of seduction, of conducting an affair. Despite their outrageous coupling only a short while ago, Christina found she could hardly think of anything but the next time they would make love.

She wondered if she and Gavin could maintain their liaison discreetly. So far, no one—not even Jenny—seemed to have guessed that Gavin had become more than simply her escort to London. And she intended to keep it that way. After all, a woman did not flaunt her lovers, nor did a gentleman kiss and tell.

Perhaps she would have to entice Gavin to her room later, or maybe he would come on his own. Anticipation shuddered through her as she unfastened her traveling gown and slipped on the gray. Though it was not the least bit enticing, it did show her collarbones to advantage, as well as emphasizing the short neckline of her shorn hair.

Oddly enough, Gavin seemed to like it.

Gavin took a walk into town and settled matters with the blacksmith. The bloody churl didn't want his illegitimate nephew, and Gavin would not turn his back on the boy, knowing his ill treatment would continue if he stayed. Perhaps it would become worse, for the child had been the cause of his uncle's humiliation.

As much as Gavin despised the executioner he'd become, he appreciated the additional training that had made it possible to strip the smithy of his whip without much difficulty, and use it to bind the man's wrists. Very few men had been recruited into Castlereagh's service, and they'd been well trained to deal with every conceivable possibility. Gavin could shoot with deadly accuracy from a distance of two hundred yards. He knew how to track his prey, how to blend in with the locals or hide if necessary. He could capture an adversary with little difficulty and knew how to extract crucial information without much trouble.

He'd been wounded a few times—twice while an officer with the Ninety-fifth, and once when he was on his own in France and an informant had turned on him. Gavin managed to survive, and learned never to let down his guard.

He was far more dangerous now—even without

a weapon—than his father had ever been. Unfortunately, Gavin hadn't possessed the necessary skills to protect Eleanor or himself from Hargrove when they were children.

He despised the kind of man who mistreated those who could not fight back.

He thought of his sister and her little daughter who was a bastard like Theo. The world was never going to hear anything of their circumstances. As far as Gavin was concerned, Eleanor had wed Mark Stafford, her soldier-lover, before he left England for duty in France. Gavin had known and liked Stafford, and did not doubt he would have married Eleanor before his regiment departed England had he known she was with child.

The fact that there had been no church service meant naught. When Gavin took possession of his Hampshire manor, Eleanor was going to be known as Mrs. Stafford, whose husband had died at Waterloo.

And Gavin dared anyone to contradict him.

It was dark when he returned to the inn, and he quickened his steps in anticipation of his supper with Christina.

Hungry for more than a meal, he went upstairs and entered the small sitting room at the end of the hall. Jenny was already there with the boy, and Christina was in the midst of pouring milk into a bowl before him.

Gavin stood in the doorway and listened as Christina spoke in a gentle tone to the lad. Her attitude was substantially different from what he'd have expected from the noblewomen he'd known in the past, including his mother. And he could not help but wonder how Amelia would have treated Theo had she been the one to come upon him in the same circumstances.

"I asked them to bring you porridge, Theo," said Christina, "because I think you ought not to eat too much right away."

The boy looked famished, but Christina was likely correct. It was all too clear Theo had not been well fed up till now and too much food would make him ill.

Christina looked up and saw Gavin, and he imagined he saw an intimate sparkle in her eyes. His body clenched tightly at her notice. "Here is Captain Briggs," she said. "Do you remember him, Theo?"

The boy nodded and spoke quietly. "He stopped Uncle Samuel from beating me."

"Jenny," Christina said to the maid, who hovered nearby, "there is no need for you to postpone your own meal. Go on. We'll be fine here."

The maid curtsied and left the room, and as Theo returned to his meal, Gavin took a moment to appreciate Christina's beauty. Even in her plain gray gown, he had a nearly irresistible urge to touch her. To touch the loose curl at her nape and steal a kiss while Theo was engrossed in his porridge.

But he held back. He intended to enjoy a great deal of touching later, after everyone at the inn settled down for the night. He focused on the matter at hand. Though he had little experience with children, he wanted this one to understand he was safe now.

"Theo."

The boy stopped eating and looked up at him with sunken gray eyes.

"I've seen to it that you need never go back to your uncle again."

An expression of puzzlement crossed the child's face. "Wh-what will I do, then?"

"The magistrate said you can come with us."

"With you . . . and . . ." He looked at Christina, clearly confused by the strangers' kindness. As well he might be, for apparently none of the damned idiots in the village had seen fit to challenge Samuel Berry's cruelty.

"You needn't worry," said Christina. "You'll be safe."

The boy put down his spoon. "Will I live with you, miss?"

Gavin answered. "I mean to have my own farm in Hampshire soon, but until then, you'll stay with my sister in London." It seemed too much information for the boy, but Gavin wanted to be sure Theo understood what was going to happen. No one had ever given Gavin that courtesy as a lad. One day, he'd lived at Seaholm Hall. The next, he was shipped off to school.

"My uncle . . . He said I can go?" the boy asked quietly.

Gavin nodded. "Aye. And the magistrate, too. Your uncle will not protest."

"Will he ever f-find me?"

Christina slipped her arm around the boy's thin

shoulders. "No. Your uncle will never be able to find you."

Theo looked at Gavin and spoke, his voice clear and resolute. "Wh-where will I sleep, sir?"

It was gratifying to note that the boy's spirit was not broken. He would do well in Hampshire. "In far better accommodations than what you have now," Gavin replied.

"You don't mind leaving, do you, Theo?" Christina asked, her tone gentle and kind.

The boy sniffed and wiped his eyes. He sat up and looked straight ahead as he talked. "I prayed that M-Mum would come for me. Or that Da would come b-back from the war. Uncle Samuel told me don't be d-daft."

Likely with a nasty clout or a sharp kick for punctuation, Gavin thought. "Then you won't miss Mr. Berry."

The boy shook his head.

Christina put her hand over Theo's small one in a comforting gesture. "Do you understand, Theo? We are going to London."

Theo looked up at her with his brows raised, and a tiny, hopeful smile softened the line of his mouth. "Will I see the king?"

Clearly, the boy didn't know the king was insane and incapacitated and *no one* saw him. "Perhaps we shall see his son, Prince George," Christina said.

Theo seemed satisfied with her answer, and finished his porridge. Then Christina pushed his tea closer, and the boy took a sip.

"Thank you, miss," he said.

"You are most welcome, Theo."

Christina did not blink at Theo's omission of her formal title. She did not correct him, either, as Gavin's mother most certainly would have done. Lady Hargrove would have expected a small boy to address her properly, without consideration of his lack of training.

But Christina had showed him compassion, when many of her peers would not. They'd have turned away and allowed the vile blacksmith to beat the child to a bloody pulp.

"Have you eaten?" Gavin asked Christina.

She shook her head and gave him a sweet smile. "I waited for you."

He rose from the table. "Then I'll return shortly. Will you be all right?"

"Of course. But Gavin, I . . ." He saw questions in her eyes. "Never mind. I will see you later."

Gavin took his leave and went to his own room. He peeled off his jacket and waistcoat, then pulled his shirt over his head, pausing for a second to slide his fingers over Christina's neat stitching. It was further evidence that she did not compare to her peers. She was a different sort of woman, entirely.

But he knew she had questions. About Eleanor, most likely. Which could wait.

After pouring water into a basin, Gavin took his shaving soap and razor from his pack, very much aware that he was shaving before a rendezvous with a woman—for the first time in his life.

* * *

Gavin had a sister.

Christina wondered about her, and about his farm in Hampshire. She'd already guessed he was planning to purchase it with his reward from Windermere, and felt more than a little bit guilty for causing a delay.

But surely he would go out of his way to assist his own sister if she needed his help. Just as Christina was doing for Lang. Gavin had to understand.

Lang's predicament, whatever it might be, was never far from Christina's thoughts. The situation with Theo was a distraction they didn't need, though she was glad Gavin had intervened.

But Lang must be in extreme circumstances, and unable to contact their father or anyone else in the family for assistance. She could not imagine what could have happened to him.

Jenny returned for Theo, and Christina instructed her to stay with the boy the following morning rather than coming up to help her dress for their day's travel. It was far more important that Theo be fed before they left. The maid took Theo downstairs with her while Christina remained in the small dining room, lost in thought.

"Is something amiss?" Gavin asked, coming toward her. He looked fresh and clean, his hair was damp, and he was wearing his other shirt.

She found herself suddenly breathless, and her hand slipped up to her throat as though that would somehow contain her lustful thoughts.

He sat in the chair adjacent to hers, not beside her, but close enough to touch. As much as she longed to do so, she refrained. Servants would soon bring their supper, and it would not do to be seen engaging in improper behavior.

"I was just thinking about Lang."

Gavin made an expression of comprehension, and Christina was struck with how well she could read him after only a few days. She might not know a lot about him, but she felt she had a far greater understanding of him than she'd ever had of Edward. But then her husband had been a master of deceit. He must have been, else Christina would have sensed something about his affair with Mrs. Shilton.

"And about the letter Lieutenant Norris mentioned . . ."

"Norris said your brother seemed disturbed by it?"

"Yes. If we knew what was in that letter, it might be a clue to help us to find him."

She noted the almost imperceptible lowering of Gavin's right brow. His reaction reminded her of his earlier assertion that he did not intend to solve her problems for her. Just because they'd become lovers did not mean she could rely on him for anything more than what they'd agreed upon, back at Sweethope Cottage.

"I do not expect you to find him for me, Gavin," she said quietly against a surprising burn at the back of her throat. "Only to help me handle the blackmailer. That was what we agreed upon."

Chapter 14

He'd ruffled Christina's feathers without saying a word.

Maybe this was the moment to try and convince her to leave Lang's fate in his own hands, rather than haring down to London to pay off—and try to capture—the damned blackmailer. If Lang was alive, which Gavin doubted, he was a grown man who ought to see to his own affairs.

One look at her told him she wasn't going to accept any such option.

"I assume your father asked Lieutenant Norris about the letter." Gavin could not help but wonder whether the man had had the audacity to kill his own friend in a scheme to collect money from his family.

Christina nodded. "He knew nothing."

"What about your friend. The viscount?"

"Lord Brundle is no friend of mine," she said with some vehemence.

"You don't care for the fellow?" Gavin asked,
though her tone made her sentiments toward the
man quite obvious.

She pulled a face. "He was simply awful when he
courted me. Fortunately, my father did not like him,
either, and refused his offer of marriage."

Gavin felt his brows rise. The man had gotten that
far in his courtship? "So Brundle was not able to offer
any more information than Norris."

Christina shook her head. "Lieutenant Norris said
he did not stay. Brundle was gone well before Lang
left the tavern."

Servants came and placed their meal before them,
but Gavin had never been less interested in food. Or
discussion. He didn't want to talk about Lang or what
Christina expected him to do about the blackmailer.
He wanted to enjoy these perfect moments alone
with her, anticipating the taste of her lips, breathing
in her scent, stealing as many secret caresses as the
moment allowed.

"You mentioned that All Hallows Church has an
undercroft," she said, dragging Gavin's attention
from the lovely hollow at the base of her throat. He
could already taste it, could already feel the weight
of her breasts in his hands.

He tamped down his lust and forced himself to
recall the design of the church. "Aye. There's an undercroft, but I've never been down there."

A small crease appeared between her brows. Her
hair shone in the candlelight, wisps of curls twining
tightly near her ears. "Do you think the blackmailer

will be able to slip away down beneath the church?"

"It's possible. There are many pathways through All Hallows. And stairs. Doors. It's possible your blackmailer could slip away unnoticed on a crowded Sunday morning."

"But if you are already inside . . ."

Gavin nodded. "I might be able to see who it is and detain him."

"I am counting on it," she replied.

Which went without saying. Gavin knew Christina didn't want anyone else to know about the situation with Lang, but he was going to have to recruit a few friends to help him cover the church's stairs and exits. He figured he would then blend in with the crowd and watch for the man. When he saw the culprit who picked up the money, he would follow him out and detain him. Simple.

Unless the unexpected happened, and Gavin had enjoyed his years of success as Castlereagh's assassin by anticipating the unexpected. It had been some years since he'd been to All Hallows by the Tower, and he hoped they would manage to arrive in London well before Christina was to leave the money in the lectern. He wanted the opportunity to recruit help and do some reconnaissance in advance of the date the money was to be left.

Gavin watched Christina push her food around her plate. He could see her thinking. Planning. Worrying. She was as bad as he. "Is there a staircase at the back of the church?" she asked. "One that leads to the undercroft?"

Gavin wondered if she was having second thoughts about her plan, which was hardly a plan at all. And too much thinking about it made her nervous.

"I don't remember it well," Gavin replied. "It's been some time since I was there."

She put down her fork. "What if he takes the money and slips away down the steps before you can reach him?"

He took her hand in his and slid his thumb along its palm. "We'll get him."

He knew what she wanted from the blackmailer, but was fairly certain she would not get it. It was time for her to face some harsh facts. "You do know that if Lang is not dead . . . he will face court-martial for desertion of his ship."

She pulled her hand from his. "Lang would never do so willingly. I know it."

"Christina, think about it," Gavin said quietly. "If he did not desert his ship, then he must be—"

"No! I know what you think, but you could be wrong!" A silvery tear slid down her cheek, but she did not seem to notice it. "He could be in serious trouble, and unable to get word to us."

Gavin sat back in his chair and said naught.

"And someone who knows about his circumstances—"

"Someone like Norris?" he asked.

Christina brushed away her tears. "Lieutenant Norris is a good friend of Lang. I cannot believe he would ever—"

"Not even if he were in dire straits?"

Color flooded her cheeks. "James Norris was introduced to our family as a man of honor, Gavin."

"Even men of honor can become desperate." He spoke quietly, but he knew he'd upset her terribly.

"Desperate enough to drag an unwilling woman to the grandfather who abandoned her?" she snapped.

Gavin clenched his teeth. "Aye."

She took a deep breath. "So, what are you suggesting?"

"If Lang was not killed in the explosion, then Norris must know exactly what happened to him, and saw it as an opportunity."

"An opportunity?" She pressed a hand to her breast. "To blackmail me?"

"To take advantage of a situation," Gavin said, though he entertained the merest shadow of a doubt. Norris and Brundle had been drinking with Lang. Brundle left the tavern, then Lang had followed sometime afterward, but Norris said he did not know how long before the explosion Lang had left.

There was a slim possibility that Norris's identification of Lang's body had been wrong. Which would only put Lang into serious difficulties with the navy.

Christina's green eyes narrowed with uncertainty. "You think I'm a gullible idiot."

"Not at all. Christina . . ."

She stood and stalked away from the table to the fireplace. He could see she was fighting for control, so he got up and followed her.

She did not turn to face him, but irritation was in

her voice when she spoke. "Lieutenant Norris would never hurt Lang. They were friends!"

"Christina." He touched her arm, but she shrugged it off.

"You just want me to give up and go back to Windermere with you."

Now it was Gavin's turn to be angry. "If I'd wanted that, I'd have brought all this up before we left Holywell House."

"I do not want to discuss this any further."

He took hold of her shoulders and turned her to look at him. "You need to face the facts, Christina. Weigh all the possibilities."

She shoved away from him and stormed out of the room, clearly unwilling to listen to reason.

"Christina."

Christina did not want to hear any more, but she barely had a chance to close her door when Gavin pushed through it and turned the key in the lock behind him. He looked dangerous.

And full of words she did not wish to hear.

"Lieutenant Norris is not the enemy, Captain Briggs," she said, angry now. "I cannot believe he would hurt Lang, and he certainly would not send threatening notes demanding money from me."

Gavin started toward her. "Your generous heart does you credit. But Norris—"

"I am not a fool, Gavin," she retorted, piqued by his patronizing tone. "I know that a man can lie straight-faced." It galled her to admit that Edward had been quite good at it, and a shard of doubt about James Norris crept into her mind. She'd met him only a time or two, but he'd seemed perfectly respectable.

"You don't know anything about James Norris or any of your brother's other shipmates, Christina."

"I know significantly more than you do."

"I doubt that very much."

She crossed her arms over her chest and glared at him. It did not seem as though he was actually trying to provoke her, but he was succeeding quite well, in spite of himself.

"You need to listen to my counsel, Christina."

The thought of one of Lang's shipmates—a man her brother trusted—being responsible for all this sickened her.

Gavin jabbed his fingers through his hair, making a mess of it. Frustration came through quite clearly in his deep voice. "This is why you demanded that I come to London with you, is it not? To benefit from my . . . my experience with military scoundrels?"

"Perhaps I don't need your assistance," she said stubbornly. "If it's Norris, as you seem to think, then I might be able to reason with hi—"

"Good God, woman. Whoever it is—Norris included—he will be dangerous. Blackmail is not to be taken lightly."

How dare he underestimate her? "Of course I don't take it lightly. But I'd planned to handle this on my own before you arrived at Sweethope Cottage, and that's exactly what I'll—"

"Christina— Oh hell."

He yanked her into his arms and kissed her, his mouth devouring hers as though he would swallow her whole.

Christina responded in kind, grabbing his lapels and pulling him tightly against her. Tipping her head for better access to his lips, she moaned, and all her pent-up longings and desires—as well as her frustrations—rose to the surface.

She felt his hands slide up her back, and then down again, pressing her hips to his. He was hard against her, and she felt as though her limbs were melting.

Suddenly, he was working on her buttons, unfastening each one, baring skin, shoving the dark fabric off her shoulders, down her arms.

Christina started to work on his trews as he pressed hot kisses to her neck and throat, then down to the tips of her breasts. She freed his hard length, encircling him with her hand, running her thumb over the sensitive tip.

He groaned and, all at once, picked her up into his arms. He carried her the few steps to the bed and laid her upon it.

"As much as I want to be inside you, Christina . . ." he growled, "this time we're going to go slowly. I want to taste every inch of you. And spend all night doing it."

Chapter 15

Gavin spent the night in Christina's bed, waking her twice more to make love to her. And then he slept with his arms around her, holding her close, as though he would never let her go.

It was a ridiculous notion, she knew, one that had not occurred to her before.

She thought of his whispered words, of the sweetly intimate urgings that were so incongruous with his hard demeanor, and was glad he'd ended their argument so abruptly and effectively. Her body trembled as though every nerve remembered the pleasure of his touch, and the incredible power of his caress.

And yet Christina could not forget about the reason for their argument. She wanted to believe Lang was alive. That he was somehow unable to contact the family.

She could not imagine what that reason could be, but it was far more difficult to think of her younger brother lying dead in a burned-out dockside warehouse. Neither circumstance was acceptable.

If Lang was alive . . . obviously, he knew there would be consequences for deserting his ship, and Christina was very much afraid they would hang him—if they ever found him. The blackmailer's note said he knew where Lang was and what he'd done. Had he deserted ship? Or had he been party to some other crime?

If the blackmailer wasn't just leading her on, Christina would find Lang and help him out of whatever difficulty he'd gotten himself into. If he needed money, she had plenty of that. If he was afraid of a court-martial . . .

Somehow, they would sort that out, too. After all, their father was not without influence. And if there had been a very good reason for Lang to drop out of sight for a time . . . Well, then . . . things might not go too badly.

She hoped.

She pressed her face against Gavin's chest and breathed deeply. Though he did not awaken, he gathered her closer, making her skin tingle when he eased his leg between hers.

How would she feel when they parted? When all was said and done in London and up at Windermere, Gavin would buy his property in Hampshire and retreat to the country. Their reason for being together would have ended.

The thought of it caused an ache in the center of her chest, but she refused to allow thoughts of their separation to intrude. They had at least three more days—two nights—together before they reached London. Before she had to face the truth about Lang.

And she was going to enjoy every minute of them.

It was far too easy to become accustomed to such lusty attentions from an attractive, but wholly unsuitable man. And too dangerous for a widowed viscountess. She was young. Her parents—and the rest of society, of course—would expect her to marry again, and marry well.

The younger son of a country viscount, a man who'd agreed to a price for doing her grandfather's bidding, was certainly not the kind of man her father would accept. Besides, she'd had a number of acceptable suitors during her London seasons, men who might still be looking for a wife when she was out of mourning and ready to consider marriage again.

Christina snuggled against Gavin's body and listened to his deep breathing. She was not sure she would ever be ready.

Christina wished they did not have to leave their quiet bower; wished she could forget all about Lang and the pain he had caused their family; wished she could forgo their trip to London, and everything that the future held.

But it would be light soon and they needed to get on the road. Whatever might transpire between them in the bedchamber, she refused to listen to Gavin's dire speculations. Lang *had* to be alive, or there was no point in all of this.

"You need not have waited for me to awaken,

sweet," he whispered, tangling their feet together. "Your touch is enough to make me ready."

"Even in sleep?"

"Oh aye."

His deep, quiet voice whispered through her, and Christina felt her womb clench when he cupped her breast. Her entire body thrummed with awareness when he nuzzled her neck.

"Why did you cut your hair?"

His question surprised her. "I did it in a fit of temper."

"Temper? You?"

Her mind might be caught up in a fog of sensation, but his sarcasm did not escape her. "That is not very amusing, Captain Briggs." She moved her head to look up at his eyes. They were mostly in shadows, but she felt him watching her intently. "I cut it after my sister-in-law, the new Lady Fairhaven, mentioned how much my late husband loved my hair."

His brows came together. "I've heard of women in foreign cultures who shear their hair in mourning."

"This had nothing to do with mourning."

"No?"

"My husband did not love anything about me—except perhaps my family connections and my youth. But certainly not my hair. Nor my company in his bed."

Christina regretted the words the minute they exited her mouth. It was humiliating to admit she had not been the woman Edward had sought for his pleasure. That he'd treated her almost like a piece of pretty furniture—pleasant and convenient, but not vital.

"The man was an idiot."

They went back to sleep until dawn, and Gavin felt nearly boneless when he awoke. He managed to restrain himself from touching Christina's curls as she slept, from slipping his fingers through the silken mass and waking her with a kiss.

Her lips were slightly parted and he could hear every breath she took. Her blanket had drifted off her shoulders, baring an enticing span of her chest.

Gavin slid quietly out of bed, crushing the lust that flared like a bright beacon over a dark sea.

He pulled on his clothes, then left her and went into his own room, reminding himself that what he shared with Christina was only sex. Truly excellent sex, but nothing more. At least, that was what he told himself as he washed and dressed for the day.

He dragged off his shirt, leaned both hands against the washstand, and took a deep breath. It was time to regroup, to think through the next few days and the events that were likely to occur on Sunday morning when he confronted the blackmailer.

And how he was going to get Christina back to Windermere. What he discovered at All Hallows Church was not going to be acceptable, no matter what it was.

Bloody hell. Gavin didn't want to argue with her anymore, and he especially didn't want to be the one to tell her what he learned from Norris—or whoever

was trying to extort money from her. She'd been so
very hopeful of finding answers she could live with.

No wonder she had argued so emphatically.
Facing Lang's demise was not an acceptable conclusion to this adventure.

Gavin could understand that. He could not imagine the pain of losing his younger sister. If there was
any doubt whatsoever—even the slimmest of possibilities that she was not dead—Gavin would move
mountains to determine the truth.

It would be all over on Sunday. Christina would
have to face the news Gavin brought her, and then
it would be his task to convince her to go back to
Windermere with him.

In spite of what happened at All Hallows Church.

If only he'd just taken Christina to Windermere
that first day—even against her will—he would not
be facing these difficulties now. He'd have his money
and already would have sent funds to Eleanor to
cover her and Rachel's traveling expenses. They
would all be on their way to Weybrook Manor.

And he would never have tasted the most enticing
woman he'd ever met.

Gavin raked his fingers through his hair. The
events of the past few days contradicted all his
intentions.

Now he was responsible for a little orphan boy, as
well as the safety of Christina's party and the valuable jewels she'd brought with her. They'd been lucky
so far, and no highwaymen had challenged them. But
a nasty crew like the one he'd subdued at Palmer's

Inn could be lurking out there on an empty stretch of road, just waiting for the right opportunity.

Christina climbed from the bed, realizing she had muscles and tendons she'd been unaware of before. She washed her chafed skin and dressed carefully, making certain to cover all the little red abrasions Gavin had made on her skin. Fortunately, Jenny would not be coming in to help her dress this morning, and Christina knew she would have to make sure her maid did not undress her that night, either.

Society would be aghast if they knew of her liaison with Gavin Briggs, but Christina felt entirely energized after her night spent in his arms, in spite of their argument.

Perhaps *because* of their argument.

But she could not think of that now—the possibilities were too forbidding to face.

Instead, she relished the moment Gavin had called Edward an idiot for failing to appreciate her. She pressed her hand against the center of her chest and willed her heart to slow. It was utter foolishness, she knew. Gavin Briggs had plans for a future that did not include her, plans he'd not seen fit to share with her.

Soon she would be out of mourning, and could marry again. But it seemed widowhood suited her far more than marriage had ever done. There had been little satisfaction in being married to Edward, and a great deal of restriction. When—if—she wed again, it would be to a man who set her blood on fire.

One who made her forget where she was and who she was. A man who respected her and would be devoted only to her.

Christina did not know if such a man existed, but she'd met precious few who drew her as Gavin Briggs did. Not even the handsome Lord Everhart, who had courted her avidly, competing with Edward for her attentions. Christina's father had objected to Everhart at the time, but perhaps when she met the good-looking young earl again . . .

She shook her head to clear it.

She'd already decided she was not going to consider remarriage for at least a few more years. Not until she gained more experience. After all, she'd already wed an attractive man approved by her father, and yet the marriage had been anything but ideal.

Life was much better with a paramour who knew how to please her.

Christina finished dressing and went to the window to see what kind of day it was. It must have rained during the night, for the road was muddy, but the sun was coming out now. Gavin walked into the stable yard with their innkeeper and another man and spoke quietly with him.

Had she ever known another man who possessed such physical prowess? Gavin was intense and masterful and yet considerate and patient.

A spark of pure longing sizzled through her.

She caught herself gawping at the man. She quickly shut her mouth and turned away to finish dressing. It was quite in her best interests to keep the affair in perspective. Gavin Briggs was a temporary diversion and nothing more.

Once they arrived in London, everything would change.

She didn't know if Gavin had a house of his own, or if he had some temporary lodgings when in Town. Wherever he intended to stay, rendezvous would be difficult. Or perhaps they would grow tired of each other by the time they reached Town.

That was a droll notion. She was insatiable for him. She could hardly wait until they reached their next stop so she could have her way with him.

It was outrageous, she knew, and though she tried to dismiss her brazen musings, Christina found she could not. The prospect of lying naked with her handsome lover, of exploring the limits of pleasure with him, was just too delectable to set aside.

By the time she left the inn to join her party waiting for her at the carriage, she felt breathless with anticipation. Utterly foolish, she knew.

"What is our destination to be this afternoon?" she asked Gavin before climbing into the carriage behind Jenny and Theo.

His knowing gaze caused her skin to heat, and she suspected he could see the marks he'd made on her neck and breast through her clothes. She could almost feel his gentle hands sliding up her legs, around her back, and on the tips of her breasts.

His voice was gruff when he spoke. "We should come close to Ledger's Mill, I hope."

"Ledger's Mill? I have a cousin who has an estate near Ledger's Mill. I know it well."

"Shall we make for it?" he asked.

Christina tried to appear indifferent, but failed miserably. She was certain every longing and desire was etched upon her face. "Of course," she managed to say. "I have not seen Avery in months. I'm quite sure he'll be pleased to see me, and happy to give us lodging for the night." And it would be a welcome comfort after the inns—and all their distractions— the past few nights.

"I'll tell Hancock to ask you for your cousin's direction when we get close."

At midday, Hancock pulled the carriage onto a side road and the women stepped out with Theo for the lunch that had been packed for them by the inn's kitchen earlier that morning. The boy sat close to Christina, and she allowed him more substantial food than he'd had that morning or the night before.

Gavin observed her interaction with the boy, her gentle manner, and her care of his injured back. She talked with him as she might with a favorite nephew, asking about seemingly inconsequential things as she ferreted out bits of information about him.

They'd figured his age to be close to five years, but he was a scrawny lad, just skin and bones. He was clean now, a good-looking boy who looked at Christina with unreserved adoration in his eyes.

Gavin wondered what his own eyes showed. Far too much interest, he supposed. Worse, his fascination with Lady Fairhaven dominated his thoughts when he should be concentrating on getting them safely to London.

"Have you heard of London Bridge, Theo?" asked Christina.

The boy shrugged, and she combed her fingers through his hair to smooth it. Gavin shivered, almost able to feel her hand at his nape, her fingers sliding through *his* hair as she'd done so often during the night.

"Would you like to see it?"

"Oh yes, miss. And the Tower?"

"Yes, they're quite close. You shall see both."

Gavin sat on a fallen log and listened to the sweet cadence of Christina's soft, feminine voice. Her laugh was contagious, and he found himself smiling. The ugly missions of his past slid away, and there was nothing but this moment, this point in time in a peaceful grove of trees. The sun was shining and there was a pleasant breeze. There were no nearby enemy troops, no targets, and no worries.

Not now.

Chapter 16

Christina had not had occasion to feel motherly before. She'd had a sense of sisterly duty toward her brothers, especially with Lang, who'd so often found himself in disfavor.

But this was different. Theo had no one at all to care for him and Christina wanted to be sure he never again felt the stinging end of a whip or a man's brutal fists. She wanted him to have a proper bed and a roof over his head when he went to sleep at night. And she wanted to see him with a little bit of meat on his bones.

The outrage she'd felt on witnessing his beating at the forge returned to her in force, and her heart swelled with more than a vague fondness for Gavin. He had not hesitated, not even for a second, flying to Theo's rescue as though he were some sort of avenging angel.

She supposed that was how she'd thought of Gavin from the moment she'd met him—why she'd coerced him into helping her deal with the blackmailer. She'd taken a chance in trusting him, but it was quite clear she'd been right. Even if it turned out to be James Norris who removed the packet of money from the lectern—which it would not—she believed Gavin would handle the situation with skill and discretion.

"You can go and play for a little while before we leave, Theo," she said.

His expression went blank at Christina's suggestion, and she realized his uncle was unlikely to have given the boy any respite from his chores. Or his punishments. "Come on, then!" she said rising to her feet. "Let's find something fun to do!"

They spent half an hour making themselves breathless playing a chasing game before resuming their southward trek. Even Jenny joined in while the men relaxed. And after their lunchtime romp, they returned to the carriage and taught some nursery songs to Theo.

It was near dusk when they came to a side road just past Ledger's Mill. Hancock had been told to watch for it, and he turned into the lane as he'd been instructed. Christina believed they must have traveled fifty miles at least, for she and Jenny were both stiff from sitting in their cramped quarters, and dizzy from the jostling of the past few hours. Theo had been asleep with his head on Christina's lap for the past hour.

"I dearly hope we're almost there," Jenny said.

"I'm sure we are," Christina replied. "As I recall, my cousin's house is not far from the northern road."

A few minutes later, they heard Hancock shout to the horses and felt the carriage turn. Christina leaned toward the window and saw a familiar church and a mill as they passed by. She knew they were in the right place, on the road to St. Ledger's Abbey.

The carriage pulled up to stop in the front drive of the ancient castle, which had generated the most romantic daydreams of Christina's life, as had her dashing cousin, Avery. She was very glad for the opportunity to visit again.

Hancock quickly jumped down from the carriage as Trevor came around to lower the steps and open the door. Christina stepped out as several of her cousin's footmen exited the castle and descended the wide granite stairs to approach her. She reached into her reticule and pulled out a card for one of the footmen to take to Avery, while Jenny collected a sleepy-eyed Theo and brought him out of the carriage.

"Take care of him, Jenny, and see that he's fed and given a place to sleep. I'll check on him later."

Gavin dismounted beside the carriage and handed his reins to a young groom, while Hancock led the horses and carriage away. He came to stand beside Christina as her cousin came out, quickly descending the stairs with his hands extended, quite obviously pleased to see her.

"Christina!"

"Avery," she said warmly, allowing herself to be taken into his embrace.

"This is a surprise! What brings you our way?"

"I have business in London, and . . ." She turned

to Gavin. "Here is my escort, Captain Gavin Briggs. Captain Briggs, my cousin Avery, Earl of Matherley."

Christina saw Gavin hesitate a moment before taking Avery's outstretched hand. She cast him a sidelong glance, and when she saw that his complexion had turned chalky, could not help but wonder what was wrong.

The weight of regret and a fair measure of dread settled in Gavin's stomach. He'd never intended to meet Amelia Winter again, and yet he knew the Earl of Matherley had become her husband. This was the man for whom Amelia had deserted him. He wished he'd realized Matherley was Christina's cousin.

"My wife will be pleased to make your acquaintance," the earl said.

"I'm very sorry I was unable to attend your wedding, Avery," Christina said before Gavin had a chance to state that he already knew Amelia. He knew her very well.

"I understand, Christina. May I offer my sympathies on your loss? It is so very hard to believe Lang is gone."

Gavin saw Christina bite her lip, a sign that could easily be interpreted as grief, though he knew it was worry that darkened her features. And with good reason.

His own emotions were far more difficult to interpret. Anger and dismay warred inside him, along with a strange sense of alarm. He had not felt this unsettled since facing his first battle in Spain, years ago.

He did not want to see the woman he'd once loved, in the presence of her husband. He did not want to see her at all.

"Let us not dwell upon unhappy thoughts," Matherley said. "Come, you must meet my wife."

"I believe your wife and I are acquainted," Gavin interjected before they went any further.

"Oh?"

"Viscount Hargrove is my father," he said. "His property and that of Lady Matherley's family adjoined."

"What a coincidence," Matherley said, quirking his brow. "Then I'm sure she'll be pleased to see you again."

Gavin doubted that, but as they continued through the entrance hall of the castle, he wondered if Amelia had told her husband about her first love. Matherley seemed to have recognized something about him at the mention of his acquaintance with Amelia.

Or perhaps it was his imagination.

Gavin took stock of her new home as they entered the large, richly furnished drawing room. Matherley sent a maid to fetch Amelia, and Gavin braced himself for their meeting. He had never expected this moment to occur, and he forced himself to ignore the jumble of emotions that roiled through him at the thought of seeing her again.

Christina and her cousin sat while Gavin remained standing near the window. He felt anxious and restless, feelings that were so utterly foreign to him, he did not know what to make of them.

"Ah, my dear. Here you are."

Gavin turned and saw Amelia enter the room. Christina rose from her seat as Matherley went to his wife, taking her hand in his.

Gavin stood stock-still.

Amelia looked the same—her hair was as golden as ever, her eyes a soft brown with thick, dark lashes framing them. She was trim and graceful in a light blue gown with long sleeves. The neck scooped low, displaying her collarbones and a generous span of flawless skin. Skin whose touch he'd once coveted as much as life itself.

She was as gracious as he remembered, greeting Christina cordially and offering sympathies to her husband's cousin over her recent losses. Her smile faltered only slightly when she turned to look at him.

"Captain Briggs," she said as she slipped her hand through the crook of her husband's elbow, a gesture of retreat—or fortification. "It has been a very long time since we last saw each other."

Gavin gave a short bow. "Aye, Lady Matherley."

"At least three years, is it not?"

With a slight tip of his head, he acknowledged that she was correct. Save for one quick visit before he'd taken Windermere's commission, he had not been back to Seaholm Hall in at least three years, perhaps longer. Still, Amelia might have written to inform him of her change of heart. She might have told him she no longer wanted to marry him when he returned home, rather than letting him learn it from his brother, who'd enjoyed the joke rather too much.

Clifford was just as arrogant, but only half as intelligent as their father. He'd always mocked Gavin's friendship with Amelia, saying that she would marry nothing less than an earl's son. And that Gavin, as a younger son, could not hope to compete.

It chafed to admit Clifford had been right.

Amelia sat down beside her husband with Christina directly across. Gavin remained standing.

"I cannot tell you how shocked we were to hear of Lang's . . ." Matherley cleared his throat and made a genteel change of subject. "How is your mother? Your father? They must be devastated."

"Yes," Christina responded as they all sat down. "It's been very difficult."

"I understand they've gone abroad with Felton and Colin."

Christina nodded, her short, dark hair a sharp contrast to Amelia's conventional coif. Even Christina's beautiful eyes flouted custom, sparkling with interest and emotion, and holding nothing back.

There in Matherley's drawing room, she was lively and expressive, nearly as spirited as when she made love. Gavin had learned that there was nothing less with Christina.

The conversation continued, though Gavin did not contribute. He was surprised to realize that whatever he once felt for Amelia had changed into something far more . . . benign. She was pleasant enough, but he felt no fiery need when he looked at her. No overwhelming desire to touch her, to taste her lips. The gentle swells of her breasts held no allure.

It was a disturbing revelation. The woman he'd spent so many hours dreaming of—Gavin realized it had been nothing more than a boyish infatuation with a girl who'd adored him. She was a mature woman now, not the young girl he'd left behind when he'd gone away to school, and then to war.

She was still comely enough, but she did not inspire any great urge to sweep her into his arms and carry her away.

Not the way Christina did.

That was a jarring thought, one he dismissed immediately. Amelia had taught him a valuable lesson about ladies of quality, one he would do well to heed. Gavin would never be more than a country farmer, while Christina was the widow of a viscount, the granddaughter of a duke. Society was hers for the taking, and take it she would, as soon as her period of mourning ended.

He needed to keep her at arm's length.

The only women in Gavin's future were his sister and her daughter, Rachel. When he collected his reward from Christina's grandfather and bought his manor house in Hampshire, they would no longer be a burden to their cousin in London. And now that he was responsible for Theo, Gavin would take the boy with them to Weybrook Manor where they all would be able to live respectably, and with ease.

Amelia and her husband engaged Christina in light conversation, carefully avoiding speaking of Lang or Viscount Fairhaven, topics that surely would be distressing to her. They spoke of the engagement of the eldest Jameson brother, and asked about his fiancée before turning to Gavin.

"How is your family, Captain Briggs?" Amelia asked.

"My father and brother are the same as always," he replied. "My sister, Eleanor, now lives in London with a cousin."

Amelia's brows dipped. "In London? I had not heard."

Gavin nodded. "She has been there more than a year."

"Well, perhaps I'll see her when we go down to Town."

"Perhaps," he said noncommittally. Of course they would not meet. Eleanor and Amelia traveled in vastly different circles these days.

Gavin was surprised to discover he did not dislike the man Amelia had wed. Matherley was genuinely affable and considerate—a far cry from the behavior Gavin had witnessed in his own father's drawing room. Viscount Hargrove was an arrogant bastard who never cared a whit about anyone but himself and his heir, the favored son, who'd been spoiled and coddled for as long as Gavin could remember.

Matherley seemed entirely different. He was attentive to his wife and Christina, and more than civil to Gavin, in spite of any inkling he might entertain of Amelia's past relationship with him.

"Well, you must plan on staying with us as long as you like, Christina . . . Captain Briggs," Matherley said. "Are you in a hurry to get to London?"

"Er . . . Yes, I have business there in a few days," Christina replied. "But thank you, Avery. Your hospitality tonight is most appreciated."

Amelia picked up a small bell and summoned a footman to the room. "Peter, please go and light the fires in the guest rooms for Captain Briggs and Lady Fairhaven. We'll follow."

Christina walked ahead with her cousin, while Gavin followed alongside Lady Matherley. "I hope you know you can ask anything of us, Christina," Avery said. "If there is anything you need . . ."

Christina shook her head slightly, far more interested in the hushed, highly personal conversation taking place behind her. Luckily, Avery kept up his friendly chatter while Christina managed to listen in on what Amelia and Gavin had to say to each other.

"You look thinner than I remember, Gavin," Amelia said.

"I'm sure it's just a trick of your memory, Lady Matherley."

Christina thought that must be so, for he looked perfect to her, and she'd seen the striking fullness of his body without a shirt, without trews . . . something she doubted Lady Matherley had.

She thought again. Perhaps she was mistaken, and Captain Briggs had had more than just a passing association with her cousin's wife. It was foolishly distressing to realize it must be so, else Lady Matherley would not speak of something so personal.

Gavin was a skilled lover, and he could not have come by his talents in the bedchamber without a good bit of experience. Why not with Amelia—with the young woman who'd known him in years past. Perhaps he'd been Amelia's first—

"Are you glad to be out of the army?" Amelia asked.

There was a pause. "Life in England is not what I'd thought it would be, but then . . . one never knows what changes will come."

Lady Matherley did not reply to Gavin's statement, and Christina tried to pay attention to Avery's remarks about the last time he'd seen Christina's parents, several months before, at a ball in London. But she only half listened, and answered vaguely, far more preoccupied with the undertones behind her, and the riot of emotions Gavin's familiarity with Amelia raised in her.

She did not want to know anything of the women who'd come before her.

It was not jealousy, but a matter of . . . of . . . priorities. She did not want to have to compete with his past. Not that she would, for Avery and Amelia seemed quite happy together. Gavin would hold no sway over her now.

Perhaps Christina's earlier assumption was incorrect, and they had simply known each other as children, for Gavin said his father's property adjoined Amelia's. Maybe that was how they could speak so familiarly with each other.

Christina might believe it if she did not sense an

agitation about him. Meeting Amelia had put him on edge.

"That is true, Captain Briggs," Lady Matherley said quietly. "Circumstances change. Decisions must be made."

Gavin did not reply, and when they reached the staircase, Lady Matherley took her leave, saying she would see them at supper. Avery saw them to their rooms, situated right next to each other. He left them, and before Christina went into her bedchamber, she turned to look at the man who'd become her lover.

"You grew up with Lady Matherley?" she asked.

His features darkened, and a muscle in his jaw tightened. He gave a quick nod.

"You . . . were close, then?" Christina persisted.

"Close? Aye. I intended to marry her."

Chapter 17

The shock on Christina's face hardly registered with Gavin. He went into his room, aware that the only emotion he felt now was a vague irritation that Amelia had not had the decency to write him of her change of heart.

He'd expected better of her, though he had to admit she'd waited a long time to wed. She was only a few years his junior and she ought to have married years ago. Five or six, at least. He'd been an inconsiderate lout to hold her to her promise to marry him at some point in the indefinite future.

She'd waited a long time without even knowing if he would survive the war and return home.

And if they'd married and she later discovered his wartime occupation, he doubted she would have been pleased. Certainly not proud. How could she condone the kind of war he'd waged? He'd been a sanctioned killer—not the same as a foot soldier or a cavalryman. Not even like a rifleman of the Ninety-fifth. He'd sought out specific targets and eliminated them—murdered them outside of any battlefield.

Gavin allowed that Amelia was far better off with Matherley, a decent sort of fellow with the means to provide her with the gracious life she deserved. Gavin's future was still unsettled until he collected the money Windermere owed him, and even then he would have no title, no prestige.

Still, it was disconcerting to realize his emotions toward Amelia were flat. His unease at the prospect of seeing her again had disappeared.

He'd thought their first encounter would play out entirely differently, but instead, he realized he'd come very close to making the mistake of his life. They were both better off with Amelia married to Matherley.

He found his heart was not broken after all.

Jenny brushed the black crepe gown while Christina undressed and thought about Gavin's startling statement. *He'd planned to marry Avery's wife.* From the little bits of the conversation she'd overheard, she inferred Amelia had been the one to cry off.

Perhaps Gavin was heartbroken.

Christina's own heart twisted in her chest at the possibility that Gavin felt crushed by Amelia's desertion. She'd heard his words quite clearly, and they indicated a dissatisfaction with life since his return to England.

His discontent must include her. After all, she'd not only shot him, but had refused to go to Windermere, thereby preventing him from collecting his reward from her grandfather. And their trip to London had been anything but uneventful. There'd been thieves and orphan boys. And . . .

And her. Christina could not help but think she had been merely a substitute for the woman who'd claimed Gavin's heart.

Yet he had bedded her with enthusiasm, and more than once. He'd given no indication that his heart was engaged elsewhere.

Not that she wanted his heart, exactly. He was a masterful lover, considerate, patient, and tender. But as long as their liaison lasted, she wanted to know she had his full attention. That she was not sharing it with another woman.

She'd done that once before.

"If you keep chewing on that nail, you'll have to let me file it, my lady," Jenny said, and Christina abruptly put down her hand. She sat on the cushioned bench at the dressing table and started to brush her hair.

Edward had wronged her in the worst possible way. She'd been his wife, and he'd humiliated her publicly. He'd essentially told the world that she was unsatisfactory.

Christina sighed, drawing her brush through her hair. She knew her silly, short curls gave her the look of a hoyden like Caroline Lamb. She wished enough of it had grown out so that Jenny could twist it into a decent chignon and she could look like a cultured lady like Amelia.

"Here now, my lady," said Jenny. "Your gown is ready."

Christina stood again and stepped into the dress, then let Jenny pull it up and fasten it for her. "What's this?"

Christina suddenly realized she'd left a dark red abrasion on her neck uncovered. "Ah . . . I think the collar of my traveling dress must have chafed my neck. I was too warm today."

"Shall I see if I can fix the seam for you, my lady?"

"Don't bother—I'll see to it myself after supper."

"If you're sure."

Christina gave Jenny a sidelong glance. "We both know how handy you are with a needle, Jenny."

Then she said nothing more about it, glad that her maid was young enough and naïve enough not to realize the true cause of her reddened skin. Even now, she could almost feel the rasp of Gavin's beard, feel his teeth and tongue and the soft kisses he'd trailed down to her breast.

Christina could not believe that he would ever be aloof when he came to a woman's bed. Or that he would perform perfunctorily. He might only be passing time in the pleasurable pursuits of the bedchamber, but she knew she was the sole focus of his attention, the recipient of his undivided interest, as she had not been with her own husband.

" 'Tis a shame you must wear your black crepe, my lady," said Jenny. "I would so dearly love to see you in your deep green silk . . . It brings out your eyes so well."

"Yes, it's my favorite, too."

But completely inappropriate for a widow in mourning. Christina did not know if she would ever wear that gown again, since it would likely be entirely out of fashion by the time she came out of mourning.

She had worn the gown only once, to a summer ball a few weeks before Edward's death. She did not think her husband had even noticed it. She remembered that he'd spent most of the evening in the card room, smoking and gambling with a number of other married men. She had not danced with him even once, and she wondered now whether he'd gone to Mrs. Shilton's house after escorting her home. He had left her at the town house alone, saying he was going to his club. Christina had assumed the men were meeting to continue their card games.

She would never be such a naïve chit again. She had learned a great deal from her lackluster marriage, and what Gavin Briggs was teaching her was at the opposite end of the spectrum.

Jenny finished fastening the gown and looked at her curiously. "If you're worried about Theo," the maid said, "he's down in the servants' hall with Trevor and Mr. Hancock. They're taking good care of the lad."

"I'm glad to know it," Christina replied. Jenny knew her well, and sensed something bothering her. Theo's well-being had been at the back of her mind, but Christina could hardly admit what direction the rest of her thoughts had taken. She hardly knew what to make of them herself.

She was over the shock of Edward's death and the circumstances thereof. There was no point in thinking about them now—unless they helped her to understand Gavin, and what Amelia had meant to him.

A lot, she guessed, though it surprised her. Gavin Briggs had not struck her as a man who would profess his undying love for a woman. He was part hero, yet part rogue. Settling down in domestic bliss seemed to be a contradiction in terms.

And yet he would soon own a farm in Hampshire.

Christina wondered what circumstances could possibly have made Amelia decide not to marry him. Had it been because Avery was a peer and Gavin was not? Did social position matter when one was in love? Had Amelia ever loved Gavin Briggs?

Perhaps not, and Christina could not help but wonder whether Amelia had fallen in love with Avery. Maybe while Captain Briggs was away, Amelia's path had crossed Avery's and she realized she did not care so very much for her former fiancé.

Christina liked her cousin Avery very much, and he seemed quite happy in his marriage. But she could not help but think Amelia had made a very grave mistake.

"Here's your shawl, my lady."

"I don't think I'll need it, Jenny."

"I just thought since you shivered— Well, never mind." She folded the shawl and put it away, then went to the door. "I'll just go on now if that's all right."

"Yes . . . or no, wait. Will you show me the servants' hall? I'd like to see Theo for myself."

"Of course, my lady."

Gavin looked at the healing cuts on Theo's back, managing somehow not to wince. He remembered the deep wounds he'd acquired at the end of his own father's belt, remembered Clifford's taunting smiles every time Gavin was punished for some typical youthful infraction. As well, there'd been a good number of times when he'd attracted his father's ire by defending Eleanor.

Someone—probably on Christina's orders—had bathed Theo properly, washing his hair and combing it out. It had even been trimmed, and when the boy was clean and dressed, he no longer looked quite the savage he had been when Christina had taken him out of the smithy shop.

She'd formed an attachment to the child. He was timid, but after only one day under her care and attention, Theo had begun to look healthier and not quite so cowed.

It had been a pleasure to watch her playing with him, running and chasing in the meadow where they'd stopped to have their lunch. Her laugh of pure joy had jarred Gavin's heart into an unsettling rhythm.

Had he ever witnessed such enjoyment before? If he had, he could not remember it.

Christina came into the servants' hall with her maid, but did not see Gavin right away. Her eyes locked on Theo, and she gave him the same brilliant smile that had hammered through Gavin at lunch. It was different from the satisfied smiles she gave him when he bedded her, and nothing like the smiles she'd given Amelia and her husband.

It showed her delight, and at the same time, was meant to reassure. "I see you are doing well, Theo," she said. "Have they fed you?"

"Yes, my lady," the boy replied, bowing, and Gavin realized someone had instructed him on the proper way to address her.

"Oh! Captain Briggs," she said when she looked past Theo and saw him.

Gavin made his bow. "We will be late for supper, Lady Fairhaven. Shall I escort you?"

She gave Theo a gentle pat on his shoulder, avoiding the injured areas of his back. For a woman who had probably never been exposed to a moment of violence, she was surprisingly aware. "Jenny will look after you, Theo. Rest well, for we have a long way to go on the morrow."

"Yes, my lady," the boy replied, putting his thumb into his mouth.

They exited the servants' hall together, Gavin thinking about how quickly she'd become attached to the lad. He wondered how she was going to react to being separated from him when he took Theo to his sister.

"I am having some difficulty imagining you with my cousin's wife," Christina said when they reached a quiet passage on the way to the dining hall.

"I was never with your cousin's wife," he said.

"Well, of course not after she became Avery's wife. But Amelia, I mean. You really meant to marry her?"

There was something in her voice that he had not heard before. Not quite annoyance . . . "Are you jealous?"

"Jealous?" Her back and neck straightened almost imperceptibly. "Of course not. Why would I be?"

He shrugged. "No reason at all."

They met Lord Matherley and his wife coming into the dining hall. After they took their seats, footmen began to serve the meal, and Amelia started a perfectly inane discussion of the spring weather.

Gavin tried to keep his attention on the conversation, rather than Christina, who sat across from him at the table, but failed. He noticed everything about her, from her dark, glossy hair to her pure, velvety skin and the subtle peaks of color on her cheeks. She did not spare him a glance.

She *was* jealous. Of a woman for whom Gavin felt nothing.

While Matherley took up the conversation and reminisced about a trip his family and Christina's had taken to Italy together many years before, Christina laughed and recalled a few anecdotes about her brothers, shutting him out completely.

Her attitude amused him. More, it put even a sharper edge on his desire for her. She wanted him as badly as he wanted her.

He noticed that the table became quiet at the mention of Lang's misadventures, and Christina's mood sobered. Her eyes brightened, her nose reddened, and Gavin realized she was coming close to tears. He took it upon himself to change the direction of the conversation. "Lady Fairhaven's parents are in Italy now, I believe."

"Perhaps it is easier for them there?" Amelia asked quietly.

Christina nodded, and Gavin knew there was conflict waging within her. He sensed it was because she could not speak of the possibility that Lang was alive, and the lie did not come easily to her.

Whereas Gavin had been lying for years, to everyone from his father to Lord Wellington. No one was to know of his actual duties once he'd been recruited by Lord Castlereagh, although he supposed a few must have known or suspected. Wellington, for instance, who'd raised an eyebrow upon learning of the sudden deaths of the French commander General Morel and his adjutant.

The general had been about to lead fifty thousand troops into Leipzig, and Gavin's orders from Lord Castlereagh had been to deal with every potential threat to the allied troops. Gavin knew Morel's death would cause chaos in his command, because his second, Colonel Beaufait, was rumored to be incompetent.

Soon thereafter, Wellington had ordered Gavin to accompany him to the battlefield at Waterloo. At least there, his role in the battle had been close to that of a

regular officer. But he had not been an ordinary officer for many years. And those years weighed heavily
on him.

Gavin glanced about the sumptuous dining room
with its silk-covered walls, and rich, mahogany furniture. There were silver serving tureens on the side-
board and expensive hothouse flowers in intricate
cut-glass vases on the table. Gavin had grown up
with such things at Seaholm Hall, and knew their
value.

They were luxuries he would be unlikely to afford,
though he would soon be well able to provide a comfortable life for himself and his . . .

Well. He'd always thought he'd have a wife to take
with him wherever he made his home. But circumstances change, as Amelia had said, and, as always,
Gavin would do what needed to be done. Eleanor
and her daughter were going to be comfortable at
Weybrook Manor, and so would Theo, though Gavin
was not exactly sure how the boy would fit into his
household.

There was time enough to figure that out. The boy
would need to spend a few weeks with Eleanor in
their cousin Hettie Mills's house—at least until he
transported Christina to her grandfather at Windermere Park. Once that was done, he could move on.

Move on without her.

He took a swallow of wine and pretended to listen
to Amelia, who was talking about a trip she and
Matherley had taken some months before. Clearly,
she had grown tired of waiting for him. And when

Matherley had come along, she had not been able to resist him and all he had to offer.

Gavin was glad she'd married the earl, even though it proved Clifford right. Being a countess suited Amelia well. She was gracious, if slightly insipid, and he knew now that he was not the best prospect as a husband.

He didn't really know if he could be a farmer, either. He was unused to settling in one place for very long, though he'd dreamed of doing just that during his long missions abroad. He'd wanted to fall asleep and awaken in the same bed every night and morning. To shave over the same washbasin every day. To eat his meals at the same table.

"My housekeeper tells me you brought a young boy with you, Captain Briggs."

He nodded. "A child who lived with his drunken uncle."

"And you rescued him, I presume?"

"Yes," Christina interjected. "He did. The uncle was beating the poor boy with a whip."

Amelia laid her hand on Gavin's arm and he resisted the urge to pull away. "You are still rescuing the helpless and oppressed, Captain Briggs?"

Gavin heard a tinge of patronization in her voice, something he'd never recognized before. Something he found quite disagreeable.

"I believe anyone with an ounce of sense would have intervened in Theo's situation, Lady Matherley," Christina said. "It was merely human kindness."

Gavin remembered Amelia's youthful laugh, and

the way it never failed to sparkle through him. Now he heard something entirely different. There was an aspect to her demeanor he did not quite understand. Or like.

He didn't know if he was the one who had changed, or if it was she, but whatever had once sparked between them was gone. It was thoroughly dead.

"What will you do with the boy, Captain Briggs?" Lord Matherley asked.

He found he was uninterested in sharing any personal information with Amelia or her husband, not about Theo, or Eleanor and her circumstances, or of his plans to buy Weybrook Manor. "I'll think of something once we reach London."

Christina caught his eye and Gavin saw that she grasped his reticence, though she could not possibly understand it. He didn't quite understand it himself.

Amelia had grown into someone he did not know. She was older and more mature than when he'd last seen her during a short visit home three years ago. Whether it had been due to her marriage or the years she'd spent waiting for him to return from France, she had lost the softness of youth.

When Christina turned to Lord Matherley and started a discussion about his mother and sisters, Gavin was grateful. It was barely necessary for him to participate.

After supper, they went into a small parlor where Avery poured glasses of sherry for the ladies, and something stronger for Gavin and himself.

Amelia clung to her husband's arm, as if making an exhibit of their closeness to Gavin. The subtle smugness in her expression gave Christina the most devilish urge to demonstrate what a vital mistake she had made in jilting her former betrothed.

Not that there was anything wrong with Avery, but he could not compare to Gavin, in any way.

The direction of her thoughts took her aback and she took a moment to recover her grounding. Whatever was between Amelia and Gavin had naught to do with her.

"Perhaps I ought to let you retire for the night," Avery said, though it was with some reluctance. He seemed to be enjoying their visit far too much to say good night.

"Not at all," Christina replied. "Besides, how often do I get to visit my favorite cousin?"

Avery turned to Gavin, which gave Christina a moment to compose herself. She was very glad Amelia had not married Gavin, and her reasons were far more complicated than she ever would have thought.

"My wife tells me you were lately in France, Captain Briggs. Under whose command did you serve?"

Christina noted yet another hesitation before Gavin answered Avery's question, and she wondered if it was because of unpleasant memories, or something entirely different. She wanted to know more about him, more than the way his calloused hands felt on her skin or the pleasing texture of his hair and the taste of his kisses. She found herself leaning forward to listen when he answered Avery's question.

"I served under General Colville in Spain and Wellington in France."

"You were in good company, then."

Gavin took a sip of his drink. "Aye."

His statement did not invite any discussion. He was the first soldier Christina had met who did not take the opportunity to elaborate on his experiences.

When Gavin said nothing more, Christina turned to Lady Matherley. "We were beset by thieves a few nights ago."

"Good heavens, where?" Avery asked.

"A long way north, near North Riding," Gavin said. He crossed his arms over his chest and his legs at the ankle. He appeared indifferent, but Christina could not help but notice the pointed look he shot her way. As though he did not approve of her mentioning the incident and speaking of his cool bravery in the face of such dire circumstances.

But there wasn't any reason not to recount what happened. It's what visitors did—made conversation exchanging stories with their hosts.

"The thieves were taken into custody and will soon stand trial," Gavin said. "It was a minor disturbance."

"What happened?" Amelia pressed a hand to her breast. "I cannot imagine such an occurrence."

"Captain Briggs saved the day, but I will admit I was more frightened than I've ever been." Christina ignored Gavin's unspoken demand that she desist.

She realized he would never boast, but it was the perfect opportunity to speak of his prowess.

"Who were these men, Captain?" Avery asked.

"The magistrate said they'd been harassing travelers in the vicinity for weeks. They were nothing special."

"There were three of them, all large, dangerous men, and Captain Briggs apprehended them." Christina was pleased to note the expression of wonder on Amelia's face.

"That is commendable, Captain Briggs," Avery said. "Three men? How did you do it?"

"They were hardly more than bumpkins. It was not such a great challenge," Gavin said.

"I disagree," Christina said. "The men came into the inn and Captain Briggs saved everyone from losing their valuables. Or worse."

"Good heavens!" Amelia said again, looking at Gavin.

"How?" Avery asked.

"The dining room was full of travelers," Christina said, relishing the tale. "Just ripe for plunder."

"Oh!" Amelia whispered.

"They were huge men, all three, and so very rough with the innkeeper. They pushed into the room demanding that we turn over our money and our jewelry to them."

"It was somewhat less dramatic than Lady Fairhaven indicates," Gavin interjected.

"I beg to differ, Captain Briggs." She turned back to Avery and Amelia. "The captain waited until the ruffians approached us, and then he upturned our table right onto them."

Amelia's eyes grew wide and she covered her mouth with her hand. "Oh my!"

"There was a terrible confusion, with shouting and screaming all around," Christina continued with a dramatic flourish, ignoring Gavin. "The villains struggled to get up, but Captain Briggs and another fellow traveler managed to confine them to a strong room in the inn."

"Astonishing," said Avery.

"You have no idea," Christina remarked, quite pleased with the reactions of her cousin and his wife.

Gavin leaned forward. "How do you know what happened, Lady Fairhaven? I believe I sent you away before the men were fully subdued."

She smiled. "As you know, Captain Briggs, I am not one to follow orders."

Chapter 18

The conversation did not become any more comfortable, even after Christina finished her recounting of the incident at the inn near North Riding. She turned to fishing for information. About him.

"I understand you grew up in the north, near Captain Briggs's home," she said to Amelia.

Amelia did not answer at once, but then she nodded. "Our fathers' estates are not far from Durham."

It had already been mentioned that the two properties bordered one another and that they'd grown up together. But she didn't add that she'd had her first dance with him, and her first kiss. Or that she had promised to wait for him when he went to war.

"It's lovely country. I visited Durham once or twice with my parents," Christina said. "You must have known the Briggs family all through your youth." Definitely prying.

Amelia shifted slightly in her chair, and Gavin

suspected she had not told Avery of her engagement
to him. Why would she? Obviously, it had been of
little import to her.

Christina's attempt to gather information would
have been amusing if he hadn't been so bloody annoyed by Amelia's aloof responses to Christina's
questions. She'd been a sweet girl, all innocence and
smiles. Gavin knew she would not have dealt well
with the truth of his wartime activities if he'd ever
seen fit to tell her.

Still, it rankled. All these years he'd planned on
coming home to her. He'd thought she would be
waiting faithfully for his return.

The jest was on him, exactly as Clifford had said.

"Of course I knew the family," Amelia said without looking at him. "When Lady Hargrove passed
away, Captain Briggs's father occasionally asked my
mother for advice on housekeeping matters and . . .
whatnot."

Gavin caught Christina stealing a glance at him
at the mention of his deceased mother. But he did
not react, nor did he contribute to the conversation.
He no longer had any connection to Seaholm Hall.
His mother was long dead, and the only ones left at
the family seat were his father and Clifford. The two
deserved each other.

"That was quite considerate of your mother,"
Christina said, and Gavin saw that she had played
out her hand. There was little else she could ask
without obviously prying.

Amelia stood just then, and her husband followed

suit. "I fear we have kept you from your rest far too long, Lady Fairhaven."

"Not at all. Thank you for the excellent company."

She bid her cousin good night with a kiss on his cheek, and went upstairs with Amelia while Gavin and Lord Matherley followed.

"Have you known Captain Briggs very long, Lady Fairhaven?" Amelia spoke in a low voice, but Gavin managed to hear her question.

"No, not very," Christina replied equivocally. "He must have been a formidable boy years ago."

"Oh yes," Amelia said. "The most handsome and daring lad I'd ever seen. He rather swept me off my feet."

Gavin was unmoved by her flattery. He knew how empty such talk could be. He was a good deal more interested in the sway of Christina's hips as she mounted the stairs before him. Her body was a perfect match to his, giving and taking equally.

"I can well imagine," Christina said, still meddling. "But then he went off to war."

"Yes." Gavin heard a sigh. "And I met my husband . . . All ended well."

Surprisingly well, in Gavin's opinion. Especially as Amelia's glimmer now paled compared to Lady Fairhaven, who'd secured his interest for the moment.

He could not even regret delaying his trip to Windermere. Not when he'd been welcomed into the bed of this stunning, amazingly fiery woman. Even now his fingertips itched to slide into her soft, curly hair. He could almost taste her.

"We will take our leave early tomorrow, I believe," Christina said, looking back at Gavin for confirmation. The curls at her nape bounced a little, shimmering in the soft light of the sconces on the walls.

He gave a quick nod and tamped down the arousal that pulsed through him. "Soon after dawn."

"I will see that breakfast is ready for you before you depart," Amelia said.

They arrived at the guest rooms and Lord Matherley shook Gavin's hand, bidding him good night. He and his wife retreated, but Gavin did not enter his bedroom.

Neither did Christina.

He leaned against the wall near her door. "Did Amelia satisfy your curiosity?"

She had the good grace to appear abashed. "Not at all."

"What else would you like to know?"

She came to stand directly in front of him, her eyes a piercing green query. "More about your sister. What happened between you and your father. Why you don't ever talk about yourself."

He straightened and satisfied the urge to touch her hair. "There is only one relevant fact, Christina."

"And that is?"

"How very much I'd like to carry you into that bedchamber and make love to you until it's time to go."

Christina should not have felt quite so rested when morning came. They'd gotten far too little sleep for that, and even now, Gavin lay beside her, his eyes closed peacefully in slumber. It was unlike him to sleep past dawn, and she was loath to wake him.

She wanted to enjoy their few moments in bed when she could look at him unguardedly. His jaw was strong and square, with a dark coating of whiskers he would shave before they went on their way. His lashes were thick and dark, and the scar at the corner of his eye was barely noticeable in the dim light. His nose was not quite straight, but the defect only added to the potency of his visage.

She resisted the urge to push back his hair and trace the line of his ear with her tongue, initiating another bout of lovemaking. They had only a few more minutes before Jenny would arrive.

He hadn't answered any of her questions the night before. And why would he? They might be physically intimate, but he kept himself separate in every other way. He knew everything about her . . . But he'd told her so little about himself, it was remarkable.

Even so, Christina knew he would protect those who could not protect themselves. He took command when necessary, and elicited confidence in Hancock and Trevor. He was an amazingly tender, considerate lover, spending more time seeing to her pleasure than she would have believed possible.

She also knew she was causing him a delay in purchasing his property. She was a little bit ashamed of blackmailing him into doing her bidding just as surely as her own blackmailer was controlling her.

She wasn't proud of it. There was little, in fact, that she could be proud of these days. From her husband's scandalous death to her manipulation of Gavin Briggs—not to mention her affair with him— she was leading anything but the proper, demure life her parents had intended for her.

Haring down to London with him was hardly appropriate, especially since he spent every night in her bed.

And yet she could not regret any of it.

The closer they came to London, the easier Gavin could breathe. They'd had no trouble on the road, not since the incident at North Riding. After their stop tonight, he estimated they would have only one more day's travel.

And then there would be no more reason for him to spend every moment of his day with Christina. Or every night.

He felt an odd twinge at the thought of leaving her at her doorstep in London. She would be alone and unprotected, but for Hancock and Trevor. She wouldn't even have the lad, Theo, to whom she'd formed quite an attachment. She had one day to sell the jewels, and they would have reason to meet only once after that, when she had the money for the packet he would place in the lectern.

Though he would have preferred that she fill the packet with newsprint rather than actual banknotes, there was a possibility that the blackmailer would elude him. In which case their trip to London would have been in vain. The blackmailer might well dis-

close whatever he knew about Lang—if anything—
which Gavin doubted was true.

In any case, scandals came and went in London,
and whatever Lang's predicament was would only
entertain society for a limited time—just until the
next scandal came along.

Like Lord Fairhaven's death in the arms of his
mistress. After that indignity, Gavin could see why
Christina did not want any more scandals to taint
her family name.

They rode unerringly south, and Gavin kept watch
over the road behind and in front of Christina's carriage. Now that they were closer to London, they encountered more travelers than before, but none was
threatening.

After a long day in the saddle, Gavin rode ahead
into Newport Pagnell. The Black Sheep Inn was a
large establishment right near the road, and Gavin
stopped to acquire lodgings for their party. He still
planned to go about the farce of letting separate
rooms for himself and Christina, but he fully intended to share her bed that night.

It was not in her best interests to make their liaison
known. He had no intention of damaging her reputation. She'd had enough to deal with in recent months.

Gavin supposed that was why he had not pressed
the matter of Lang's death. Her brother was surely
dead, but Christina's hopes had been raised, and
Gavin didn't want to force his more realistic ap-
praisal of the situation down her throat.

He went into the inn and took a look around. There was no one about but a couple of serving maids, though he heard voices in a taproom behind a staircase adjacent to the travelers' dining room. The maids went about their tasks as Gavin walked across to the taproom, in search of the innkeeper.

Instead, what he found was a man who looked quite like the one who'd reminded him of Baron Chetwood. He was leaning back in his chair, and holding court with a group of avid followers.

This time, it actually was Chetwood.

Chapter 19

Gavin tipped down his hat and turned right around before Chetwood had a chance to look up and see him. He slipped away to a spot behind the adjoining staircase and looked carefully at the men, studying their faces for future reference.

He could not be sure, but it looked as though Chetwood's companions were his own cronies and not just random travelers he'd encountered at the inn. Black Sheep, indeed.

All of the men were well dressed, and most were clean shaven. One man had a wide black mustache and a large, dark blemish high on his cheek, and another didn't look old enough to shave. A third was a redhead with the pointed features of a ferret, and the others had their backs to him, so Gavin could not see their faces. One of these two was fair-haired, the other mostly bald.

Gavin's position provided cover for the perfect shot. If he'd had his Baker rifle, he could have picked off the baron and slipped away with no one the wiser.

But the war was over, and he was done with killing, even if the target was one of the most immoral, despicable churls in the kingdom. He made a quick exit from the building, going through a side entrance, then mounting his horse and galloping toward the road.

He did not think it was any accident that Chetwood was there. They were about fifty miles from London, and the Black Sheep Inn was a likely place for Christina to stop.

If the baron had stopped there for the purpose of encountering her, he would have to have known she was headed to London, and not to Windermere and her grandfather.

Gavin wondered what Chetwood knew and how he'd found out about their journey south. He searched his memory for some clue, some incident that would have revealed Christina's movements, but could think of none.

But it was no coincidence. Gavin's instincts were quite clear on that. While he'd been tracking Christina's sister, Chetwood must have hired men to follow up on what they'd learned of Christina. The baron might even be aware of the change in Windermere's will, but some nefarious motive drove him to pursue Christina in spite of it.

Gavin could have stayed and confronted Chetwood at the inn, but that would only confirm to the baron that he was close. And Gavin would not kill another man unless his own life—or that of someone he cared for—was at risk.

No, the best course was to direct Christina's party to the next town, and find lodgings far off the main road, whatever they might be.

Christina knew something was wrong. She heard the shouts and leaned forward to look out the window, just as the carriage increased its speed. Theo awoke from a long nap and pulled his thumb from his mouth when the carriage jerked them nearly off their seats. Christina saw the alarm in his eyes and hugged him close.

"Don't worry. Mr. Hancock is a very good driver."

"I wonder what could be the matter," Jenny said.

Christina gave a slight shake of her head. She did not know, but she trusted Gavin to keep them safe, and she didn't want to alarm Theo.

Gavin had said he was riding on ahead to secure their rooms, but clearly, something had changed his mind. And if Gavin thought they needed to travel faster and farther, then they would do exactly that, and hold on to their seats as they rode.

Christina had been lulled almost to sleep just a few moments before, but now, all her senses were alert. She felt energized, if a bit worried. She didn't know if she'd ever ridden in a carriage behind galloping horses, and it was not an experience she hoped to repeat. She held on to Theo with one hand and the carriage strap with the other as they bounced along the road.

Hancock kept the carriage upright and on track for the next few minutes as they continued past the town where they had agreed they would stop.

Eventually, the carriage slowed to a more reasonable speed, and so did Christina's heart. Hancock turned the carriage in a westerly direction into a street in a busy little town. She did not see Gavin, and assumed he must be riding ahead.

She could not imagine what had happened to spur the kind of race they'd just run. It did not seem that anyone had been pursuing them, or surely there would have been a confrontation by now.

It was something else.

When they were deep within the town, the carriage stopped and Gavin came to the door. He opened it, but stopped her from stepping out of the carriage. "We're going to take rooms here, but we cannot use our names—at least, not mine or Lady Fairhaven's."

"What's happened?" Christina asked.

"I'll tell you once we're inside. For now, you will be . . . Mrs. Crocker. I'm your husband, and this is our son, Theo."

"My word," Jenny said, under her breath, and Christina's heart quaked in her chest. She could not imagine what . . .

Baron Chetwood? Highwaymen had not chased them, so what else could it be?

A chill ran through her.

"I assure you the ruse is entirely necessary to keep Lady Fairhaven safe, Jenny." Gavin turned to Theo, and put his hand on the boy's head. "Theo, do you understand? You are to call Lady Fairhaven Mama. Just for tonight."

He nodded, and Christina's heart clenched in her chest. It was much too easy to imagine that Theo was Gavin's son . . . and hers. She took a deep breath of shock and stepped away from the carriage.

"We're agreed, then," she heard Gavin say. "I'll go get rooms for us. Wait a few minutes, then come in with Trevor and Hancock."

How absurd. She would have suitors aplenty after her year of mourning was done. Earls and viscounts had courted her before, and maybe even a duke's heir would come around once it was known that she was Windermere's granddaughter. Now that she had some experience—both within her marriage and without—there were certain things she required of a husband.

Fidelity was one of them. Respect was another.

Gavin went into the inn, and Jenny came over and spoke quietly to her. "Do you think it's entirely proper, my lady? Pretending to be Captain Briggs's wife?"

Christina managed to remain composed. Of course it was not. Nor was it proper to spend every night in his arms. But she'd learned quite painfully that the appearance of propriety was not always accurate. At least she was not hurting anyone by her liaison with Gavin.

"There is some danger to me, Jenny," she said without even blushing. "You know about the jewels . . .

The situation is too complicated to explain now, but I'm sure Captain Briggs only intends to keep me safe."

Jenny's eyes widened, but she only said, "Well, if you're sure."

Christina was only sure that she wanted this last night with Gavin, because once they reached London, she didn't know what would happen.

They started for the inn, with Theo's hand in hers.

Gavin took rooms for all of them at the King's Head Inn. It was not the highest-quality lodging house Gavin had ever seen, but its location was exactly right. It was far from the North Road, and nestled a good distance off the main street of town.

He put Jenny and Theo in the room next to Christina's, with Hancock and Trevor flanking the other side. They'd understood the need for Gavin to stay in Christina's room at Palmer's Inn, and when he explained the dangers now, he knew they would appreciate the same kind of necessity.

Gavin did not think Chetwood had seen him, but he could not be sure. He believed the subterfuge of traveling as Mr. and Mrs. Crocker with their son and servants would go a long way if the baron managed to track them this far into Milton Keynes. Gavin doubted he would, though.

Chetwood had seemed entirely relaxed, as though he was certain everything would play out exactly as he had planned. Gavin just wished he knew what the bastard intended for Christina.

He ordered a meal to be brought up to Christina's

room, where she would dine with her maid and Theo. He and the men would spend the evening in the tap-room, keeping watch, in case Chetwood or any of his minions came along. He explained to Trevor and Hancock as much of the situation as they needed to know, describing Chetwood so they would recog-nize him. Then he established a schedule for them to rotate watches throughout the night.

He shared a quick meal with the two men, then said he would take the first watch. He figured if Chetwood were to come around to the King's Head, it was likely to be earlier rather than later. First, he went up to check on the women and Theo, and found that all was well.

It looked as though they had already supped, and now they were engaged in a rhyming game. Gavin watched for a moment, and saw that the game had drawn Theo out, and he was laughing at Christina's silly verses.

"Go on with your turn, Jenny, while I talk with Cap— er, *Mr. Crocker.*"

Her smile belied the potential danger they faced. If the baron knew Christina was en route to London, he guessed the man would show up on her doorstep at some point.

He would deal with that after they reached London, when Christina was safely entrenched at her home.

"What happened?" Christina asked him quietly. "Why did we come here instead—"

"I saw Chetwood," Gavin replied. "He was sitting

in the taproom of the Black Sheep Inn, the best-look-ing inn near the road at Newport. It was the most likely place for us to stop for the night." But only if Chetwood knew where they'd stayed the previous night.

She went pale, and Gavin suppressed the urge to take her in his arms. But it would not do for Jenny and Theo to see him embrace her. He satisfied his longing to touch her by taking hold of the door frame beside her head.

"Trevor, Hancock, and I are going to take turns keeping watch downstairs," he said. "I don't expect Chetwood to find us, but if he comes around, we'll be forewarned. I'm taking the first watch. I'll come up later."

Christina nodded, and as he turned to exit the room, she took hold of his arm. "Please be careful."

"Aye." Her kiss would take away the sour taste of seeing Chetwood at the Black Sheep, but that would have to wait. Perhaps later, when he returned to the room, he would be inconsiderate enough to wake her.

Christina found it surprisingly difficult to fall asleep. She was tired from the long day of uncom-fortable confinement in the carriage, and the threat from Baron Chetwood was only vaguely real to her.

It was thoughts of Lang that kept her awake. No matter what they learned from the blackmailer, it was not going to be good. She desperately hoped Lang was alive, but that in itself was going to pose serious problems for him, and for their family.

Of course, her parents and brothers would want to know Lang had not been killed. But there would be scandal. A court-martial. She swallowed thickly. A hanging?

Perhaps Felton's fiancée would be compelled to cry off.

She moved restlessly in the bed, turning this way and that, missing Gavin. She'd grown accustomed to losing herself and drifting to sleep in his arms, his body curled around hers after a delicious bout of lovemaking.

It was yet one more worrisome thing.

Theirs was not exactly a conventional relationship in which expectations were clearly delineated. They were not betrothed, they were not even friends. Gavin's assistance with her blackmailer was solely for the purpose of ensuring that she would go back to Windermere with him.

She didn't even know if she would go with him when they were finished in London.

It was unethical, and unfair, she knew. But she had no interest in taking a long trip north to the Lake District to meet the grandfather who had abandoned her and her sister when she needed him most. She owed nothing to the old duke.

But she did owe Gavin. He'd come this far with her, and he would not renege on his promise to help her. Nor would she go back on her word to return to Windermere with him.

Fatigue finally overtook her, and she drifted off. She might have slept until morning, but for the lovely sensation of Gavin's hard chest pressing against her back sometime during the night. She sighed and turned to face him, sliding up to meet his kiss.

"No sign of the baron?" Christina asked, drawing back to take a breath.

"No. Come here."

She skimmed her hands up his chest, delighting in the crisp hair and the solid feel of him.

His hands roved over her, their light touch arousing. Sensations flowed through her, at once satisfying and frustrating. She wanted more, she wanted to give him pleasure.

Feeling pleasantly drowsy, she pushed him back to the mattress and moved on top of him, pressing kisses to his neck, then his chest. "You must be exhausted."

"Aye."

She slid her hand downward, finding him hard and ready. Encircling his manhood with her fingers, she stroked him as she moved ever lower, feathering kisses to his chest, her breasts brushing against his abdomen, then his thighs. She looked into his startled eyes as she touched her lips to the tip of his shaft, then swirled her tongue around it.

He closed his eyes and groaned, and she relished her sensual power, pulling him fully into her mouth.

It was incredibly arousing. Christina licked and sucked, driving Gavin relentlessly, as he'd done to her many times before.

She heard his deep groan and felt his hands cupping her head, exhorting her to continue.

She was close to her own climax, but she wanted to take him to the brink and back first. When she finally took mercy upon him, she shifted, moving up to straddle his hips. In one quick plunge, he joined their bodies together. Christina dictated the rhythm, so ready, and yet so keen to make it last. She leaned forward, her breasts swaying over him, and he caught one pebbled nipple in his mouth.

That sharp sensation pushed her over the edge, and she climaxed wildly, pleasure bursting through her body like the surf in a wild storm. Her heart roared and every muscle flexed.

And then a new, intense fire rushed through her as he drove into her again and again.

He altered their positions and she was suddenly under him. He thrust into her with an intensity that belied his fatigue, and his power became her own. His breaths were harsh pants in his throat, and he lowered his body fully against hers when he came. A savage, exquisitely visceral sensation sped through her as Gavin growled and thrust one last time.

Then a dangerous thought intruded, but Christina pushed it aside. Now was not time for thinking, but for pure rapture. That's what her liaison with Gavin was about, and not . . .

Well, it certainly was not about anything else.

Gavin did not want to move, but he was too heavy to stay where he was. He slid off Christina, but pulled her close and kissed her forehead before nestling her under his chin.

The thought that he might not be able to protect her from Chetwood worried him. There was no functional reason the baron should be able to get to her once she arrived at home, but he had resources Gavin did not. He had help. And he had strong motivation, it seemed.

But what could it be? By now, Chetwood had to know the will was changed. Certainly Windermere had seen to it. Could it be anger? Revenge? But for what? For being a legitimate heir to the duke? For having the right to a portion of Windermere's estate?

Gavin supposed that was likely it, especially for a man with the extravagant tastes—as well as the debts—he was reputed to have. Chetwood would have been infuriated by the loss of a significant portion of wealth that he'd come to believe would be his. But he could not possibly think he could get away with causing any harm to Christina.

"You built up the fire," Christina said.

"Mmmm." She snuggled close, fitting him so perfectly. Her warm, womanly scent surrounded him.

"You don't think Baron Chetwood turned up at Newport by chance, do you?" she asked.

"No."

"I don't understand. If Windermere changed his will . . ."

"It doesn't make a lot of sense. Chetwood would have made himself available to receive news of your grandfather's demise, so I'm sure he was informed of the change in the duke's will." But Chetwood was a scoundrel of the first order. If the rumors were to be believed, he and his wife had squandered most of their own fortune, and were now dining out on the certainty of Windermere's imminent demise. But nothing Chetwood did could alter Windermere's bequests to Christina and Lily.

Gavin was missing something. For years, he had made a point of knowing what his enemies wanted. He knew their motivations, their resources, their weaknesses. He'd been able to anticipate their moves, which was what had made him so effective, and what had kept him from losing his own life.

His lack of information regarding Chetwood chafed. After witnessing the man's near violence to his wife at Windermere, Gavin should have realized the baron would have no qualms about hurting Christina or her sister. They'd been his only competitors for Windermere's wealth, and now they'd seen to it that Chetwood did not inherit everything. He had to be as angry with them as he'd been with his wife that afternoon Gavin had seen them together at Windermere Park.

"I'll keep you safe, Christina."

"I know you will," she said sleepily. He felt her drift off, but found it difficult to do the same.

He needed facts. He wished he had a few men to circle back to Newport Pagnell to keep an eye on Chetwood and to report his activities. But he could not send Trevor or Hancock—they were needed to drive the carriage and protect Christina.

Gavin tried to put together the pieces of the puzzle. If the baron had discovered Christina's identity—as he surely had done, for he had resources Gavin had not possessed—he would know where to find her in London. Gavin wondered if Chetwood had been tracking her for long. Maybe he knew about the blackmailer.

No. Christina had not told anyone about it—except him, whom she'd asked to help. So Chetwood could not have any idea why she was hurrying down to London . . .

But he must. He had been ahead of them at Newport Pagnell. As though waiting for them.

Gavin was too tired to think clearly. He settled in close to Christina, aware how important it was for him to get some sleep so he could be fully alert on the morrow, for who knew what the day would bring.

Chapter 20

The gravity of Christina's situation came back to her with force when they reached Town. The weight of grief and responsibility for whatever had happened to Lang burned in the pit of her stomach. She would confirm that he was dead, or have to deal with the consequences of his desertion.

Looking back at Gavin as he tied his horse at the front of the house, Christina knew he did not intend to stay, not even for a short while.

And her misery grew.

She blinked back a sudden spate of tears and took Theo's hand. It was so absurd, allowing herself to become attached so quickly. It was just an affair, after all, and she would do well to remember the limits of their liaison.

She started for the door, but Gavin stopped her.

"Christina."

She looked back at him—so handsome, so capable—and reined in her instant flash of desire.

"I planned to take Theo with me," he said.

"Right," she said, though her heart was in her throat. She felt her lip begin to quiver and bit down on it to stop. Gavin had said from the first that he would take Theo to his sister. This ought not to be a surprise.

But she'd become so accustomed to having the little boy near, and . . . it was as though this parting were some pale foreshadowing of her eventual separation from Gavin. She swallowed and managed to mask any sign of her foolish distress.

"I . . . I thought he could stay here until . . ." *Drat.* If only her voice did not betray her.

Gavin's jaw tightened for an instant, then gave a quick nod. "Aye. Keep him here with you for now."

"Where will you be?" she asked, but felt no calmer.

He followed her into the house, but went no farther than the entryway as the servants worked around him, bringing in luggage. "I need to pay a visit to my sister," he said with a quick glance at Theo, "then scare up a few friends to help with what must be done these next couple of days."

Christina's heart skittered in her chest. The fear she'd felt last night when they'd evaded Baron Chetwood returned in force. "You'll go to the church?"

"Aye, I need to refresh my memory. But I want to locate Chetwood first."

She could not hide the panic that must have shown on her face. If Chetwood was as dangerous as Gavin seemed to think, then he just ought to avoid him. She was in her father's house now. And safe. "Gavin, no."

He ignored her protest and put a hand on Theo's shoulder. "Theo, listen to me. For now, you'll stay here with Lady Fairhaven, all right?"

"Yes, sir," the boy replied, and Christina saw signs of worship in the child's eyes. She took great care not to show any such emotion in her own. Or her fear.

"Gavin, I don't think it's such a good idea to broach the lion in his den."

"He is no lion, Lady Fairhaven, but a tiny foul snake."

"Small snakes can bite, too."

"I'll see this one's fangs blunted."

She closed her eyes and took a deep breath. "Will you come back tonight?"

"I doubt it."

He said it so offhandedly, his casual manner yet another warning for Christina to rein in her emotions. What she believed had passed between them the night before must have occurred only in her imagination.

She retreated, taking a step back. "Well, then. I . . ."

"I'll return tomorrow." He ruffled Theo's hair. "I'll see you then."

He was gone so quickly, Christina barely had time to realize the door had closed behind him. She gathered her wits and introduced Theo to the housekeeper, who took Gavin's exit as a signal to approach.

"Mrs. Wilder, please send for my father's tailor to come and make a few sets of clothes for young Theo. He'll need to be dressed from the skin out. For . . . for country living." Gavin might have rescued Theo and taken responsibility for him, but there was no reason Christina could not see that the boy was properly outfitted.

"Of course, my lady. I will see to it immediately."

Jenny came downstairs and collected Theo. "Come with me, young man, and I'll show you the nursery."

"Thank you, Jenny. Bring him to me in the parlor when you've shown him his room."

Christina went to her own bedchamber to change out of her traveling clothes. She put on a gown of dark red—not quite mourning, but not overly colorful or frivolous, either. Besides, she was not expecting any callers.

Not even Gavin.

A night apart was no catastrophe. She could certainly sleep alone—she'd done it her whole life. A few days in Gavin Briggs's arms had not changed her so very much.

Besides, this was the way lovers conducted affairs. Edward had not gone to Mrs. Shilton every night— Christina recalled many evenings when he'd stayed at home. Perhaps it had been his way to keep his distance from his paramour, to keep their association well-defined.

It hurt to think that was what Gavin had just done. Truly, there was much for him to do before he placed the money in the lectern at the church on Sunday morning. Besides, she hated to correlate anything about Gavin with Edward's actions. The two were nothing alike.

She paused at her dressing table, turning her

thoughts to what he intended to do. The danger would be when he came into contact with Baron Chetwood.

Christina knew she ought to trust him, trust his judgment. Just because he did not trumpet his abilities didn't mean he was without them. She'd boasted to her cousin of the way he'd dealt with the thieves at North Riding. And she'd seen him disable Theo's uncle with barely a twist of his wrist.

But Lord Chetwood . . . She suspected the man was pure evil.

After all, he'd sent killers to murder her sister, a woman who was innocent of anything but having the misfortune of being a recipient in Windermere's will. Gavin was right. Chetwood truly was a snake.

Theo needed to become accustomed to Eleanor and Rachel, but Christina was not ready to let him go, and Gavin had not had the heart to take him from her. She was under too much pressure now, and he would not add to her distress.

But there would come a day when he would take the boy and part ways with her. In frustration, Gavin rubbed his tired eyes and decided he could not dwell on it now. There was much to do before he took her packet of money to the lectern at the back of All Hallows by the Tower.

More reluctantly than he ought to have felt, he left Christina at Sunderland House and made his way through the streets of London to the home of his cousin, Hettie Mills.

Hettie had been more than generous, taking Eleanor in when her pregnancy could no longer be hidden and she had nowhere to go. When Gavin learned of her predicament, he'd sent money whenever he was able, but he doubted it was ever enough.

That would change once he had his money from Windermere. Fortunately, he'd made a contractual provision that he was to be paid whether or not the duke lasted long enough to meet his granddaughters. All Gavin had to do was get Christina to Windermere Park to reap his reward.

Gavin sincerely hoped events on Sunday did not interfere with their journey back to Windermere. If the blackmailer turned up, Gavin was sure he could apprehend him, and the rascal would then admit to lying about Lang being alive. It would be a blow to Christina . . . and he feared she had not prepared herself for disappointment.

She was much too full of hope.

On the other hand, finding evidence that Lang was alive was going to complicate matters, not the least of which would be a court-martial and possible hanging.

Gavin dreaded the thought of it, for Christina's sake. He would not wish such a horror upon anyone's sister . . . but especially his sweet Christina. She'd been through too much already.

Gavin did not want to think of complications now. He had not expected to develop such an extraordinary connection with Christina . . . and he was not quite ready to put an end to it. He was not the fool her husband had been.

He arrived at Hettie's house, and Eleanor greeted Gavin with a tight embrace, clearly happy to see him. "It's been weeks, Gavin!"

He smiled at his younger sister. "Pursuing a good cause, I assure you."

"Well, come in, dear brother, come in!"

Eleanor was a conventional beauty, five years Gavin's junior. Her hair was long and light brown, and neatly pinned at her nape. It was lovely, but predictable; nothing at all like the dark, whimsical curls that had so captivated Gavin. Or the full lips that held him in thrall.

He stifled his thoughts of Christina and took pains to put aside the memories of their nights together. But it was not easy. Their bed play had been astounding.

He'd told himself it was just sex, and he'd truly believed it, until last night. Something more was developing . . . something he could not—nor did he want to—define. His original mission had become more complicated than he liked, but this visit to Eleanor would go a long way to helping him to put matters in perspective.

Gavin took a purse full of coins and put it in Eleanor's hand, but she protested its weight.

"This is too much Gavin. You must have need—"

"Soon, neither of us will be in need. In a few days, I'll leave for Windermere again and collect my payment from the duke."

"Then you'll buy the house in Hampshire?"

He grinned. "Aye." And there it was. Everything

he'd striven for these past few weeks during his search for the Windermere granddaughters.

"Oh, Gavin, I can hardly wait. Rachel will love the country."

Gavin shrugged and followed his sister into the small kitchen where their spinster cousin, Hettie, was keeping an eye on Rachel, Eleanor's nearly two-year-old daughter. Gavin hoped the country would suit them, and he would finally be able to put his past behind him.

As would his sister. Gavin knew Eleanor had been devastated by the news of Mark Stafford's death, not just because she was pregnant with his child, but because she'd truly loved him. They had planned to marry as soon as Stafford returned from the war, but a French bullet had kept him from her.

Stafford had been an honorable soldier, a light horseman who'd faced his enemy head-on. He'd been nothing at all like Gavin.

"Gavin, lad, we didn't expect you!" Hettie cried, taking Gavin's hand in hers. "Look Rachel, here is your uncle!"

Sweet little Rachel smiled up at him and Gavin was humbled by her utter trust in him. He hated to think how she would have been treated had Eleanor been allowed to stay in their father's house. Just like Theo, no doubt.

"We'll soon have an addition to our little family," Gavin said.

Eleanor smiled broadly. "Oh my dear heavens, Gavin! You're taking a bride? How wonderf—"

"*No!* No, not at all," Gavin said.

Eleanor looked puzzled. "What, then? Who?"

"A young boy," he explained. "We took him from his uncle before the old man could beat him to death."

"Oh dear!" Hettie cried.

"How old is this boy?" Eleanor asked.

"We're not exactly sure. He's older than Rachel, but small . . . probably about five years or so," Gavin replied. "And much too quiet. Guarded," he added, more to himself than to his sister. But at least he'd started to come out of himself under Christina's care. "Can you make room for him here for a few weeks while I'm gone to Windermere?"

"Of course," Hettie said. "There's space for a pallet in the parlor. I expect the lad will be more than comfortable there."

"Thank you, Hettie." Gavin excused himself and his sister, taking Eleanor's arm to draw her into Hettie's small parlor for a private chat. They sat on two threadbare chairs near a window with no view but that of a dark alleyway.

"Will there be trouble with the boy's uncle, Gavin?"

Gavin shook his head. "No. Even the local magistrate favored us taking the boy."

"Us?"

He wondered if the magistrate would have been so quick to give him Theo if Christina had not used her influence. She'd acted quickly in the boy's best interest. He admired her for it.

"Aye. Our party. Lady Fairhaven's group."

"Lady Fairhaven? *She* is . . . the duke's grand-daughter?"

"She is."

Eleanor was quiet a moment. "I've heard of her. There was a good deal of gossip about her a year ago."

It disturbed Gavin to hear that people had been talking about Christina—likely after the outrageous manner in which her husband died. It was just the kind of thing that would create a stir, and cause innuendos about her wifely inadequacies.

Yet he knew Christina possessed not the least imperfection. She was blameless in her husband's indiscretions, and the man had been a fool not to know what a treasure waited for him in his own house.

"Her husband died," he said. "I'm sure there was talk."

"I believe Lady Fairhaven left Town for a time."

"Circumstances brought her back to London. I . . ." He hesitated, unwilling to cause Eleanor any worry. "I'll be taking her to meet her grandfather in a few days."

Eleanor nodded. "We'll take good care of your young charge, Gavin. What is his name?"

"Theo."

"Why was he being beaten by his uncle?"

"No reason except for being a bastard orphan. The proverbial whipping boy."

"Oh, my dear brother." She smiled. "Always so tenderhearted."

Hardly. "I'm not the least tenderhearted, Eleanor, and you need to know it. I'm not even sure if it's such a good idea for me to live with you and Rachel. I'm thinking of buying the house and then—"

"Nonsense. I would have my daughter know the only honorable uncle she has."

Gavin clenched his teeth, all too aware that Eleanor barely knew him anymore. He was no more honorable than their elder brother. Perhaps even less, for Clifford had never sat in the crook of a tree with his rifle on his shoulder, waiting for his prey to walk into his sights.

"There will be plenty of money as soon as Windermere pays me what he owes me. It's just a matter of time."

Eleanor frowned. "What's troubling you, Gavin? Is there some complication with Windermere?"

He shrugged. "It's nothing I can't manage. In a couple of weeks, I'll have ten thousand pounds in my possession—more than enough to buy the manor and get you and Rachel established in the country. And Hettie, if she will come."

Her eyes still held questions, but Gavin preferred not to worry her with talk of Chetwood. Nor could he explain his affair with Christina. As of this morning, he hardly understood it himself. He doubted she was aware of it, but she'd raised their lovemaking to the next degree. And while he'd thoroughly relished it, he wasn't sure he liked it.

What he needed was distance. Perspective.

A woman like Christina ought to be properly

courted by a peer, with flowers, and pretty trinkets, and promises for her future.

Unlike Theo, Gavin was the one who deserved a whipping for drawing a virtuous woman into an illicit affair.

"I'll be gone for a few days," he said, "but I'll bring Theo to you before I leave for Windermere. He's an easy lad to deal with, and quite grateful to be away from his uncle."

Eleanor nodded.

"And use that money I gave you," Gavin said. "Buy some cloth to make dresses for yourself and Hettie. And Rachel."

Eleanor's eyes glistened with tears of appreciation, and Gavin took it as his signal to leave.

"I'm sorry to be such a watering pot," she said. "But I've worried . . ."

"All is well, Ellie. I'll see you in a few days." He stood, and when she followed suit, he gave her a quick embrace, then went to the kitchen to bid farewell to Hettie.

He had a lot to do before morning, and forced himself to concentrate on the hours ahead, not on the sensual interludes he so foolishly craved.

He left Hettie's house and rode north, toward Marylebone, where one of his old friends had lodgings. Former lieutenant Robert Osborne was a younger son of an earl, and sure to know of Chetwood—where he lived and where he played. Once Gavin had that information, he intended to contact two or three more friends, and have them help him keep an eye on the baron's house and club.

He had no intention of leaving any stones un-turned where that scoundrel was concerned. Espe-cially not when Christina's safety depended upon it.

Christina found herself awash in banknotes after the jewelers came and went. The blackmailer had stipulated that his payment was to be in notes from the Bank of England, which the jewelers had on hand. All but one, who said he would secure the notes and bring them to her on the morrow.

She'd raised a good deal more money than she needed, but decided it was just as well to divest her-self of the jewels, in spite of what the jewelers might think of her. No doubt they wondered if she'd fallen on hard times.

Their opinion was of no interest to Christina. The jewels meant nothing to her, but information about Lang was of the utmost importance.

She waited for Gavin, in case he decided he didn't want a night apart any more than she did. All the while, she tried not to let the thoughts that niggled at the edges of her mind trouble her. But no matter how she tried, she could not stop worrying about the dangers he would face on her behalf. With Chet-wood . . . and the blackmailer . . .

She could not bear it if he were injured in any way, and wished it could all be over. She'd had no right to involve him in her troubles. He had responsibilities that did not involve her—a sister, and now Theo. And if something happened to him, what would they do?

She could not dwell on it. Gavin was more capable than any man she'd ever met. She knew nothing would befall him. It just couldn't.

Too nervous to eat any supper, she went in search of Theo and Jenny, and found them in the kitchen, sharing a simple meal. Christina joined them at the table, and was gratified to note that Theo was relaxed and smiling.

No child should have had to endure all that he had, no matter what the circumstances of his birth. His uncle had been a brute and a bully to treat him so viciously.

"I believe there might be some of my brothers' toys in the attic, Jenny," Christina said. "Perhaps we ought to make a trip up there and see what we can find for Theo."

She believed Gavin had rescued the boy just in time. He was much too thin, and far too reticent. And one more beating like the one they'd witnessed at the smithy might have killed him. She shuddered at the thought of it, realizing that she'd become much too attached to the boy.

Gavin was going to take him away to Hampshire.

Her lungs deflated when she thought of it, of Gavin going away with Theo and making a home in the country with his sister. It made her feel quite empty inside.

So she would spoil him a bit in the meantime.

She went up to the attic with Jenny and Theo and found a number of choice toys, perfect for a little boy. Christina did not want to overwhelm him, so they brought down just a few and then watched with amusement as he carefully lined up Felton's tin soldiers on a shelf in the nursery.

He took the fiercest one—the figure who held a rifle at his shoulder—and placed it in the midst of the others. "This is Captain Briggs," he said.

"Oh yes, it surely is," Jenny responded with a smile. "He is the bravest of all the soldiers, isn't he?"

Theo nodded, then spoke quietly. "No one ever stopped my uncle Samuel from hurting me. No one but Captain Briggs."

Christina's heart clenched. "No one will hurt you ever again," she said. Gavin would see to it. She didn't know quite how he intended to fit Theo into his household, but the boy would most certainly grow into a fine young man under Gavin's care.

After a while, Jenny put Theo to bed and Christina retreated to her mother's small parlor to read. She curled up in a soft, overstuffed chair, but was unable to keep her attention on the pages before her. Theo and his enjoyment of the toys had diverted her for a time, but now she could not ignore her worries.

She knew she was allowing herself to think too far ahead, when Gavin and Theo would be gone from her life. But she could not help herself. She thought of Gavin's growls of satisfaction when she'd made love to him last night, or the way he'd wrapped her so tightly in his arms before falling asleep.

And yet with their arrival in London, his demeanor had changed most distinctly.

Christina's throat thickened and burned at the realization that he'd purposely put up an invisible wall between them. She suspected his intention was to end their affair. He would live up to his commitment to deal with the blackmailer at the church, and then remind her of her promise to return to Windermere with him.

It filled her with a sort of desolation she had not felt even on the occasion of Edward's ignominious death.

It was very late when Christina realized she could no longer sit up pretending to read. She gave instructions to Edgar the footman to admit Captain Briggs if he should happen to arrive, no matter how unlikely such an event was.

Chapter 21

With Osborne's help, Gavin recruited three of their old friends who'd served with them in Spain in the Ninety-fifth Rifle Regiment, to help him keep surveillance on Chetwood's London residence. Gavin positioned himself with Philip Caldwell in the square across from Chetwood's house. Osborne and John Mason kept up surveillance at the back, near Chetwood's stable. A fifth man, Arthur Andrews, was free to move about as needed, but especially to carry messages between the two groups of observers.

They all had an excellent view of the house. No one could enter or leave without being seen.

They saw no signs of Chetwood's wife, but the baron himself arrived well after dusk. The house remained mostly dark, except for the servants' quarters at the back, and a lamp that illuminated the drawing room.

Less than an hour later, the drawing room went dark, and the men at the back of the house saw the

light move through the rooms toward them. They
had a clear view of the baron going all the way to a
room at the back and sitting down near a window
to smoke a cheroot. Soon afterward, the back kitchen
went dark and the light followed Chetwood up the
stairs to his bedchamber. They saw no other activity
and knew the baron had remained inside through
the rest of the night.

Gavin had hoped to catch Chetwood leaving his
house in the dead of night and attempting to broach
Christina's residence. Then he would have caught the
bastard red-handed, and dealt with him once and for
all. It grated to know that keeping watch all night
had been a wasted effort.

As soon as dawn broke, Gavin and his men left
Chetwood's house, agreeing to meet later. They all
needed a few hours' sleep, and Gavin . . .

Gavin wanted to see Christina. Needed to see her.

It was unwise, he knew. But even though he'd
put some space between them, the physical distance
did not seem to matter. He felt an elemental craving
for her. He needed to see the sparkle in her clever
green eyes, and smell her delicious scent. He was
compelled to feel the softness of her skin against his.

It was a fool's errand, he knew. He'd made all the
arguments, told himself all the reasons why he ought
to stay away.

He could let a room for himself somewhere, bunk
in with one of his friends, or even return to Hettie's house. No doubt the parlor that would become
Theo's bedroom would do for a few hours.

Besides, all would be well at Christina's house. Hancock and the butler, along with Trevor and the other footman, were there to keep the house secure. Gavin knew for a certainty that Chetwood had not left his own dwelling. No harm would have come from that quarter, and naught would happen during daylight hours.

In spite of all his rationalizations, Gavin found himself riding in the direction of Sunderland House. He was admitted to the house by Trevor, who was just returning from the market with a basket full of groceries.

Christina came to the door, and when her eyes flared at the sight of him, Gavin thought for a moment that she might step right into his arms.

They felt acutely empty when she did not. She greeted him warmly, though, with utmost civility, and invited him in for breakfast.

"I am not very hungry, Lady Fairhaven," he said, except for one thing—something he ought not even to be considering. "But if you can—"

"There is a bedchamber upstairs where you can rest, Captain Briggs," she said as she studied him. "And you look fatigued. If you would rather sleep than eat, that is perfectly acceptable."

Worry marred her brow, and she looked as tired as he felt. Gavin wished they had the privacy to allow him to pull her into his arms and reassure her, but he could hear the servants' voices and knew they were close by.

Besides, such an act clashed with every argument

he'd employed during the night and all the way to
Sunderland House.

So far, Christina's reputation remained intact, and
he intended to keep it that way.

"Thank you," he said. Her mouth was so soft and
pink, he found it difficult to take his eyes from them,
and restrain his wayward thoughts. "I have no news
to give you. Nothing has changed from the moment
we parted yesterday."

She walked with him to the staircase. "Ah, but it
has. I sold the jewelry, so you will have something to
place in the lectern tomorrow morning."

Gavin nodded and followed her up the stairs.
There was no sign of anyone in the upstairs corridor, and when they reached the guest room where
he would take his rest for a few hours, he could not
resist touching her face. It was an innocent gesture,
a gentle cupping of her jaw, but her eyes fluttered
closed and she leaned slightly toward him.

Gavin could not resist bending and touching
his lips to hers. It was not enough, but he managed
to step back and place some space between them.
He didn't want to think about Chetwood or James
Norris or All Hallows Church.

Christina fully occupied his mind.

She took a deep breath and somehow maneuvered
him into the bedchamber. "Sleep awhile, Captain
Briggs. We'll talk when you are rested."

The news spread through Mayfair like the Great
Fire of London. Lady Chetwood was dead. It was

said she, as well as one of Chetwood's menservants, had been killed in her own house by thieves who had broken in. The baron's desk drawers had been opened and a few valuables dropped on the floor as the thieves made their way out of the house.

Christina had thought her own troubles bad enough. But now there was this worry.

She sent Hancock out to hire two strong footmen whose sole duty would be to guard Sunderland House during the night. She hadn't really wanted any more people underfoot in the house, because it would likely prevent her being able to slip into Gavin's room during the night. But it could not be helped.

A murder in Mayfair was unheard of. And troublesome. Christina could not help but wonder if it had anything to do with the dangers that had worried Gavin at the Black Sheep Inn. She sent Jenny out to the neighbors' to see if she could glean any more information about the situation, and then went into the drawing room to wait for Gavin to awaken. She found herself pacing.

The morning wore on interminably, in spite of Theo's presence and the games they played together. Christina was anxious to see what Gavin thought about Lady Chetwood's death, but she would not disturb him yet. She knew he'd had little sleep during their last night of travel. And he'd looked exhausted this morning. He'd said there was no news, but Christina could see in his tired eyes that he'd stayed up yet another night. It must have been for some very good reason.

What that might have been, she could not say.

Jenny returned more than an hour after going out, with a great deal to report.

"Oh my lady! Her poor husband found her."

Christina stopped Jenny from speaking in front of Theo. She called for Maycott, the butler, who took him to the kitchen for a cup of milk.

"What happened, Jenny? Where were the servants?"

"Lord Chetwood told the police magistrate that he came home late and sent everyone to bed. Sometime after, burglars must have come into the house, and the valet tried to stop them. The baron said he is a sound sleeper, but Lady Chetwood was not. He believes she must have heard a noise . . ."

"How did they get in?"

"An open window," Jenny replied. "Lord Chetwood said he stayed up to smoke. That his wife didn't like the smell of his cheroots in the house, so he had a window open. He admits he must have forgotten to close it."

Christina had never heard of servants who would retire before their master. The least they should have done was to wait until they heard Lord Chetwood retire, and then secure and straighten the house.

"Lord Chetwood said he awoke just before dawn and felt something amiss." Jenny swayed on her feet.

"Come and sit down, Jenny," Christina said, but the maid ignored her, and remained standing, wringing her hands, her eyes unfocused, distant.

"He got up to look in on Lady Chetwood and found her bed empty. Oh, it must have been horrible!"

"What next, Jenny?"

"He went to look for her and found her at the bottom of the stairs." Jenny put a hand up to her mouth as her eyes filled with tears. "Her throat was cut. And his . . . his valet was on the floor near the window. Stabbed in the heart."

"Jenny, sit down before you fall down."

Christina felt quite ill herself. Whatever Baron Chetwood's intent toward Christina, she did not believe the man deserved to lose his wife so hideously. And the poor valet . . .

"I'm all right, my lady," Jenny said. "I'll feel better if I keep busy. I'll just go and see about Theo . . ."

Jenny made for the door, and Christina saw Gavin standing just outside it, frowning. The maid made a small curtsy and went on her way.

Gavin came into the drawing room. He crouched down in front of Christina's chair and took her hands in his.

"Burglars did not kill Lady Chetwood or the valet," he said.

"What do you mean? How do you know?"

"Five of us watched Chetwood's house all night long, front and back." A feeling of abject horror came over Christina as Gavin spoke. "Chetwood went in at midnight and did not go out. No one else entered the house."

"What are you saying, Gavin?"

He hesitated a moment before speaking. "I'm saying the only possibility is that Baron Chetwood killed his wife."

Chapter 22

Gavin wished he'd positioned himself closer to Chetwood's house. Then he might have had a better idea of what had transpired there during the night.

He had absolutely no doubt that Chetwood had been responsible for his wife's death. No intruders had entered the house. He was certain of that. One of the men watching the back had noticed a window slightly ajar, but no one had gone in or out through it. Gavin hadn't thought much of it until now.

It was a ruse. Chetwood had set the stage for the magistrate to believe the drama he had created. No doubt the man would report some valuables missing, too.

"Why? Why would he kill his own wife?" Christina asked. The color had drained from her face, and her expression was both somber and shocked.

Gavin placed one of his hands on each of the arms

of her chair, the closest thing to an embrace he could manage in her parlor.

"What?" Christina asked, her voice hushed with worry.

"The man is a member of the Hellfire Club, notorious for all sorts of offenses. Maybe his wife discovered something incriminating and threatened to use it against him."

"I don't understand."

A libertine like Chetwood would have no deep connection to a wife, no matter how long they'd been wed.

"They were arguing when I first saw them at Windermere Park."

"About what?"

"I don't know . . ." But Lady Chetwood's words—*You wouldn't dare*—came back to him now. He'd assumed she meant Chetwood would not dare strike her. But perhaps she'd meant something different. He wouldn't dare kill her? Wouldn't dare what? Eliminate Windermere's granddaughters?

Whatever she'd meant, they'd clearly been at odds.

He touched Christina's chin, raising it so that she would look at him. "All this proves just how dangerous Chetwood is."

Her lips started to quiver, but Gavin did not regret frightening her. Knowing the truth meant she would not take the threat lightly.

"My guess is that the baron sent his servants to bed, and then he used some ruse to lure his wife downstairs. The valet must have seen what happened, forcing Chetwood—"

"To murder the valet, too." She pressed her fingers to her lips to stop the tremor.

"I'll keep you safe, Christina," he said. "We'll deal with your extortionist tomorrow morning, then I'll get you back to Windermere."

She looked away for a moment, distraught. Overwhelmed by his theories on Lady Chetwood's murder, and probably also by his mention of their trip to Windermere. "Wh-what are you going to do tomorrow? Do you have a plan?"

"The four men who stayed with me at Chetwood's house last night—they are committed to helping me capture the blackmailer at the church."

"I will pay them any sum if they can help me bring all this to an end."

"We won't worry about that now. These men are trustworthy and reliable. They'll cover the stairs and entrances of the church, so there's no chance of missing your tormenter. We could have him before services even begin, and you will find out what he knows about your brother."

"Oh Gavin," she whispered, wiping away the moisture that filled her eyes. "I don't know what's gotten into me. Just that the news of Lady Chetwood is so horrible."

Gavin nodded. "She was no innocent, love. There have been tales of her cruelty . . ."

"I'd rather not know." She swallowed and put her hand on his.

"And you might not know any more about your brother tomorrow than you do now." He hated saying so, but she had to be aware that Norris or whoever was extorting money from her could be leading her down a blind alley. The man might know nothing at all about Lang.

Or they might find out that the information they'd received three months ago—that Lang had been killed in the explosion—was irrefutably true.

Christina bit her lip and he wanted to kiss away her worries. So much for putting some distance between them. It seemed he could not stay away.

Christina wished Gavin would hold her.

But they seemed to be miles away from the days of roadside inns where he felt something for her beyond getting her safely to Windermere. It was surprisingly disappointing, especially in light of the terrible news he brought her.

"You need to hire a few extra men to keep watch over the house until this thing with Chetwood is settled," Gavin told her.

She took a deep, shuddering breath and gathered a modicum of composure around her like a cloak. "I already did. When I heard about Lady Chetwood this morning, I sent Hancock to hire two strong footmen to help keep watch over the house."

"Good. I want to meet them before I leave," he said, his manner firmly businesslike.

A sensation of calm washed through Christina at his words, and she could not help but lean forward and brush her lips against his, in spite of his apparent coolness. He did not withdraw, and she sensed a war being waged inside him. He was not entirely impervious to her attentions.

She drew back and spoke softly. "The new men are touring the house with Hancock."

Gavin's gaze dropped to her mouth, as though he could not help but remember the pleasure she'd given him. She saw him draw in a tight breath, and realized she wanted him to remember. Every time he saw her, she wanted him to think of the intimacies they shared.

Averting his eyes, he stood abruptly and held out one hand to her, just as he would if he were master of the house, responsible for her and everyone else in it.

The gesture was telling. Gavin took command in a way that made her feel confident and secure.

"You'll need to keep the extra men until I figure out what to do about Chetwood."

She agreed. "They will stay until you tell me they are no longer needed."

His strong jaw clenched tightly for an instant, and she wondered what he was thinking.

She touched his arm. "Gavin . . ."

The butler interrupted anything she might have said. "My lady?"

"Yes, Maycott?"

"A caller just arrived."

"Who?" She had not expected any visitors but Gavin, and she would hardly call him a visitor, not when they were so intimately—

" 'Tis the Earl of Everhart."

Christina frowned. "Lord Everhart? Is here?"

"Yes, my lady."

"Who is Lord Everhart?" Gavin asked.

"He is just a . . . Well, he is a former suitor." She felt her face heat with unaccountable embarrassment. The last person she wanted to see now was the man she'd once hoped would be her husband. The Earl of Everhart had been charming, handsome, and oh so engaging, but her father had objected to him on the grounds that he was too young, and not prudent with his money. Sunderland had believed Edward would make a much better husband.

Christina had not been in love with Lord Everhart, but she'd come very close to it. In the end, she'd respected her father's opinion in the matter, and married Edward. And to Lord Sunderland's credit, he'd admitted to being wrong about Viscount Fairhaven.

Her father could be forgiven, of course. There'd never been a hint of any irregularity about Edward, and Christina's father had also felt somewhat betrayed by the manner of his son-in-law's death. He'd promised to heed Christina's preferences when it was time to marry again.

"Get rid of him, Maycott," Gavin said.

"No," Christina objected. "That will only cause speculation we do not need. I . . ." She wanted to see him. Wanted to see if the handsome young man who'd once vied for her hand still had the potential to make her heart trill with interest. He'd been very charming, and quite obviously taken with her.

Gavin stood still for a moment, that muscle in his strong jaw flexing again. "Go then. I'll check on Hancock and the new footmen."

He bowed, and she returned his bow, though perhaps a bit stiffly. All was as it should be, though the forced sense of detachment made Christina feel raw inside.

She smoothed her skirts and started for the drawing room, but turned back for a moment. "Perhaps he'll have heard something more about what happened to Lady Chetwood."

Gavin's expression remained impassive, but he did not move when she started back to the drawing room behind Maycott.

Gavin found the footmen Hancock hired satisfactory. Turner and Chandler were solid men, who seemed to be very clear on their responsibilities. As Christina visited with her former suitor in the drawing room, Gavin spoke to the servants, emphasizing the need for caution. He could not yet speak openly of his suspicions regarding Chetwood, but the household seemed fully cognizant of what it meant to have murderous burglars afoot. The Ratcliffe murders might have taken place several years before, but the grisly killings would not soon be forgotten by any Londoners.

"Where is Theo?" he asked.

"Gone to the attics with Mrs. Wilder," Trevor said. "They are choosing a few more toys from Lady Fairhaven's brothers' collections."

Gavin thought about going up and seeing how the boy fared, but knew that if he had any sense at all, he would leave now, before his better judgment escaped him entirely. Those moments alone with Christina when her eyes filled with tears had nearly been the undoing of his resolution to keep his distance.

He found himself lingering in the back kitchen, aware there was no need for him to return to the front of the house, or stop in the drawing room. His horse was in the stable at the back, and all he needed to do was make his exit through the door adjacent to the kitchen.

But he found himself heading toward the sound of Christina's voice.

"Oh my dear Lady Fairhaven," Gavin heard her companion say. "I would have come sooner, but . . . I was abroad when . . . Well, I cannot tell you how sorry I am about . . . well, everything."

"Thank you, Lord Everhart," Christina said. Gavin walked into the drawing room just as she removed her hands from Everhart's grasp.

Gavin looked in only to assure himself that her old friend Lord Everhart was not one of the men he'd seen with Chetwood at the Black Sheep Inn. It was not beyond the realm of possibility for Chetwood to send one of his minions into Christina's house, though he did not think the baron would try to harm her openly.

The earl looked up as Gavin entered the room and quirked his brows at him, as though he had no right to intrude.

In that, Everhart was correct.

Christina introduced Gavin, then indicated the earl should take a seat. He did so, right across from her.

Everhart was tall and fair-haired, his skin ruddy, as though he spent a good deal of time out of doors. Gavin supposed the man was good-looking, perhaps even attractive to women. Judging by the way Christina smiled at him, she found him favorable.

Gavin found him to be no such thing. He wondered if Everhart had been one of the men whose faces he'd been unable to see at the Black Sheep Inn. Certainly not the bald fellow, but there'd been one man with light hair in the group whose face Gavin could not see. He decided to see what he could discover about the earl.

"Briggs, you say? Captain Briggs?" Everhart asked. His expression was puzzled; he looked as though there was something he ought to remember, but could not.

"Aye." Gavin searched his memory for some recollection of the man, but he was quite sure they had never met.

"I'm sure I've heard the name."

" 'Tis not an unusual one," Gavin remarked, concerned he might be playing some sort of charade. He might not know the Hargrove family name, but if Everhart and Chetwood were accomplices, he would surely recognize Gavin's name.

It would not be too difficult to find out if the man had actually been out of the country as he claimed.

"To be sure," Everhart remarked, although some

puzzlement remained on his face. He turned to Christina. "My dear Christina, I'm sorry to think of how difficult these past months must have been for you."

She nodded gravely. "It has not been easy, Lord Everhart, but I'd rather not speak of it."

"I understand."

He said nothing more, depending upon Christina to carry the conversation, even though his comment quite obviously caused her some distress. Even Gavin recognized the gaffe. Of course she did not want to talk about her dead husband or the loss of her brother. Even the dullest dolt would have thought of that before speaking. The man ought to have redirected the conversation.

Gavin intervened. "You were abroad, Lord Everhart? On the continent, I assume?"

The man leaned forward, his knees coming far too close to Christina's. Gavin felt his jaw clenching almost painfully. "I was in Greece, yes."

"Oh, what took you to Greece?" Christina asked with polite interest.

Gavin barely heard the earl as he droned on about his travels. He didn't like the way the man's gaze rested upon Christina's mouth, or slid down to the fullness of her bodice.

Bloody hell. He was *not* jealous. Gavin intended to be long gone when Christina chose her next husband. And once he settled at Weybrook Manor, their paths would not cross again.

Gavin's mood became more sour by the minute

and he knew he had to take his leave. There were things he needed to do.

He stood abruptly, causing Christina and Everhart to look up at him quizzically. "Lady Fairhaven . . ." he said.

He had no intention of making an arse of himself, but he found himself on the verge of it. "My lady, if you will forgive me, I have business to attend to this afternoon." He glanced at Everhart, but continued speaking to Christina. "I will return later to . . . pick up the package."

She nodded, lifting her hand for him to take, and he bowed over it.

Then he made a quick acknowledgment of the earl, more anxious than ever to take his leave. He should have gone ten minutes ago. "Lord Everhart, it was a pleasure," he lied.

Everhart stood and shook Gavin's hand. "Wish I could remember where I'd heard your name, Briggs."

"Don't let it bother you." He turned to Christina. "Until later, Lady Fairhaven."

Gavin had a number of things that needed to be done before morning, and watching Everhart fawn over Christina was not one of them. He wondered how serious a suitor the earl had been . . . and why Christina had turned him down. Had Everhart gone so far as to offer for her? He supposed it did not matter, since she'd chosen Fairhaven.

In any event, Everhart's visit quite effectively demonstrated the social gap that existed between Gavin and Christina. Her future would be with an upstanding peer of the realm, not a former assassin for the crown.

And that was an end to it.

Gavin did not allow himself to dwell any further upon Christina and Everhart as he went out to her stable. Perhaps he would not return to Sunderland House later. He'd seen the delight on Christina's face while visiting with the earl. Gavin thought perhaps he ought to bow out now and give her a chance to rekindle the association they'd once shared. She did not seem at all opposed to this suitor, as she'd been with the other—the one who'd spent time in Plymouth with Lang.

Muttering a low curse under his breath, he mounted his horse and rode to Fleet Street, where he was to meet the men who'd stood watch with him the night before. They'd all fought together in Spain, and Gavin trusted each one implicitly. All were good men with excellent instincts, and their reconnaissance at All Hallows Church now would go a long way toward making their venture on the morrow a success.

Gavin was the last to arrive at the tavern, into the midst of a discussion of what they ought to do about Chetwood and his blatant lies to the magistrate. He collected a mug of ale and carried it to their table and sat down, glad for something else to occupy his mind besides Christina and her solicitous caller.

"The man's in line to become Duke of Windermere," said Osborne, the fourth son of an earl. A gentleman to his core, Osborne still possessed some respect for the nobility. From all that Gavin had heard, Osborne's sire was nothing like the maggot Gavin's was.

"I'll admit the thought of Chetwood with a duke's status and power takes me aback," Andrews said.

"How do we know the magistrate will believe us?" Mason asked. "Chetwood is quality. And we're naught but—"

"We're soldiers without any prospects," Caldwell finished for him.

"We *don't* know if he'll believe us. Or even listen to us." Andrews took a swallow of his drink. "But we've all got honorable reputations. Why wouldn't the man hear us out?"

"Because Chetwood will soon become a duke, a prince of the realm. His word trumps all others."

"Ah, but his reputation can't have escaped the magistrate's office," Gavin said. "Even *I* am aware he's a member of the Hellfire Club. How would it be possible the authorities do not know?"

"True enough," Caldwell remarked.

"Shall we go to All Hallows?" Gavin asked. "We can figure out what to do about Chetwood later."

The men all assented. It was time to get the lay of the land so they would be prepared for whatever happened there the following morning.

"I know it is a painful topic, Christina," Lord Everhart said, sitting forward in his chair so that his knees were a breath away from touching hers, "but please be assured I would do anything in my power to ease your distress."

"Thank you, my lord." She wondered if he referred to the disgraceful manner in which Edward had died.

But of course not—no gentleman would make reference to such an indelicate situation, especially to the offended lady. Likely, he meant Lang's death. His *supposed* death.

She found herself sliding back in her chair to avoid making accidental contact with him.

"Perhaps you should have gone to Italy with your family."

His hazel eyes were so understanding, so sympathetic. But Christina felt no affinity toward him. No attraction whatsoever, no matter how kind or how handsome he was. "I had reasons for remaining here in London," she said.

He reached out and took her hand, and spoke in a quiet, cosseting tone, as though he thought she might crumble into pieces at any moment. "Your parents are well?"

Everhart was nowhere near as charming as Christina remembered him. She extracted her hand as she lifted her chin and looked into his eyes. "They are as well as they can be under the circumstances, my lord."

"I understand. I hope—" He snapped his fingers suddenly. "Now I remember."

Surprised at his quick gesture, Christina looked at him inquisitively. "Remember what, my lord?"

"Where I heard of Briggs."

Christina swallowed, curious, but a little bit

worried about what he might say. Gavin had shared so little of his background with her, she hardly knew him.

"He is the son of Viscount Hargrove, of Durham."

"Yes, he—"

"More important, they're saying Captain Briggs was the hero of Waterloo."

Chapter 23

Wh-what do you mean?" Christina stammered. "I thought Lord Wellington was—"

"Oh, of course Wellington, but there was said to be a sniper—a certain Captain Briggs under Wellington's command—who arrived just ahead of the Prussians and started picking off the French artillerymen."

"Picking off?"

"Shooting them. Disrupting their line."

Christina was not familiar with the word *sniper*, although she gleaned its meaning from Everhart. She shuddered. "And you think this man was Captain Briggs?"

"He is Gavin Briggs, is he not?"

Christina nodded, frowning. Of course he'd never said anything about it. He'd been surprisingly reticent about speaking of his wartime experiences. "That is his given name, yes," she said, looking at Lord Everhart doubtfully.

"Well, I only recount to you what I've heard. Briggs has eyes so sharp, he caught sight of a French rifleman who was about to take a shot at Lord Wellington. Your friend felled the man before he was able to pull his trigger."

Gavin spent an hour at the church with the others, deciding on a few hand signals, where they would position themselves, and how Gavin would apprehend the bastard who was taking advantage of Christina's loss. And while they inspected the premises, Gavin considered the course he would take with Baron Chetwood.

He toyed with the possibility of sending Osborne or one of the others to Sunderland House to collect the blackmail money, but knew he would be the one to go back. Because no matter how much distance he knew he should put between them, he could not stay away.

Besides, Baron Chetwood had proven how brutal he could be. He might have sent proxies to do away with Christina's sister, but he'd clearly demonstrated how twisted he was, and how capable. Gavin knew that only someone as deadly as he could thwart the bastard.

Lady Chetwood's words rang in Gavin's ears. *You wouldn't dare.*

Clearly, her husband would and did. The baron must have used the information Gavin discovered about Lily and Christina while he searched for them. Chetwood paid men to find Lily and kill her, and it was quite likely that while Gavin was searching for Lily, Chetwood had sent men to find Christina. Whatever Lady Chetwood thought her husband would not dare to do—it seemed he had done it.

Gavin had no doubt that the baron had cut his wife's throat and left her body at the bottom of the staircase, then set the scene to look like a burglary. The man's viciousness reached heights even Gavin had not touched during his years as Lord Castlereagh's pawn. It turned his stomach.

Chetwood's presence at the Black Sheep Inn still rankled, and Gavin wondered what the baron would have done had Christina taken lodgings there. He was sure it was not mere happenstance that put the man at the inn at that moment, just as Christina completed her day's journey. Chetwood had to have been aware of her progress toward London.

He must have had a man following them all the way from Holywell, and reporting their progress. It infuriated him to know someone had gotten past him without his knowledge.

No one was going to get past him tonight. If Chetwood could kill his wife so callously, there was every chance the man would be just as brutal with Christina for interfering with his inheritance, even though the disposition of Windermere's wealth was not her decision.

Gavin had to stop the bastard before he could do any more damage.

"Let's go to the magistrate's office in Westminster," Gavin said when they were finished at the church. "It's time to speak with him about what we saw last night."

Christina stood to indicate an end to her visit with Lord Everhart. The earl took her hand in his, bowed over it, and placed his lips upon it. "Will you allow me to escort you to church on the morrow, my lady?" he asked.

The invitation seemed inappropriate. Her parents were away, and she was in mourning. He ought to know she could not accompany him to church or anywhere else without causing talk.

"If you'll forgive me, I think not tomorrow, my lord."

He was not quite successful at masking his disappointment, and Christina supposed she ought to feel flattered. Everhart was still a very eligible bachelor, handsome, and possessed of numerous prosperous estates. Her father's objections to his suitability would surely be moot now that she was a widow—not that her father would have quite so much to say about her next marriage.

Thanks to a generous settlement Sunderland had negotiated with Edward before her marriage, she had her own funds as well as Sweethope Cottage and a house near Ullswater. When she married again, she would be certain to make arrangements so that her new husband would not have free access to them.

She knew it was rather a callous approach, but she'd learned her lesson with Edward. Not so much with money, but with trust. Christina was no longer the green girl she'd been on that February morning at St. George's Church when she'd signed the papers that bound her to Edward until death parted them. She knew better now.

"Then will you allow me to call on you again tomorrow afternoon?"

Christina paused. Everhart must realize that if he proposed to her, there would be some delay in their nuptials because of Lang. Her mourning period for Edward would be over soon, but Lang had been gone only three months.

But neither his patience nor his attentions thrilled her as they once would have done. Her life and all her expectations had been drastically altered by her sham of a marriage, and now Lang's . . . disappearance.

That was how she had to think of what had happened to her brother, at least until someone proved otherwise. How could she do anything but hope Lieutenant Norris had been wrong about Lang's death?

"I think not yet, Lord Everhart," she said quietly. "It has been only three months since Lang . . ." She swallowed and looked into his eyes. "Forgive me. I am not yet ready."

She exited the drawing room alongside Lord Everhart, and entered the foyer just as Maycott responded to a knock at the front door. The butler opened to yet another suitor whom Christina had not seen in the nearly two years since her marriage. Word of her return to Sunderland House had spread far too quickly for her peace of mind.

Christina stopped short. "Viscount Brundle," she said with some surprise as the man stepped inside. Brundle was one of the last people to see Lang alive.

"Good God, gel, what happened to your hair?"

"What sort of question is that, Brundle? 'Tis quite original, I think," Everhart chided, his tone chilly. It surprised Christina, for she'd always thought they were friends. Or, at least, on friendly terms.

Perhaps not when they saw each other as competitors.

"Well, you're quick, Everhart," Viscount Brundle said. "I'll say that for you."

Christina chanced a quick glance at Everhart's face and found him reddening. He *had* been rather quick, although Christina would never mention it. She had too many other pressing issues on her mind, one of which was the realization that she would not need to go all the way to Plymouth to ask Brundle what he remembered about the night Lang was . . . the night of the explosion.

Christina wished Gavin was present to do the asking, for she wanted as little to do with the viscount as possible.

The man was as distasteful as ever. He'd been obtuse and incredibly boorish during the season of Edward's courtship, and Christina had found him intolerable. She'd tried to discourage his suit, but he'd ignored her gentle rebuffs and offered for her anyway. Christina had begged her father not to consider his suit, and he had agreed. He hadn't cared for Brundle any more than she had.

Christina found it strange that the viscount did not mention one word of sympathy for her losses. He knew about Lang, obviously—had even had some close connection to Lang's demise. And yet he said nothing. He was as dull-witted as ever.

"I don't notice you hesitating, Brundle," Everhart said, bristling in response to the viscount's remark.

Christina wanted them both to leave, but Brundle took her hand and kissed the back of it. His heavy mustache brushed unpleasantly against her skin, and she found herself unable to suppress an unpleasant shiver at his touch.

She pulled her hand away.

"Of course I do not hesitate," Brundle snapped, though he smiled at Christina. "Came to pay my respects, of course."

Brundle's eyes had always sparkled with a bit too much eagerness, and his thick mustache seemed to twitch at inopportune moments. Christina could not envision kissing such a furry lip.

"I appreciate your visit, my lord, but—"

"Dashed bad luck in your family these days," Brundle said, turning over his walking stick and hat to Maycott.

Christina gasped at the man's rudeness and once again found herself wishing Gavin were there. He would have booted the viscount from the house in no uncertain terms, and likely Everhart as well. Gavin was a man who could be counted upon to deal with whatever situation arose.

"Shall we . . . go inside?" Brundle asked, raising his brows inquisitively.

Christina clenched her teeth. She had no intention of entertaining the beastly man now, or at any other time. If he wanted to crow like some old gossipmonger over her misfortunes, he could do it elsewhere. Gavin would find him and question him if it became necessary.

"I am so sorry, Lord Brundle." She spoke without the slightest hint of civility in her tone and beckoned Maycott to return the viscount's walking stick and hat to him. "I was just going out."

"Allow me to escort you, my lady," Everhart said.

She shook her head. "No, my lord. But thank you for the offer." She turned and started back to the drawing room. "Maycott will see you both out."

It was late afternoon when Gavin's men reached Chetwood's residence. Two policemen guarded the door, and they observed another two men exiting the house. Gavin guessed one was the coroner, and the other, the magistrate himself.

Naturally, the highest official in the magistrate's office would personally look into Lady Chetwood's death. The woman would have become the Duchess of Windermere, and her murder would not have been left to anyone of lesser rank or stature.

Besides, such violence did not occur in Mayfair. Ever.

Gavin looked closely at the two men. "Is that Colonel Watkins coming out of the house?"

"Looks like him," Andrews said. "Nobody else could be as gaunt as all that and still live."

"And that head of red hair . . .," Mason added.

Gavin dismounted and tied his horse, silently agreeing with Andrews and Mason. His unit's former colonel was as tall and thin as a reed, his hair as bright as a copper coin.

"I haven't seen him since Buçaco," said Osborne.

"Nor have I," Gavin remarked as the four men started toward the house. He'd been a lieutenant under Watkins in Spain, and already one of Wellington's sharpshooters. "If I remember correctly, Watkins was badly wounded there."

The others nodded in agreement, searching their memories for details of the battle that had taken place six years before.

"It's a bit of luck for us," said Sergeant Caldwell. "Watkins was a devilish good cove back then."

"Let's see what he's like now."

Watkins stood in front of the house, deep in conversation with the other man. But when he caught sight of Gavin and the others, he squinted and watched them approach. Gavin noticed the minute recognition dawned.

"Briggs?"

Gavin nodded and shook the colonel's hand, and brought his companions forward. "You remember Andrews and Osborne? And here are Caldwell and Mason."

Watkins looked pleased to see them, but puzzled. "What brings you to Cavendish Square this afternoon, gentlemen?"

"If I might have a private word with you, Colonel Watkins?"

The colonel's prodigious red brows came together. "Has this aught to do with the . . . er, situation in this house?"

"It does."

"Gentlemen, come inside."

Gavin and the others followed Watkins and his associate into the house. They walked past a large bloodstain at the foot of the stairs and went into the adjacent drawing room. Clearly, the rumors about Lady Chetwood's cause of death were true.

"This is Mr. Gell, our coroner. Anything you have to say to me, you may say in his presence."

He introduced Gavin and the others.

"Briggs? Captain Briggs?" Gell asked.

Gavin nodded. "Formerly captain, but I am no longer in His Majesty's service."

Gell shook his hand vigorously. " 'Tis a pleasure to meet you, Briggs. Your reputation precedes you."

Gavin took no notice of Gell's remark. "Is Baron Chetwood in custody?" he asked Colonel Watkins.

"No, he is not," Watkins replied, his expression one of puzzlement and concern. "Beyond having questionable associates in his damned Hellfire Club, I have no reason to arrest him. I allowed him to leave in order to make arrangements . . ."

Gavin believed Chetwood had made certain the

servants—all but his valet—had retired for the night before taking a knife to his wife. So his story of burglars would not be contradicted by any witnesses.

The thought of Chetwood on the loose when Christina had only a few young footmen to protect her in her father's house was disturbing.

Lord Everhart might also be with her, but the kind of protection the earl might provide would not be effective in the least. Not with those soft hands and that pampered manner.

Clearly, Chetwood was a twisted bastard, his actions proving he was more than just a little desperate. Gavin needed to get back to Sunderland House. Needed to assure himself that all was well there.

"For reasons I will explain later," Gavin said, "these men and I had reason to keep this house under surveillance last night."

Gell's narrow gray eyes seemed to light up. "Reasons?"

Gavin gave him a nod. "Aye. We came at dark—Caldwell and I out front in the square, and Osborn with Mason near the stable in back. Andrews was free to move between us. We had the entire house in our sights all night long."

"Then you would have seen the burglars who entered—"

"There were no burglars," Osborne said.

A look of unease passed between Watkins and Gell.

"No burglars?" Gell finally asked quietly. "What do you mean?"

"Baron Chetwood arrived here just after we did," Gavin explained. "The five of us had only just gotten into position when a hackney coach left him at his door."

"About what time of the evening was that?"

"Just after dark. We saw a light here." Gavin walked to the front window to verify that what he said was accurate. "Definitely here in the drawing room. The draperies remained open, so we could see the lamp in the window. It remained burning for a short while—perhaps half an hour, wouldn't you say, Caldwell?"

"Aye," said Caldwell. "Then it faded and the front of the house went dark."

"We saw some activity near the servants' quarters at the back of the house, but then everyone seemed to go to bed," Osborne added.

"No one came into or left the house after Chetwood's arrival," Gavin informed them.

"What are you saying?" Watkins inquired.

"I'm saying . . . that unless one of the servants murdered Lady Chetwood and the baron's valet, the only possible killer was the baron himself."

Gell dragged one gnarled hand across his face. "Bloody hell."

"How do you explain the open window at the back of the house?" Watkins asked.

"We saw Chetwood open it," Mason said, and Osborne concurred. "He pulled up a chair and smoked for a few minutes. We could see the hot ember of his cheroot."

"But no one came through that window, either in or out," Osborne said.

"We've all heard Chetwood's account of his activities when his wife was killed," Gavin said, "but we five are witnesses that the baron lied about his comings and goings last night."

"You are absolutely certain of all this?" Watkins asked, looking at each man in turn. "You would swear to it?"

Gavin nodded gravely. "I only wish we'd positioned ourselves closer to the house in order to give you better details of what happened."

"You're speaking of a peer, Briggs. Baron Chetwood is heir to the Duke of Windermere."

"I am all too aware of it, Colonel," Gavin said. "And it gives him far more influence than he deserves."

Gell looked at him thoughtfully, hesitation in his eyes. "We'll have to question the servants again. It could have been one of them."

"I suppose it's possible," Gavin said. "But not very likely." Not with all Gavin knew about the baron.

"The lamp in the back kitchen went out before Chetwood finished his smoke," said Osborne. "The servants retired before the master."

"Sit down, men," Watkins said. "You'd better tell me everything—I want to know why you were watching the house."

The delay did not sit well with Gavin, but he had no choice. Everyone took seats in Chetwood's drawing room and Gavin started his explanation with a recounting of his visit several weeks before to Christina's grandfather at Windermere Park. He very carefully omitted any mention of Christina's brother and his disappearance, or the blackmail plot against her.

But he did give details of Chetwood's attempt to have Christina's sister killed in order to keep her from inheriting any portion of her grandfather's estate.

"How do you know this?"

"Because I was hired to find both granddaughters," Gavin said. "Chetwood sent two assassins to make sure the first one could not inherit. The second one—"

"Good God, man," said Gell, "do you know what you're saying?"

Chapter 24

The wounds on Theo's back were healing well with careful tending. Christina watched as Jenny put salve on them and wrapped them in cotton, and thought of Gavin taking Theo and going away without her.

She felt a sharp twinge of loneliness. It was hardly explicable, given that she'd known them both for such a short time.

And yet she felt a more tenacious connection to Gavin than she'd ever experienced with Edward. It hurt to think of him moving on without her.

She took Theo up to the nursery before bed and read him stories from one of Lang's books, wishing she'd had the wherewithal to ask Viscount Brundle about that last night with her brother. According to her father, Brundle hadn't had much to add to Norris's account of the evening, but perhaps he hadn't asked the right questions. Maybe Christina would ask something that had not been asked before.

She finished the last story and tucked Theo into his bed for the night. Returning downstairs, Christina distracted herself with her basket of mending and started to repair the sleeve of a chemise Gavin had torn accidentally a few days ago. Stopping suddenly, she pressed the delicate garment to her chest, letting out a long, shuddering sigh at her recollection of the incident. It had happened at Ledger's Mill, in her cousin's house.

Gavin had awakened her during the night, kissing her and gently twining her short hair around his fingers. All of a sudden, he'd made a low growl and pulled the chemise from her shoulders. He'd bent down and kissed her breasts, licking and suckling, making her mindless with need.

And then he'd been inside her, pulling her legs around his hips, and rocking her fiercely. He'd raised his chest off hers, and braced himself on his densely muscled arms, looking into her eyes as she shuddered with unspeakable pleasure.

Christina had felt that unique bond with him then, a connection that had felt so very unbreakable.

On reflection, it was more than a little frightening, for she doubted he'd felt any such thing, not even at the King's Head Inn when she'd pushed him beyond all restraint. He kept a portion of himself separate, as though he could not make that bond.

She wondered if he was unable to, or just unwilling.

Questions abounded, although most of them would likely remain unanswered. But at least there was one thing she could find out.

Setting aside her sewing, she went into her father's small study and searched for a dictionary. When she found it, she sat down at the desk and looked up the word Lord Everhart had used. *Sniper.*

A marksman who shoots at individuals as opportunity offers, from a concealed position.

Frowning, she read it again, then closed the book and rested her elbows on the desk, covering her eyes with her hands. Though she knew little about the military, Christina had made assumptions about Gavin's role in the army. He'd been an officer—she'd supposed he'd commanded a company of soldiers.

He'd been a marksman—a very good shot. She recognized that word from her father's hunting parties.

Christina wondered what it meant to be a sniper in the army. Had Gavin worked alone, or had he commanded a company of snipers whose function was to conceal themselves and shoot the enemy from afar?

Had he killed many men?

Lord Everhart had called him the hero of Waterloo. And yet she'd heard nothing about it. Which shouldn't have surprised her, given Gavin's reticence.

What she knew about him, she'd learned by chance. He had a sister, and Christina doubted he would have mentioned her if not for Theo. She knew his father was Viscount Hargrove, but only because of her mother-in-law's familiarity with the Briggs family and their subsequent visit with Amelia at St. Ledger's Abbey. He'd spoken briefly of the property he intended to acquire, but that had been an end to it.

He kept himself from her. For him, it was enough merely to bed her.

Christina stood abruptly, feeling so tense it seemed her bones were at risk of breaking. Her tension and worry were entirely foolish, of course. Gavin had become her lover, that was all. They had shared an enjoyable interlude during their travels from Holywell to London, and once they discovered where Lang was to be found, Christina would go back to Windermere with him. He had no obligation to discuss his family or his sniper past with her.

But she dearly wished he would.

Gavin spoke privately with Colonel Watkins of his experience with the men sent by Chetwood to follow him in his search for Christina's sister. "The old duke made no secret of his plan to include his granddaughters in his will. I believe Chetwood started searching for them well in advance of my arrival at Windermere Park."

Watkins frowned fiercely.

"He meant to have Lady Ashby killed," Gavin said with the stark truth of the matter. "He wanted to make sure she did not inherit anything from her grandfather."

"'Tis a bad business," Watkins said, shaking his head. "And you say the other granddaughter is Lady Fairhaven?"

Gavin nodded. "I have reason to believe Chetwood's wife had some idea of her husband's intentions toward Windermere's granddaughters."

"Bloody hell," Watkins muttered. "That would be quite a sufficient motive for murder, would it not?"

Gavin gave a curt nod. "Colonel, I am . . . responsible for Lady Fairhaven's safety. The Earl of Everhart came to visit her today. Do you know anything about him? Is he another Hellfire member?"

Watkins shook his head. "Not that I've heard. Why? Do you suspect he's a part of—"

"Not necessarily," Gavin interjected. "I only want to be sure he's no threat."

Watkins scratched the back of his head. "Peers do not usually come to my attention for any reason, Briggs."

Gavin nodded. He did not doubt that, even if the men were scoundrels. Their status always protected them. "He told Lady Fairhaven he'd been abroad of late. I wonder if it's true. If not . . . Well, it would be a lie, which might make him suspect."

"I can look into it, Briggs, but you understand this Chetwood business is my priority."

"Of course. But you might run across information about Everhart during your investigation. I only ask that you keep your eyes open for it."

Watkins called back the servants to question each one individually, and he sent policemen out to locate Baron Chetwood, either at White's or any of the known haunts of the Hellfire Club.

Gavin had a feeling they would not find him, having more faith in his own four comrades. The men set out on their own for various parts of London to see what they could discover about the man in question.

It was full dark by the time Gavin left Chetwood's house. He and his men had agreed to meet at the Tower at dawn, then go on to the church where Gavin would place Christina's packet of money in the lectern. They intended to get into position early, to be ready for the blackmailer when he arrived. But his concerns about the church were secondary now.

Ever since learning of Lady Chetwood's murder, Gavin had been anxious to get back to Sunderland House. It was impossible to know what the baron might do once he learned that the magistrate wanted to question him again. It was certain the man would understand that suspicion had turned in his direction. He might panic.

And there was no telling what the bastard might do then.

Christina knew it was pointless to worry about the morrow and what would transpire at All Hallows Church when her blackmailer attempted to remove the packet of money from the lectern.

Gavin would seize him. She suspected he had talents she knew nothing about. He was an experienced soldier, which was why she'd thought of asking—or rather, coercing—him into helping her in the first place. He had commissioned assistants to help him cover the vulnerable areas of the church, so it was quite unlikely the man would get away.

Still, there was so much that could go wrong. The

blackmailer could wield a knife, or perhaps draw a pistol—

Her heart thudded painfully in her chest. She could not think in terms of disaster. Gavin would do what he'd set out to do, and there would be no trouble, no injuries.

Christina found herself biting her thumbnail, and made a conscious effort to stop. She didn't care about the money. The scoundrel could have it if only she could discover where Lang was.

She wished she knew why her brother had felt it necessary to hide from their family. There had to be good reason for it—and not what Gavin and everyone else thought. Lang hadn't been killed. Christina refused to believe it. Maybe he was ashamed of something he'd done and was reluctant to face their father. Lord Sunderland had never been unclear about his expectations for his offspring . . .

She clenched her hands around her arms and rubbed away the sudden chill. What would cause him to be ashamed? Surely he had not disgraced himself on *The Defender,* or one of Lang's superiors would have said so to her father.

Her head began to ache at the contradictions. Either she believed he was dead, or he had something to be ashamed of. She didn't want either one to be true.

Now that it was dark, Christina's footmen were diligent about making sure the house remained secure. They took turns, much as soldiers on guard duty, changing places every hour, looking out the windows, checking all the locks. "All is well here, my lady?" Hancock asked after his quick knock on the study door.

"Yes, Hancock. I'm fine here."

But she was not. Christina thought she might go mad from the confinement as well as the worry. If Baron Chetwood had murdered his own wife, and Gavin was keeping watch on his residence . . .

She'd told Lords Everhart and Brundle she intended to go out, but that was clearly impossible with the dangerous baron about. She shuddered. If he'd actually killed his own wife, he would have no compunction against hurting—even murdering—*her*.

She wished Gavin were with her. Christina did not know when to expect him, but fervently wished he would come to her soon. As horrible as Lady Chetwood's murder was, she was far more preoccupied with what Gavin had planned for the morning rendezvous with her blackmailer. She was anxious for the scoundrel to be caught and forced to tell what he knew about Lang.

The man would be desperate, of course. The blackmailer of a widowed viscountess would not be treated with leniency by any court in the land. Once found out, he would surely be transported for life, if not hanged. She became more convinced he would be armed, and unlikely to care whether he hurt innocent churchgoers in order to escape into anonymity.

Christina took a deep breath and calmed herself. She had to believe Gavin would not be harmed. He had been far more than an adequate protector as they traveled, and he would successfully manage the situation at All Hallows Church on the morrow.

Unable to dispel her worry entirely, she took her stack of banknotes from her father's safe and stayed busy wrapping them in thick paper. She tied each packet with string, then returned them to the safe, the task done far too quickly for her peace of mind. Now, all she could do was wait for Gavin.

She needed to see him and touch him, more than anything.

Gavin was anxious to assure himself that naught had happened at Sunderland House since he had left earlier in the day. And though he did not care to admit it, he wondered whether Christina would be somehow different after her visit with her former suitor.

Gavin felt a low growl build in his throat at the thought of the earl touching her—even just to kiss her hand. Everhart seemed like a pretentious imbecile who probably hadn't the intelligence or the skill to tie his own cravat, much less keep his lady safe. Worse, he wouldn't know the first thing about giving her pleasure, but take his own pleasure from her, just as Gavin suspected her husband had done.

Gavin's entire body clenched in anticipation of touching Christina again, even though he knew he should not. He knew better than to allow himself to feel that sort of need, or expect her to leave behind every—

Good God, what was he thinking? He could not ask

her to leave anything behind. Gavin had joined the very dregs of mankind when he accepted his commission from Lord Castlereagh. He had not even worn the uniform of his brigade, but blended into the scenery in order to kill his prey from hidden perches and crannies.

There was no honor in what he'd done.

Not even Amelia would have been able to stomach his deeds, and they'd known each other since childhood. With his violent history, Gavin wasn't even sure he ought to live in the same house with Eleanor and her daughter.

He rode slowly past Christina's house. It was late, and only one lamp was still lit. Gavin went on to the far end of the street and tied his horse, then moved stealthily behind the last house. He circled around to the back of Sunderland House, looking for signs of anyone else watching the house.

When he saw no one and nothing but the appropriate animals and grooms in all the stables in the vicinity, he went back to collect his horse. He stabled it, then walked up to the servants' entrance of Sunderland House and knocked.

One of the new footmen admitted him to the house, but not until he'd ascertained who was outside. The process was done exactly as Gavin had instructed. "I believe Lady Fairhaven is in her father's study," the man said when Gavin came inside.

Chapter 25

Christina closed the safe just as Gavin entered the study. He shut the door behind him.

"Gavin!" she cried, happy and relieved to see him.

He pulled off his gloves and dropped them on a chair, and Christina noted a curious light in his eyes.

"Is there anything more about the baron? Have they—"

"No," he said, coming toward her. He always walked with purpose, but now his gait seemed predatory.

Christina wanted naught but to feel his arms around her, but he'd kept his distance ever since their return to London. It was as though their affair had never occurred.

"They do not think he did it?" she asked, unsure of his purpose. "Or they have not been able to question him?"

"No, they have not found him. But when they do, they'll believe it soon enough."

She bit down on her lip, wishing things did not have to change between them. Not yet.

She went to the safe and took out the money she had just placed there. "Here are the packages of banknotes. There were too many for just one . . ."

He took them from her and set them on the desk behind her.

"Is s-something . . ." She swallowed. She did not understand the gleam in his eye—whether he was angry or annoyed, or perhaps frustrated with Baron Chetwood's evasion of the authorities. "Gavin?"

"Did you enjoy your visit with Everhart today?"

"Everhart? What has he to do with anything?"

He stepped very close and started to unfasten the buttons of her bodice.

Christina flushed with desire, with relief. He wanted her as she wanted him.

He opened her gown, his fingers trailing deftly down the bodice, causing her heart to beat furiously in her chest.

He touched his lips to her neck, slipping her gown from her shoulders, causing her to shiver, but not with cold. She had missed him desperately the night before, and most of the day.

Christina reached up and pushed his coat off his broad frame, then pulled at his neck cloth, wanting him as bare as she. A moment later, she slid her hands up inside his shirt and felt the firm, warm flesh of his chest against her palms.

He moved suddenly, his breath harsh against her neck as he lifted her onto the desk and parted her legs to stand between them.

There was an urgency to his movements, an intensity that gave rise to a scorching heat in the core of her being. She wanted him closer.

Christina touched his hard, flat nipples and he kissed her mouth, pressing his body against hers, demanding a degree of contact they could not accomplish there in her father's study, and certainly not while clothed.

He moved suddenly and dragged her skirts out of the way, and then he was hard against her, and struggling with the fastenings of his trews.

Yes! He was exactly what she wanted.

Her heart thudded in her chest. Neither the inappropriateness of the setting nor the hard wood of the desk thwarted her desire. "Now, Gavin. Quickly!"

She needed him desperately. Needed to feel him inside her, wanted to feel the familiar, exquisite connection of their bodies and souls.

Suddenly he was there, his powerful thrust making her shudder with pure bliss. He was so much a part of her, she could not imagine letting go.

"More," she whispered, clasping her hands over the edge of the desk to hold on as he moved.

He indulged her, watching her intently, his eyes a hazy blue in the dim light of the study.

She would have wished for a bed, would have pressed kisses across the thick muscles of his chest and licked his hard nipples. She'd have gone down on her knees and plundered him with her mouth as she'd done once before, arousing him in a fiery, explosion of sensuality.

But he put his hands on her, opening her, creat-

ing a flurry of sensation, a battery of flexing pleasure that pulled him in so deeply, Christina could
not breathe. Gavin became her universe. Her very
existence depended upon him as her body tensed
and contracted around him.

He suddenly shuddered with his own climax and
caught her lips with his own, his kiss madly intoxicating. She clasped him to her, unwilling to lose their
intimate contact . . .

Even though it terrified her. Their union was not
what it had been only a few days ago. It had become
something more, just as her emotions had grown
and expanded. She had allowed herself to become
vulnerable to a man who needed—wanted—only to
deposit her at the home of her despicable old grandfather. And then he would be done with her.

To her horror, her eyes filled with tears. She
blinked them quickly away, before he could have any
inkling of her distress. Somehow, when he withdrew
from her and helped her off the desk, she was relatively composed.

She turned her back and fastened her bodice, as-
suming he was righting his own clothes.

"You'll want to take the money—"

"I will."

She had not expected him to say anything more.
But his reticence—though she had not minded it a
few days ago—rankled now. She picked up the packages and turned to face him. "Take them. I'm sure
you'll want to go early to All Hallows tomorrow."

The right side of his brow dipped over his eye, as

it often seemed to do when something troubled him.

"Christina, this . . . I—"

A loud crash and shouts of alarm erupted at the front of the house, interrupting whatever Gavin was about to say, and he made a quick exit from the room.

"Stay here," he ordered.

But Christina had always had trouble following orders.

Gavin heard footsteps racing toward the front door from every direction in the house. He did not know how he managed to move after his fiery encounter with Christina, but he made it to the foyer as one of the new footmen wrestled with a strange young man, leaving the front door ajar.

The intruder was a competent fighter, and nearly managed to overpower the footman, but when Gavin lent his assistance, the fellow found himself outweighed and overwhelmed. They had nearly subdued him when he heard Christina cry out.

"*Lang!*"

Gavin could not believe his ears, not even when Christina fell to her knees beside him. He had no intention of releasing the intruder.

"Get them off me, Tina! Christ almighty!" the young man growled. Clearly, it wasn't Chetwood, but he was too shabbily dressed to be a Jameson brother. But *Tina*? Who but a brother would address Lady Fairhaven so informally?

"Stop, Gavin!" Christina cried. "It's my brother! It's Lang!"

Hancock and Edgar arrived in the foyer at that moment, and their shouts of surprise at seeing Lieutenant Jameson gave Gavin good reason to drop the fist he had been about to plow into the young man's face.

"Gavin!" Christina cried again.

The new footman pushed himself up to his feet, and Gavin helped Jameson stand. Then he caught sight of someone hovering just outside the door. A young woman, holding a ragged bundle.

"Good Christ, what is going on here?" Jameson demanded. "Cannot a man come into his father's house without being molested by strangers?"

Christina threw herself into her brother's arms, and the sight of her tears tugged at something deep inside Gavin. He knew she was feeling relief and joy, but when he thought of the agony Jameson had put her through, he wanted to lay that good, solid punch right into the young whelp's jaw.

"Where have you been?" Christina cried.

Jameson extricated himself from her arms and went to the door, drawing the horrified young woman inside. "It is a very long story," Jameson growled as he cast a dangerous look in Gavin's direction, "and I do not intend to tell it while standing here in the entrance hall, surrounded by brutish strangers."

Christina wrung her hands together, seemingly at a loss for words. "Of course you don't understand. So much has happened, not the least of which . . ."

Jameson bent down and picked up his key. Gavin surmised he must have been entering the house of his own accord when the new footman realized someone was breaking in. Gavin was surprised the young man hadn't just knocked like every other nobleman he'd ever known.

Christina's brother put his key into his waistcoat pocket just as a screeching sound emanated from the bundle in the young woman's arms.

Lieutenant Jameson put a protective arm around the young woman, ignoring the pitiful wail. "Shall we go inside? I could use about a gallon of Father's whiskey."

"Lang!" Christina protested. She stopped him from taking another step and pulled away the top flap of the bundle held by the young woman. "There is an infant in here!"

Jameson's female companion looked frightened and ill at ease, not to mention pale and drawn.

"I am Lang's sister, Christina Warner," she said to the woman. "And you are . . . ?"

Jameson gave a shake of his head, as though he still could not believe all that had happened. "Tina, this is my wife, Eva Jameson. In her arms is my son, Geoffrey."

Christina felt the blood leave her head, then Gavin's arm sliding around her waist to steady her. She did not think she'd ever appreciated him more than at that moment. Gavin was absolutely dependable, especially when she was in need.

Gavin apologized for the misunderstanding in the foyer and introduced himself to Lang, who shook his hand. Their clash was apparently forgotten.

But Christina was still in shock. Her brother was not dead. He was with her there at home, alive and well. And he had a wife and son. It was all too much to comprehend.

"Lang! We thought you were dead!" She raised her hand to her brother's cheek and touched it, hardly able to believe he was standing before her.

"Well, I'm not, am I?" Lang replied curtly, obviously still incensed by the attack on his person when he entered the house.

"Let's go into the small parlor, shall we?" Gavin said, calmly taking charge once again. "I'm sure everyone has questions."

And answers, Christina hoped.

Once she was seated across from Lang and his wife—*his wife!*—Gavin poured her a generous draught of sherry, and a glass of whiskey for Lang.

"I think brandy for your wife, Jameson?"

Eva sat close to Lang on the narrow settee. She looked small and pale, and though Christina did not mean to be unkind, she thought Lang's wife appeared sickly. Lang gave a nod of agreement to Gavin's suggestion of brandy.

The little bairn did not seem much healthier than his mother. Christina guessed he was not far past newly born. He'd given out that one harsh cry, then only a few small whimpers afterward. Surely newborns were lustier than this.

"Where is everyone?" Lang demanded.

Christina looked at him in disbelief. "No," she

said, suddenly feeling incredibly angry. "The question is: *Where have you been, Lang?*"

Her brother frowned at her. She'd seen him behave in this very same manner every time he'd been called to task for one infraction or another. Annoyed and defensive.

"Oh no," she said ignoring her glass of sherry. She settled her fists onto her hips and faced him squarely. "*You* are the one at fault here, not the family for being absent when you happened to turn up."

He at least had the grace to appear slightly abashed. "As I said, it's a long story, Tina."

"And I will soon hear it, dear brother, but clearly, your wife and child are exhausted." She swallowed her questions, clenching her jaws almost painfully. As much as she wanted to hear Lang's reasons for putting their family through agony, there were priorities.

"There is an infant crib in the attic," she said to Eva, keeping her voice calm and as cordial as possible when speaking to her sister-in-law. "We'll have it brought down to Lang's room, then you and the child can go up and rest."

She looked at her brother, still furious with him, but very concerned. Something was decidedly amiss.

Gavin went to the door. "I'll summon the housekeeper and send Trevor for a doctor."

Lang slipped his arm around his wife's shoulders. "Aye. If you would."

"Take your family up to your bedroom, then,"

Christina said. She would hear his story later, after Eva and the bairn were settled.

Lang stood and took the bairn from his wife. "What are *you* so angry about?" he asked, his tone harsh. "I wrote to tell you all where I was. But no one ever replied."

His statement took her aback, and she pressed one hand against the center of her chest, frowning. "You wrote? We never received a thing from you."

"I sent a letter to Father. Sent it here, to Sunderland House. And another one to Commodore Hammond on *The Defender*."

"Your letter never arrived here."

"*What?*"

"Oh Lang," she said as her throat thickened with joy as well as sorrow. Thank heavens all their worry had been for naught. She embraced him tightly for a moment, taking care not to squeeze her nephew, so relieved she could barely breathe.

"Your letter must have got lost in the mail," she said, releasing him and turning back the blanket to look at the infant's tiny face.

"I didn't send them by the mail," Lang snapped. "Didn't trust it with such a crucial message."

"Well, what—"

"I gave them both to an old friend of yours to be sure they were delivered."

His words stunned her. "Oh no, you do not mean . . . Was it Viscount Brundle?"

"Aye," Lang said. "I'd seen him earlier, in Plymouth. Norris and I had stopped for a drink in a dockside tavern after we picked up our letters. Norris had . . ." He cast a quick glance at Gavin. "Norris met up with a young lady . . ."

Christina's heart sank. Lieutenant Norris had not mentioned anything about a woman, at least not that Christina had heard.

"So you split up," Gavin said.

Lang nodded. "I'd had a letter from Eva and needed to get to her as quickly as possible. Brundle offered me one of his horses so I could ride to Tavistock." He set his jaw and looked directly at Christina. "She was in dire need. I had to go."

Christina's throat clogged with tears. "Your letter never came." And Brundle had not mentioned it when he'd called earlier in the day. The scoundrel.

Gavin spoke then. "There was an explosion, Jameson. On the dock. They thought you were in it."

Lang shook his head, puzzlement shadowing his features. "You mean they found someone who . . . They were wrong about me, but good God . . ." He swallowed thickly. "I left with Brundle to go to his estate and collect the horse. I . . ." He looked at Christina. "I didn't know."

"We thought you were dead. We've mourned you all these months."

She wiped her tears with one hand as Gavin took the other and gave it a squeeze.

"Oh God," Lang said, going pale with a sudden thought. "If Brundle didn't bring you my letter, he must not have taken my explanation to the commodore, either."

Chapter 26

Jameson took his wife from the room, and Gavin observed as Christina gathered her composure and took charge of the situation, giving Mrs. Wilder her instructions.

She'd had a moment's shock when the bairn had made its presence known, but her backbone was as strong as a steel saber. Not inflexible, but solid and resilient.

"Brundle, then?" he asked, though he felt certain it must be.

Christina's cheeks flushed with color and her eyes narrowed. "No one forgets to deliver a letter."

"If Brundle's estate is near Plymouth, he must have known about the explosion and fire in the town. And he would have known about Lang's body being identified."

She clenched her hands into fists. "He had no right to do this to our family."

"Was he angry when you refused his suit?"

"Not half as angry as I am now." She crossed her arms and stalked to the fireplace.

Gavin would have smiled at her pluck but for the gravity of the situation. She had her brother back, no thanks to Lord Brundle's negligence.

Or was it something more than mere negligence?

"Christina."

She stopped her pacing and looked at him. "He might have been angry at the time," she said. "But I cannot be sure because I did not see him afterwards."

"If he was angry enough—"

"He came to call today. Lord Brundle." Her gorgeous eyes were troubled. "He came while Lord Everhart was still here."

Gavin felt a growl building deep in his chest. Soon all the damned lords in the kingdom would be swarming around Sunderland House. Christina was a woman of property, and now Windermere's heiress, and the loveliest woman to be found west of the channel.

But Brundle—he was another puzzle altogether, the pieces of which Gavin had yet to put together.

"I've got to go," he said abruptly.

Christina looked at him with bewilderment, but he did not waver. He exited the room, walking past Hancock and Edgar, who still looked stunned by Lang Jameson's appearance at the house with a wife and child in tow. Trevor and Maycott remained near the front door, and Gavin told them that naught had changed. They were to keep the house closed up and locked for the night. Chetwood was still afoot, and the danger to Christina had not abated.

And now there was another twist. Lord Brundle. He'd known all along that Lang was not dead. It only remained to be seen whether he was the blackmailer, or if someone else knew, too.

Gavin went for the door, but felt a moment of hesitation. He turned to catch a last, quick glance at Christina before leaving the house. While the taste of her was still on his tongue.

He saw her in profile as she crouched down to comfort Theo, who'd crept down the stairs unnoticed at all the commotion and stood hiding with his thumb in his mouth behind a small table. She gathered him into her arms and offered a few quiet, reassuring words, for the boy looked frightened.

Gavin's throat went dry, and the loud thrum of his pulse sounded in his ears. One day, she would bear children of her own—magnificent black-haired, green-eyed beauties—and she would be a superb mother.

But the children would not be his.

Christina put Theo to bed, then paced outside Lang's bedroom while the old Scottish physician who'd treated their family for years examined Eva and the child. She heard Lang question the man, and when they came out, the doctor gave instructions to Mrs. Wilder to provide plenty of sherry and beef tea to Mrs. Jameson.

"I'll send you a wet nurse," he said, "and you're to allow the woman free access to feed the bairn if he's to survive, Lieutenant Jameson. Your wife isna strong enough."

Lang's expression was a troubled one, but he gave the man a nod of agreement and returned to his bed-chamber while Christina walked Dr. MacRae down to the door. "She's in quite a precarious state, Lady Fairhaven. The next few days will be crucial to her survival, as well as the bairn's."

Christina felt speechless. Lang was found, but the circumstances were shocking. More shocking, even, than the blackmail plot against her. She needed to send a message to her parents, and summon them home as soon as possible.

And then it occurred to her that nothing had changed for Gavin. *He'd said he would deal with her blackmailer, and so he was still going to All Hallows in the morning!* He was going to put himself in danger for no reason.

Gavin thought the blackmailer must be Viscount Brundle. Christina had to admit he was likely right, unless there was someone else who knew where Lang had been, and what his situation was.

But why would he extort money from her? And such outrageous sums! How he must have despised her for declining his proposal.

She felt all at sea. It seemed everything was coming to a frightening climax, a coalescence of di-vergent events, all of which made her feel more than slightly ill.

There was a tense hush over the house that added to her disquiet. Hancock and Trevor worked quietly to arrange Lang's bedroom to suit his small family, while Mrs. Wilder went down to the kitchen to prepare a meal for Lang and the beef tea for his wife. Christina sent for Jenny, and asked her to sit with Eva. Then she took her brother's arm and drew him from the room.

"Lang . . . If I could speak to you in Father's study . . ."

"Tina, I—"

"Just for a few minutes." She would not be gainsaid. There were too many unanswered questions.

"What's all this?" Lang asked when he entered the room and saw the packets of banknotes.

"This?" Christina repeated. She worked to control her anger and frustration and surveyed the desk where Gavin had thoroughly ravished her only a short while earlier. Three of the packages had fallen to the floor, and one had split open.

She picked up the bundles and placed them on the desk. "This is two thousand pounds in banknotes, which I collected in order to pay some anonymous scoundrel to find out whatever had happened to you."

"What? I don't understand."

"I was being blackmailed, Lang."

"Blackmail?" His expression became one of shock. "As in . . . You're talking about extortion?"

She felt her composure begin to crumble. She needed Gavin. Wanted him there to bolster her as she confronted her rascal of a brother. "I don't know if the terms are interchangeable, but yes. Someone claimed to know where you were—*and what you'd done*—and he demanded money from me to keep it quiet."

"I've done nothing."

She sat down before her knees gave out. Her relief at knowing he was alive was mixed with so many other emotions. "Nothing?"

"Well," he smoothed back his hair as he always did when upset, "I did not return to my ship as I was supposed to do."

"So we gathered. But you had good reason, hadn't you? And you sent word . . . though your letter could not have been delivered, or we'd have heard of it. Tell me what happened, Lang. Eva, of course. I understand that much."

Lang took the chair across from her, so handsome with his dark, coppery hair and strong Jameson features. His eyes were intensely blue, but their magnificence did not compare to Gavin's. No one's did.

"*The Defender* put into port, and Norris and I took a day's shore leave. There was no time for me to go to Tavistock—Eva's home—much as I wanted to." He swallowed thickly. "Norris and I picked up our mail, and Eva's letter was there . . . She wrote she was with child. I could not just ignore her."

His features twisted with distress. "We'd planned to marry, but I needed some time to prepare Father, so I delayed. She is the daughter of a tailor. Not exactly . . ." He pinched the bridge of his nose with his fingers.

Christina's heart began to soften. "I understand."

As fair-minded as Lord Sunderland was, Lang's trepidations were not unfounded. Their parents expected all their children to marry well. A marquess's daughter for Felton, heiresses for Lang and Colin.

"Eva was disgraced," Lang continued. "Her father put her out when her pregnancy became too advanced to hide. She had no one. She was forced to rely upon the charity of the parish . . ."

Christina leaned forward and put her hand on Lang's forearm. "I'm so sorry she had to go through that."

"What could I do but leave Plymouth? Leave *The Defender*? I hardly thought twice when Brundle offered me a horse. I left with him and went immediately to go find her in Tavistock."

"And you married?"

He nodded. "As soon as we could. Geoffrey was born early and the midwife did not think he would live. Eva's labor was long, and she . . ." He stood abruptly and jammed his fingers through his hair. "I never knew what women went through. If I'd known—"

The thought struck Christina that even now, she might be carrying Gavin's child. It took her breath away.

"I knew Father would be disappointed," Lang continued, "but I sent the letter. I wanted him to know about Eva, about what I was going to do. I had a little money. But the pregnancy was difficult. Eva was ill. I spent every last shilling on shelter, food, and the midwife."

"Oh, Lang."

Anger colored his tone. "I cannot believe that bastard Brundle did not bother to deliver my letters."

Which proved she'd had good reason to refuse his proposal. She'd never liked or trusted the man.

"When Father did not come or send help," Lang continued, "I could only conclude that he was angry. I'd hoped he had not disowned me; that once he met Eva—"

"He did not know, Lang. He'd have come—we all would have come to you immediately."

"I knew no one in Tavistock—only Eva, and she was entirely without resources."

Christina despised Lord Brundle more with every word Lang said. "Why didn't you write again? At least, to me?"

"You had your own problems, Tina. What was I to—"

"*Anything*. You are my brother, Lang. You know I would have helped you, no matter what my circumstances."

He glanced at the desk. "I see that. I'm sorry to have put you through all that. First, to have thought I died. And now—"

"Now I know you are alive, and there is nothing anyone can say against you. Captain Briggs—"

"You mean the goliath who took me to the floor in the foyer?" He rubbed his elbow, and Christina realized he must have been injured at least slightly during the altercation.

She could not worry about that now. "Captain

Briggs was to take this money—the *second* payment of its kind, I might add—and put it in a designated place at All Hallows Church tomorrow."

"But you needn't do it now. I'm here, and there is nothing to keep secret. Right?"

But Gavin would want to apprehend the scoundrel who'd already taken a thousand pounds from her, no matter how dangerous a task it would be. He'd want to see the man punished.

She shuddered. "Captain Briggs thinks it's Lord Brundle."

"Thank God you didn't marry the bloody bastard."

Christina could not believe the man's brass, visiting her when he'd been the one to put her through such difficulties during recent weeks.

"Eva and I—we had no choice but to come home, even though Eva was really too weak to travel," Lang said. "The trip took a great deal out of her. But we had to risk it. I could not take care of her in Tavistock."

"Yes," Christina replied, hoping to reassure him. "You did the right thing." It could not have been an easy decision to travel all this way with a sick wife and a weak newborn. But it was done, and they would make the best of it. They could only pray Dr. MacRae's treatments would produce a happy result.

"Why did Brundle demand money from you, and not Father?" Lang asked.

"They've gone to Italy."

Lang stood. "Dash it all."

Again, Christina wished Gavin had not left the house. His bravery was deep and true, his prowess unaffected, his judgment sound. He was nothing like the men who'd courted her, nothing at all like her glib and shallow husband.

He was so much more than just a paramour. Christina had come to rely upon him . . . to need him quite desperately. "The whole family went away t-to mourn you. Father doesn't even know about the blackmail."

She felt more than a little light-headed at the realization that she wanted more from Gavin Briggs than a short, intense liaison.

He had gotten her safely to London in spite of all their difficulties on the road. She could not imagine him worrying about his father's ire had the mother of his child been in need.

Christina shook her head to clear it, then looked up at Lang. "I'll write Father and Mother and tell them what's happened."

"No, I'll write. I owe them nothing less, especially after . . ." He ran a hand across his mouth. "What a bloody mess. How long has it been? Two months?"

"Three." Christina replied distractedly. She needed to intercept Gavin, wanted to convince him his trip to All Hallows was no longer necessary. She did not care if Lord Brundle was the culprit. She would not have him put himself in danger, now that Lang was safely home.

She went to the door and called for Hancock, who came to her immediately. "Do you know where Captain Briggs went?"

"No, my lady. He did not say."

Chapter 27

Seeing Lang Jameson alive was entirely unexpected. Gavin had been quite certain Christina's brother must have been killed—the most obvious culprit being his friend Norris. It was the only thing that had made any sense whatsoever—the only reason Lang would not have contacted his family.

But now Gavin knew Viscount Brundle was involved in the blackmail plot. He was glad to have that information, but would deal with Brundle in the morning. The greater threat at the moment was Baron Chetwood, and Gavin rode to the baron's house, hoping to find Colonel Watkins or Mr. Gell still there, and some word on Chetwood.

"Captain Briggs," the magistrate said as he came down the steps.

"Any news on the baron?" Gavin asked.

"Not yet. I've sent men to check at his club and a few other places he and Brundle are known to frequent."

"*Brundle?*"

"Aye. You know him?"

"Not exactly," Gavin replied, his mind racing. Chetwood and Brundle together?

"I understand the two are thick as thieves. If they're together, Brundle will be remembered."

"For what reason?" Gavin asked.

"He's a rough-looking character. Tall and thick-set with heavy black mustaches and owlish brows."

Aye, Gavin remembered. He had seen a man fitting this description at the Black Sheep Inn. If only he'd realized then that it was Brundle, he'd have made the connection so much sooner.

"Oh, and he's got a sizable mole just under his eye," Watkins added. "We'll find him if he goes anywhere about Town."

"Damnation," Gavin muttered.

"What's that?"

"Nothing, Colonel," Gavin said. "Will you send word round to Sunderland House if either one of them is found?"

"Will do, Briggs. You do the same, eh?"

Gavin considered what he ought to do. Perhaps make the rounds of London's darker corners himself to try and locate Chetwood and his lackey. It seemed quite clear that the two of them had conspired together to make Christina's life hell.

Disgusted by thoughts of such a dark and devious scheme, Gavin decided to return to Sunderland House. He bid farewell to the magistrate and went across to the square where John Mason and Philip

Caldwell were getting set to keep watch in case
Chetwood appeared.

He turned to inform the two men of Brundle's part
in all this when a fancy landau rolled into the square,
driving slowly past Chetwood's house.

As the landau drove by, Gavin could see the driver
clearly in the lamplight. It was the man Watkins had
just described. Viscount Brundle.

Gavin stayed out of sight until the landau was
gone. Then he quickly mounted his horse. "I'm going
to follow him," he said to his men. "No need to go
to All Hallows in the morning. Make sure the others
know."

Gavin rode out to Henrietta Street, then loitered a
moment before following the landau to Oxford, keeping some distance between himself and it. He wondered why Brundle had turned up at Chetwood's
house. Perhaps the viscount had come to see whether
Watkins had posted guards there and intended to
report back to Chetwood.

That was the only thing that made any kind of
sense. Chetwood had been overconfident and hadn't
considered the possibility that he would be suspected of his wife's murder. He'd concocted a fiction
he hoped the magistrate would believe, unaware that
Gavin and his men had been watching the house all
through the night.

Peer or not, he would hang for the murders.

And Gavin could not think of a more appropriate
fate for the vicious bastard. Christina would never
again have to be wary of the man—which was fortu-

nate. Because Gavin would not be there to protect her.

She would have Lord Everhart, or someone like him, a peer of the realm, to take care of her. The man Christina wed would be able to hire as many strong men as he deemed necessary to keep her safe, while keeping his own hands clean.

Gavin's were anything but clean. Even now, with regret for his past years of service to the crown burning in his craw, he would not hesitate to put a ball of lead between Chetwood's eyes if he had the opportunity.

He lost sight of the landau when it turned into Oxford Street, but when he caught up, there was a second man in the carriage beside the first. Gavin's hackles rose. The man had been there all along, but hiding.

He could not positively identify Brundle's companion, but knew it could not be anyone but Chetwood. The baron must have wanted to gain entry to his house, but the presence of the magistrate's policemen prevented it.

And so they'd driven on.

The landau continued down Oxford Street but soon reached Stratford Place—where Sunderland House was located. When it turned into Christina's narrow street, Gavin had a very bad feeling.

He knew he had to act, and quickly.

Christina's household was quiet and dark, but for one sconce burning near the bedrooms. The wet nurse had come and fed Eva's child while Mrs.

Wilder made sure Eva herself took some nourish-
ment. Soon afterward, everyone settled down for
the night, with the wet nurse and tiny Geoffrey in a
separate bedroom, giving Lang and Eva the opportunity for some much-needed, uninterrupted sleep.
It was obvious they were exhausted.

Christina made herself ready for bed, but knew
she would not be able to manage a wink, not when
Gavin was out, probably looking for Baron Chetwood. She wished they could leave for Windermere
on the morrow. Just ignore the blackmailer and his
demand for payment, and get away from Town
before anyone knew where they'd gone. Her father
could deal with Viscount Brundle personally when
he returned from Italy.

She and Gavin did not need to go directly to Windermere. She was quite sure he had said he would
receive his payment whether or not her grandfather
was still alive when he got her there. So there was
no great hurry. They'd delayed more than a week
already, and . . .

Christina wanted a few days alone with him. She
wanted to spend them in a quiet cottage somewhere
away from Town, far from worries of blackmailers
and murderers, just the two of them.

But something was different about Gavin. Christina had felt it when he'd returned to the house
earlier, when he'd taken her so hard and fast in her
father's study. There had been a growling intensity
about him that she had not understood. Almost as
though he'd been angry with her.

He'd mentioned Everhart, but Christina had been so caught up in his fierce seduction, she had not tried to understand.

Until now.

Lord Everhart was not even half the man Gavin was. And yet he must believe she would choose the earl—

Christina suddenly had a sensation of pure vertigo. She felt as though she was falling from a great height—from the top of the house, or perhaps off one of the high fells near her house at Ullswater. The trust and respect she wanted was there, in Gavin. He might not hold a title, or possess any great estate, but he was honorable and true.

And she loved him. She loved him quite completely and perhaps a little desperately.

She sat down on the bed to catch her breath and regain her bearings. Falling in love was not something she'd planned to do. Not something she'd wanted. And yet—

There was a quiet tap at her bedroom door and her heart leaped at the possibility that it was Gavin coming back to her. She rose to her feet and dashed to the door, but it was Theo.

Concern for the boy trumped her disappointment. He'd been frightened by the altercation at the door with Lang's arrival, and when Christina had gone into his room to say good night, he'd still been restless.

He'd asked her where Gavin had gone.

For both their sakes, Christina wished she could

have said Gavin had only gone out to the stable for a moment, and that he would be back momentarily.

She crouched down before him. "What is it?"

"I had a dream," Theo said in a whisper. He was trembling again, and Christina knew the evening's events haunted him even now.

She put her arms around him. "A bad one?"

He nodded. "I could not sleep."

"Maybe we ought to go down for some tea. Would you like that?"

The boy nodded.

"Let's go to the kitchen and brew some for ourselves." She put on a thick wrapper and left the room, keeping his hand in hers. She wasn't going to be able to sleep, either. Not until she saw Gavin.

Christina wanted to tell him how she felt, but she did not even know if he shared her feelings. Just because he had not seemed pleased with Lord Everhart's visit did not mean he thought more of her than he did any other mistress.

The thought of Gavin with another woman shook her, but not the same way Edward's betrayal had done. Christina was in love with Gavin. She wanted to meet his sister, wanted to know all his thoughts and dreams, and what it meant to be a marksman in Lord Wellington's service. She wanted to be a part of him, wanted to be a part of his life when he took possession of his country home.

Society and a "good" marriage could go hang if it meant another match like the one she'd made with Edward.

One of the new footmen was in the kitchen keeping watch near the door, and Christina assumed the other guarded the front door. Her own three footmen were about, as well.

She ought to have felt secure, but with Gavin away, could not relax, and it was not entirely due to the threat from Chetwood or Brundle. Their interlude in the study had been so hard and fast and desperate because Gavin intended it to be their last time together. Somehow, Christina knew he was trying to give her the distance he believed she needed . . .

And yet he had not been able to stay away.

The stove was still warm, and she put the kettle on it while Theo took a seat at the table.

"Shall I do that for you, my lady?" the footman asked.

"No, it's all right, Turner," she replied. "Theo and I do not intend to be any trouble. I see all is well."

Turner nodded. "Quiet as ever."

Christina took the pot and cups to the table and sat down beside Theo. She skimmed his hair back from his forehead. "Do you feel better now?"

He nodded. "Yes."

"Your dream woke you?"

"It was Uncle Samuel's face. He was . . . I was scared of him." He took a deep, shuddering breath, and Christina hugged him to her.

"Your uncle has no idea where to find you, Theo."

Theo nodded. "When will Captain Briggs come back?"

Christina wished she knew. "We'll see him in the morning."

She tried not to think of what might happen at the church, and concentrated on Theo. "Soon you'll—"

A loud rap at the door interrupted what she was about to say. Turner checked the lock. "Who is it?" he asked without opening it.

"Lord Everhart," was the reply.

Turner looked at Christina for instruction.

She did not know what to do. The earl had never meant her any harm, but it was incredibly odd for him to come calling so late. "Ask him what he wants."

Turner did so.

"Just let me in, man. My carriage sprung a wheel. It's late, and I'm too far from home to walk the distance."

"Is he in his cups?" Christina asked Turner. His words sounded slurred.

She got up from the table, and Theo came with her. It was bad enough that she was in the kitchen in her nightclothes, but to have Lord Everhart arrive in this manner was unwelcome as well as unprecedented.

"Most likely he is, my lady. Should I—"

The door suddenly crashed open, and it was not Lord Everhart who entered, but a dark-haired man with a thick mustache.

"Here now!" Turner protested, but he suddenly dropped to his knees, clasping his chest. When his hands dropped away, Christina saw that they were bloody. She stifled a scream as she looked at the in-

truder and saw Lord Brundle coming toward her
with a knife in hand.

"Theo—"

"Stay where you are, boy," Brundle snapped. "And
be still. If you rouse the house, someone else will
die."

Theo whimpered and wrapped his arms around
Christina, who held his trembling body close. She
looked past Brundle at Turner, who lay supine on the
floor, but still breathing. Perhaps if Dr. MacRae saw
to him right away—

Brundle grabbed Christina's arm, shoving Theo
aside. "Stay there," he ordered him.

"No! Let him—"

"He's no concern of yours."

"What do you want?" Christina cried. He yanked
her against him and held the knife to her neck, so
there was no possible way to escape him.

"I've only wanted one thing, but you would deny
me now, just as you did two years ago."

Christina felt tears burning down her cheeks.
"Lord Brundle, we . . ." She took a tremulous breath,
at a loss for what she could possibly say to him. "You
know we did not suit," she said weakly.

Brundle's mustache brushed against her ear. "It
no longer matters. You are naught but a barrister's
daughter."

"H-how do you know that?"

He started pulling her to the door. "My good
friend Chetwood knows everything. And he's going

to get his due, no matter what Windermere does with his will."

"His due?"

"Aye. You've been a good little pigeon, paying him whatever he demanded."

"What *he* demanded? I never paid—" The air whooshed out of her. "*Chetwood* was the blackmailer? But you! You tricked Lang!"

She raised her hand to slap him, but he caught her wrist and she felt a burning pain at her neck. She cried out, bracing herself for him to slice her throat, just as someone had done to Lady Chetwood.

"Enough talk. We're going for a little ride with your cousin." He shoved her outside.

"Cousin?" She felt terrified as well as confused.

"Aye. Baron Chetwood."

Christina felt a scream building in her chest, but when she tried to let it out, no sound came out.

"Briggs!"

Gavin pulled up short when he heard the hushed call of his name. It was Colonel Watkins and two of his men. They were running toward their horses, which had been tied at the opposite end of Christina's street. "Watkins?"

"Keep on moving, man," the colonel ordered. "They've gone around to the back of Sunderland House! We'll follow!"

Gavin raced to the end of the street, then turned into the alleyway behind it. He dismounted even before his horse halted, checking his pistol as he sprinted toward Sunderland House. It was quite dark in back, with only a bit of light from a partial moon to guide him.

He'd dealt with worse conditions, although he wished he carried his Baker rifle, because it was a much more accurate shot. But the pistol would have to do. He moved quickly but stealthily to Christina's house, and when the kitchen door fell open, Gavin retreated behind one of the pillars at the back of the house next to hers.

With growing dread, he watched Brundle drag Christina outside and shove her toward the stable. And when he saw a quick glint of metal at her throat, he realized the bastard wielded a knife.

His heart pounding in his ears, Gavin raised his pistol and prepared to fire, but there was too much movement, and Christina was too close to his target. It was the most important shot of his life and his hand shook at the thought of missing Brundle.

Gavin would not be able to live with himself if Christina was injured, even if it was due to his inaction. Somehow, he had to thwart the man who held her. He had to get her away from the knife.

Gavin lowered his pistol and started to follow them, but a sudden burst from the door surprised him, especially when he saw that it was Theo. The boy rushed at Christina's captor and caught him, throwing his arms around the man's leg.

Brundle gave out a shrill cry, and lost his hold on Christina, giving Gavin the opportunity he needed to get off a shot. He didn't need to kill the man, after all—only disable him so he could do no further harm.

Christina scooted away and Gavin quickly took aim. He squeezed the trigger, firing, and putting the ball into the villain's shoulder. The bastard howled again and fell to the ground.

Just as he did, the landau Gavin had followed earlier bolted out of the stable and raced down the alleyway, with Baron Chetwood driving. Colonel Watkins and his men fell into pursuit behind the landau, chasing it out to the street and beyond.

Gavin paid them no attention.

He rushed to Christina's side and caught her in his arms before she fell, kissing her face, her eyes and forehead, and then her mouth.

"Gavin," she said softly, just before she fainted. "I knew you'd come."

Theo came to Gavin's side and, with his thumb firmly in his mouth, took hold of the edge of Gavin's jacket. "You are a little hero, you know that, Theo? You saved Lady Fairhaven from this worthless scoundrel."

Gavin left the mustachioed villain bleeding on the ground and carried Christina into the house, but the sight that greeted them was not a good one.

Christina's brother stormed into the kitchen, his hair askew as he yanked on his travel-stained shirt. Hancock was right behind him, while Trevor and the other new footman knelt over Turner, who lay bleeding on the floor, just inside the door.

"Someone go for MacRae," Lang ordered. "Hancock, get a fire going. We'll need hot water. Where's Mrs. Wilder?"

Lang looked directly at Gavin and then lowered his gaze to his sister, unconscious and cradled in his arms. "What in hell is going on here?"

Chapter 28

The sharp smell of vinegar woke Christina, and she found herself lying on a settee in her mother's parlor. The first thing she saw was Gavin's face, uncharacteristically pale. He was holding something firm and warm at her neck.

Everything that had happened suddenly came to her—except how she'd come to be lying on the settee. But a reassuring warmth slid through her as Gavin took her hand and kissed the back of it.

"Christina." His voice was soft and gentle.

"How is Turner? Will he live?"

"MacRae thinks so. He's done what he can for him, and now we'll have to wait and see."

"And Brundle?"

"The idiot in the back garden?"

She nodded and tried to sit up, but Gavin would not allow it. "He'll live, too. Unless his shoulder becomes infected . . . And I'm not so sure about his leg."

"What happened to his leg?"

Gavin grinned, the first time Christina had seen him truly smile. "Theo bit him. Took a large piece of flesh from his calf."

"I daresay he deserves it. Poor Turner."

"What about me?" Gavin asked quietly.

Christina felt a moment's panic at the thought that he had been injured. But he appeared to be undamaged. "What about you, Captain Briggs?"

"My heart. I thought it would stop when I saw Brundle pull you out of the house. And when I saw this cut on your neck—"

She cupped his jaw in her hand. "I love you, Gavin."

The expressions that crossed his features were no more readable than they'd been earlier in the evening, when he'd made love to her in the study.

He closed his eyes and swallowed. When he looked at her, his eyes were hard. "Christina, I am not the man you need. I'm not who you think—"

"You are."

He shook his head. "You have no idea."

"Of course I do," she countered quietly. "In spite of what you have not told me about yourself, I do know you, Gavin."

"No. Christina . . . I've done some despicable, wicked things . . ."

"No, Gavin. Never. You could not."

"Aye. I could. And did. I was in Lord Castlereagh's service in Europe." He said it all in one breath, as though the words were painful to articulate. "As his agent, I killed so many—"

"Like any soldier is required to do."

He took her hand from his face, but did not let go of it. "Not like any soldier. Good God, I didn't even wear a uniform. I was anything but an honorable adversary, shooting my targets from rooftops and behind barrels."

"Gavin—"

"They never knew it was coming. I was the angel of death in a peasant's clothes."

She could not bear the agony in his eyes. "You saved Theo from his uncle."

"As would any—"

"As would only an honorable man. People in that town must have known what was happening to that little boy, and yet no one did anything."

"Chris—"

"You saved an entire roomful of travelers at Palmer's Inn, when you could have let the thieves hurt whomever they pleased while they took everything of value."

"I was not the only—"

"And the day we met, you did not drag me to Windermere when that was exactly what you wanted to do," she said as she sat up and took his hand in hers.

"You gave me no choice."

Her brows came together. "We both know you could have overpowered me. You didn't. You assisted a damsel in distress. You are a better man than you think, Captain Briggs."

Gavin shook his head and started to protest, but

Lang came into the room, interrupting anything he might have said.

Her brother appeared bewildered and exhausted, and Christina was glad he had not come downstairs any sooner, or everything might have played out differently. He could have been hurt.

"Good. You've come to," Lang said. "How is your neck?"

It stung a little. "Not too bad, I think." She kept hold of Gavin's hand, wishing they had more time alone. More time for her to convince him of what she knew about him. But that would have to come later.

Christina couldn't help but wonder how her barrister father would have argued her point to Gavin, for she intended to win her case with him. He was the most worthy man she'd ever met. He was her anchor, her love, and she could not fathom letting him go.

Lang took a seat. "I gave my explanations earlier. Now perhaps you'll finish with yours."

Christina gave her brother a brief account of her relationship to the Duke of Windermere, and why Gavin had come for her, eliciting a low whistle from her brother in response to the tale.

Gavin filled in a few more details. "Baron Chetwood is Windermere's heir, and I believe he intended to prevent Christina and her sister from inheriting anything he believed was rightfully his."

"Even after the will was changed?" Lang asked.

Gavin shrugged. "I think he was outraged by the

duke's decision to leave his unentailed property to his granddaughters. And he has been playing out his anger ever since learning of it."

"So, this blackmail business . . ." Lang frowned. "Brundle was in on it from the first?"

"Once Magistrate Watkins questions Brundle and Chetwood, we'll have a better understanding," Gavin replied. "Christina's grandfather was not exactly quiet about summoning me and making his wishes known. Chetwood was deeply in debt, and infuriated by the loss of such a large portion of Windermere's wealth."

"You think he decided to get it any way he could, then? And got Brundle to help him?" Lang asked.

"I think his friend Brundle intended mischief when he ran into you at Plymouth. He saw an opportunity to have his revenge on your sister for her refusal of his suit."

Lang stood, clenching his fists. "His *mischief* nearly cost my wife and son's lives. Even now . . ."

"They will be all right, Lang," Christina said gently. "I'm sure of it."

"Brundle and Chetwood are Hellfire cronies, the most depraved of men," Gavin continued. "The baron must have been delighted with Brundle's trick. And while I was occupied tracking Christina's sister, they concocted this plan to make Christina's life miserable as well as recoup some of Windermere's wealth for Chetwood."

Lang rubbed his head, disheveling his already mussed hair, and when he spoke, his voice cracked.

"Do you think Brundle would have killed my sister?"

Gavin shook his head, still feeling more than slightly raw himself. "I think he intended only to threaten her and take her to Chetwood. Then Chetwood . . ." He swallowed, unwilling and unable to think what would have happened had Brundle succeeded in getting Christina to Chetwood's landau.

"So, now you will go to Windermere to collect the bequest from a grandfather who disowned you when you were a child, in the greatest need of his help?" Lang asked.

"No," she replied. "I won't."

Gavin looked at her blankly for a moment, then with an expression of resigned disappointment. Christina squeezed his hand. "I'll only go so that Gavin can collect his reward for finding me. And to meet my sister. But I want nothing from that horrid old man."

"Christina . . ."

At that moment, Hancock brought Colonel Watkins into the parlor and announced him. "Magistrate Watkins to see you, my lady."

Watkins entered the room looking as battle-weary as the entire Ninety-fifth had felt after the fighting at Buçaco. He bowed to Christina, then turned his gaze toward Lang and Gavin. "Perhaps we gentlemen can adjourn for a moment while—"

"I will not hear of it," Christina countered. "Be seated, Magistrate."

Gavin's chest swelled with emotion. His Christina was as fierce as Boudicca must have been.

And she loved him. Her words rang in his ears, so incredibly impossible.

Watkins nodded and took the seat offered to him. "It was Baron Chetwood in Lord Brundle's landau."

Gavin nodded. "I thought so."

Watkins tapped his fingertips against his knees. "When you shot Brundle, Chetwood took the landau and raced out of Stratford Place and into Oxford Street. From there, he dashed westward at breakneck speed, the carriage bobbing wildly. We thought he would overturn in the street."

Lang raised his brows and started to ask a question, but Watkins continued.

"We pursued him all the way to Hyde Park, where he lost a wheel. The carriage became airborne."

"What happened?" Gavin asked.

"It flew into the Serpentine, with Baron Chetwood underneath it."

"Good God," Lang breathed.

Watkins nodded. "He drowned."

There was much more to be said, but now was not the time. Watkins indicated that Brundle was being taken to his home and would be kept under guard until he could be questioned about his role in Baron Chetwood's crimes.

"I'm going to bed," Christina's brother said when the magistrate had left.

Gavin was not sorry to see Lang and Watkins leave. He wanted Christina to himself, wanted to hear the words again. He wanted her assertion that he was as decent as any other man in spite of all he'd told her about his past.

And then he wanted to take her to bed and hold her until morning.

"Sleep as long as you can tomorrow," Christina said before Lang took his leave. "I will write to Father, and—"

"No, I already told you—"

"Because I have something else—something very important—to tell him."

"What could that possibly be, my dear sister?" Lang asked wearily.

"News of my upcoming nuptials."

"Gesu, Christina, will you speak plainly? I am far too tired to try to decipher—"

"I am going to become engaged tonight, and late this summer, I intend to marry Captain Briggs."

As improper as it was to lie with Christina in her bed under her father's roof, Gavin gathered her close and kissed her mouth.

God, how he loved her.

He slid his thigh between hers. "You did not listen to anything I said, did you?"

She slid her hands down his chest, lingering at his most sensitive spots. "You are a hero, Gavin. *My* hero."

"I'm no one's hero, Christina," he said. "But I've fallen so hard and so deeply in love with you, that I cannot find the strength to argue."

She smiled up at him. "I am very glad to hear that.

Because there are much more enjoyable things to do than argue."

He groaned with pleasure when she dipped her head and swirled her tongue around his nipple. Her hands made a tingling path down his belly and found what they sought, hard and ready for her.

"Mmmm . . ." The sound came from the back of her throat just before she took him into her mouth, and he knew she derived a great deal of pleasure from the act. Perhaps as much as he.

"Christina," he groaned.

She drove him nearly mad with her mouth and tongue, then arched up and straddled him. "You are my hero, Gavin Briggs. And never forget it."

Epilogue

Windermere Park. Late August 1816

This was not a visit Christina looked forward to, but Gavin deserved it. He'd earned every shilling of the prize Windermere had promised him, and she was going to see that he got it. And then they were going to Ashby Hall to meet her sister, whose husband did not want her to travel while she was with child. Christina wanted to meet her before her own pregnancy became too advanced.

Her wedding to Gavin, one week after the anniversary of Edward's death, had been a quiet one. Only her family, Gavin's lovely sister, and their closest friends had attended. And Theo, of course. He walked ahead of her now, between her parents as they ascended the steps of the mansion at Windermere Park. They had accepted Christina's little hero into their circle without question—just as they had Christina. And Gavin.

Gavin took her hand, sensing her nervousness, the way he seemed to sense all her moods. "He's just an old man with regrets, Christina. At least he's got them."

"Unlike your father."

Gavin shrugged.

Christina knew he thought his father a lost cause, and would never forgive him for abandoning Eleanor. The irony that Eva and Eleanor shared the same plight was not lost on Christina. She did not judge either woman, and had fallen in love with Gavin's little niece as quickly as she had Theo.

Christina now understood Gavin's reasons for wanting to buy his farm. He'd wanted to assure Eleanor and Rachel's security at Weybrook Manor. Which Christina had delayed.

She assuaged her feelings of guilt by putting up the funds to purchase the manor as soon as he told her his intentions. Weybrook was the perfect home for Eleanor and her daughter.

Gavin squeezed her hand. "Don't worry. The old man is too weak to bite . . ." he said. "Although I might be tempted to sample a morsel later . . ."

Christina felt her cheeks suffuse with heat and knew they'd turned as deep a red as the gown she wore. "You are one wicked man, Captain Briggs."

"That's *Baron Dartmoore* to you, my lady."

Christina laughed as her father turned and called to them. "Come along. There's no sense in delaying this."

Lady Sunderland turned and smiled reassuringly at her daughter. She knew how much Christina dreaded this meeting and had insisted on traveling with her daughter to meet the old curmudgeon. Christina learned that the Windermere title would now become dormant, for there was only one possible heir, and he had immigrated to America some years before.

What happened to the title was of no interest to Christina. The last Duke of Windermere had not behaved with honor, and she had already decided she would never call herself his granddaughter. She was Christina Jameson, now Baroness Dartmoore, since Gavin had received not only medals of honor from the crown, but letters patent for saving the life of Lord Wellington at Waterloo, and on at least one other prior occasion.

She was exceedingly proud of her husband.

"There is an old woman in London," Gavin said, perhaps to distract her from the meeting she was about to face. "She was your nurse at the time of your parents' deaths."

"You met this woman?" Christina asked, her brows furrowing with curiosity.

Gavin nodded. "Aye. When I was following leads to locate you and Lily. Miss Thornberry is her name."

Christina had tried not to think too much about her mother and father, or their drowning deaths. She had not wanted to recall anything she might have felt during those dark days when she and her sister were separated and taken away from their home.

But she felt a little light-headed now. The old nurse

could probably tell her and Lily about their parents, about their life in London before . . .

Gavin spoke again. "I know my visit worried her."

Christina stopped and pulled Gavin to the far side of a pillar on her grandfather's portico. "And now you're concerned for her?"

He touched a curly wisp of hair near her ear. "What would it hurt if you were to write her, you and Lily—to reassure her?"

Her heart swelled with love for this man who was so considerate of an old woman he barely knew. "Do you know how very much I love you, Gavin Briggs?"

"If it is half as much as I love you, my lovely wife— then it is enough."

Christina slid her hands up her husband's broad shoulders and pulled him down for a kiss. He was not the terrible brute he thought he was, but the kindest, most honorable man she could imagine.

And he was all hers.

Their kiss was brief, considering where they were. "Look, Christina," Gavin said when they moved apart.

Christina's heart nearly stopped when she saw what . . . *who* stood at the top of the portico.

A woman who looked exactly like her. Except that her hair was longer, and her midsection was somewhat thicker. Christina put one hand on her own slightly rounded abdomen and returned Lily's beaming smile, pleased that her sister had come to Windermere instead of waiting for her at Ashby Hall.

"Come on, love. It's time you met your sister."

978-0-06-184132-3

978-0-06-202719-1

978-0-06-206932-0

978-0-06-204515-7

978-0-06-199968-0

978-0-06-201232-6

At Avon Books, we know your passion for romance—once you finish one of our novels, you find yourself wanting more.

May we tempt you with . . .

- **Excerpts** from our upcoming releases.

- Entertaining **extras**, including authors' personal photo albums and book lists.

- Behind-the-scenes **scoop** on your favorite characters and series.

- **Sweepstakes** for the chance to win free books, romantic getaways, and other fun prizes.

- Writing **tips** from our authors and editors.

- **Blog** with our authors and find out why they love to write romance.

- **Exclusive content** that's not contained within the pages of our novels.

Join us at
www.avonbooks.com

AVON

An Imprint of HarperCollins*Publishers*
www.avonromance.com

FTH 0708